Sherlock Holmes

Consulting Detective

Volume Eleven

AIRSHIP 27 PRODUCTIONS

TM

Sherlock Holmes: Consulting Detective, Volume 11

"The Scotland Yard Murder" © 2018 I.A. Watson
"The Adventure of the Artful Forger" © 2018 Lee Houston Jr.
"The Adventure of the Manhunting Marshal" © 2018 Jim Doherty
"The Adventure of the Conundrum King" © 2018 Greg Hatcher

Cover illustration © 2018 Laura Givens
Interior illustrations © 2018 Rob Davis

Editor: Ron Fortier
Associate Editor: Gordon Dymowski
Production and design by Rob Davis
Promotion and marketing by Michael Vance

Published by
Airship 27 Productions
www.airship27.com
www.airship27hangar.com

ISBN-13: 978-1-946183-34-7
ISBN-10: 1-946183-34-2

Printed in the United States of America

10 9 8 7 6 5 4 3 2 1

Sherlock Holmes
Consulting Detective
Volume XI

TABLE OF CONTENTS

A woman's mutilated corpse is found in pieces stashed away in the foundation site of what will become the New Scotland Yard. When the police are baffled, Holmes is called into the affair solve the mystery.

The missing painting of a deceased woman send Holmes & Watson on a merry chase leading to murder and conspiracy.

U.S. Deputy Marshal Cordrell Vance has come to London chasing a vicious killer but he'll need the help of Sherlock Holmes and Doctor Watson to catch his deadly prey.

Holmes and Watson are challenged by a sadistic killer who leaves them puzzles before each of his murders. Only by unraveling his latest riddle can they save the next victim.

Sherlock Holmes

in

"The Scotland Yard Murder"

By

I.A. Watson

A consulting detective's role is to be called upon when other professionals need guidance or support in their detection. Much as medical cases too complex or unusual for a regular practitioner are referred to a consultant doctor, so my friend Mr Sherlock Holmes is relied upon by the forces of the law when all other resort is exhausted.

One reason for referral is Holmes' discretion. Although he can be unconscionably rude in social settings, indifferent to the mores of our age or the conventions of human interaction, he is remarkably good at maintaining confidences and in resolving matters with a minimum of scandal and publicity.

That was undoubtedly why he was called upon again by one of his oldest clients, the grizzled Detective Branch investigator Tobias Gregson, on the case of the Scotland Yard Murder.

Rather, it was the New Scotland Yard Murder.

Ever since the *Metropolitan Police Act 1829* instituted the police force as we know it, a small cadre of plain-clothes Inspectors had operated from the back entrance of Whitehall Place police headquarters, a small square known as Scotland Yard. By 1888 the number and function of these detectives had increased so that new premises were required. Land was purchased to build a tailor-made headquarters down by the river, the New Scotland Yard.

You may imagine the pain and embarrassment then for Inspector Gregson and his colleagues to suffer an unsolved mystery in their own new facilities before the buildings were even completed; a mystery which thwarted their best efforts to resolve, and which eventually had to be laid before the world's only consulting detective.[1]

"It's not that we wouldn't get to the answer eventually," Gregson insisted defensively as he led us past the hoardings that fenced off the work-site. "Except we are under pressure from the Home Office, hounded by the

---

[1] Our present story draws upon the real life "Whitehall Mystery" which stirred press and public in October 1888. Many of the names of characters and the evidence they present are borrowed from the coroner's inquest at the time. The usual caveat about this being a work of fiction which does not seek to accurately represent any actual person of course applies.

damned press. New Scotland Yard is the Home Secretary's pet project.[2] He approved the funding, selected the site, picked out the architect. So he takes an unexplained corpse on the premises as a personal affront. He wants results quickly, and so we must resort to…"

"To Holmes," I suggested.

"To special measures."

Holmes and I followed through a wooden gate that was now, belatedly, guarded by a posted bobby. Inside the barrier was the scaffolded front wall of what would eventually be an elegant four-storey building. For now all was site rubble and construction dust, shouting workmen and rumbling pulleys.

"It is two weeks since the discovery," Holmes complained. "Two weeks for the site to be danced upon by every curious hob-booted labourer and idle journalist. Two weeks for evidence to be lost and forensic methods to have been rendered meaningless."

He meant it had been two weeks of boredom for Sherlock Holmes. September of that year had been a remarkable one even by the great detective's standard. Along with minor investigations such as the Manor House Case and the matter of the French Will, Holmes has looked into the singular circumstance of the Greek Interpreter, the complicated puzzle of the Sign of Four, and the monstrous affair of the Hound of the Baskervilles.[3]

---

2   The Home Office is the branch of British government that administrates matters of justice, law and order. Its responsibilities include the police, military intelligence, and at Holmes' time also included the prison service. The Home Secretary, fully titled Her Majesty's Principal Secretary of State for the Home Department, is the politically-appointed head of the Home Office. He is selected by the majority party in power from existing Members of Parliament and sits as a member of the executive Cabinet who run the nation. The post is considered one of the "Great Offices of State" along with the Foreign Secretary and the Chancellor of the Exchequer, and since the 20th century with the Prime Minister (which is quite a new office compared to the other three).

3   The first two investigations are referenced in "The Greek Interpreter" in *The Memoirs of Sherlock Holmes*. *The Sign of Four* and *The Hound of the Baskervilles* occupy volumes of their own. Watson shows his own discretion in not mentioning here a blackmailing case upon which Holmes was also working during the Baskerville adventure.

The other major news story at the same time was the murder on 30th September 1888 of prostitutes Elizabeth Stride and Catherine Eddowes, the fourth and fifth killings of Jack the Ripper. For a short while the Scotland Yard Corpse was speculated to be another victim of Bloody Jack, but this connection was soon dismissed after examination of the evidence.

The Canon makes no mention of the Ripper. This is unsurprising given the topicality and newness of his horrendous real-life crimes. For Arthur Conan Doyle to have depicted Holmes investigating would have been in poor taste. Half a century and more later, however, when the Ripper was blurred to gruesome Victorian legend, Holmesians were at liberty to consider whether the great detective had stirred to address the serial killings that shocked all London. Holmes' biographer W.S. Baring-Gould devoted a whole

I had been unexpectedly diverted by the discovery of Miss Mary Morstan, who would eventually do me the honour of gifting me her hand and becoming Mrs Watson. October, by comparison, had raised few puzzles that had engaged the interest of my friend's ever-active mind.

"We had hoped to have solved the crime by now," Gregson grumped.

"But you have not," my friend pointed out with unflinching precision.

The carpenter had told his tale many times before, but never for so intent a listener as Sherlock Holmes.

"It was a Tuesday," Fred Weldbore recounted. "I remember particular because that's when my missus packs me trotter sandwiches, and that is what was in my lunch bag that day. Trotter and a bit of pickle."

Holmes shifted irritably. "Unless your culinary habits are relevant to your testimony you may pass on, Mr Weldbore. It was Tuesday, 2nd October 1888 and you were employed as a carpenter by Mssrs Gurner & Son in the construction of the new Cannon Row police headquarters upon the Victoria Embankment. Take your statement from there."

The workman nodded, cowed. "Well, it were the day before, really, the Monday. Cheese and chutney day, that was. We'd been fitting out some of the cellar rooms left over from when there was going to be that theatre there."

"The site was previously intended as a Grand National Opera House before lack of funding brought building to a close," Holmes told me. "Extensive cellars laid down for prop storage and dressing rooms are being incorporated as foundations for the new construction."

"Aye, that's it," Weldbore agreed. "There's a proper warren of rooms down here. The deepest ones go right down below the level of the river. You know the old Thames once ran over the site, 'till they made the Embankment to pen it up? It's reclaimed land, and the cellars were built while they were filling in the banking to 'old back the river."

section of his work *Sherlock Holmes* to such an investigation, hypothesising that Holmes secretly uncovered the killer to be no other than Inspector Athelney Jones (who does not appear in the Canon after November 1888, time of the last of the Ripper's depredations). Many other writers have likewise set Victorian Britain's best-known crimefighter against its most infamous real-life monster.

Since Doyle chose not to reference the Ripper, the current author has elected to follow his lead. Those with other preferences are at liberty to imagine the great detective feverishly working on that case alongside his other endeavours recorded in the present tale. Further discussion on this matter may be found in I.A. Watson's article "Sherlock Holmes vs. Jack the Ripper" in *Sherlock Holmes, Consulting Detective volume 7*, ISBN 0692387196.

"Monday or Tuesday," Holmes prompted.

"Monday. It was Monday morning. I'd left my tools locked away in one of the little rooms down the east side corridor of the second basement. I don't always lug 'em home, that bag being cruel heavy for a man of my years. But I always sees 'em hidden a bit and locked tight. We still get tramps creeping in for a night's accommodation sometimes, like they did in the months the place was abandoned before work started again."

"You locked your tools away when?" Holmes interrogated.

"Saturday afternoon, when we knocked off. Except it wasn't me as locked up, it was my labourer, Dickie. Richard Lawrence, that is. Good lad but careless with a lathe. It was six on the dot when I started work of Monday and went to pick up my bag. But it wasn't there."

"What did you do?"

"Well, I had a good poke round for it. Not that I found it there, of course, for Dickie had already come in and taken it up to where we'd be working. Meaning well like, but the lad's not got a brain in his head to tell me 'afore I want traipsing down into the dark. But as I was poking round in the corners I first saw that there bundle, didn't I?"

Holmes leaned forward. "What did you see, Mr Weldbore?"

"Not that much, then. There's a fair old bit of debris had collected down there in the time the place was empty, and digging mess from a drain we were making. I thought it was just more rubbish that had been dumped. A black rag wrapping something, or maybe it was an old coat. I thought perhaps someone had thrown away a rotten ham. You'd be amazed what gets tossed onto a building works, sirs, and them navvies will bundle it anywhere to avoid having to shift it off-site. I didn't bother looking 'cause it wasn't my tool-bag. I didn't give it no thought."

"It was there by 6 am on Monday 1st," Holmes noted. "Would Lawrence have noticed it if it had been present on the Saturday?"

The carpenter shrugged. "I can't honestly say, sir." He gestured around him at the vaults where he worked. "You can see 'ow gloomy it is down here, even in daytime. The room we used as lock-up is darker still, with no proper windows. That's why we thought it was safe, see? Anyway, the bundle was in a recess in the darkest bit of the room. I might not have seen it meself if I'd not been hunting for my kit."

"Did you apprehend anything else about it at that time? Any odour?"

"Nothing. And that night, Monday night, about fiveish when we was knocking off, I came back to put my tools safe and it was still there. Arthur Cope, he was with me and I pointed it out to 'im. 'We should tell foreman about that,' I says. 'If it's rotten meat we'll have more rats than ever.' And I did strike a light to 'ave a better look at it, but it was just a black bundle. That's what I thought, then."

"That takes us to Tuesday again," Holmes observed. "Were you the one who opened the storeroom and retrieved your possessions?"

"I believe I was, sir. I was reminded to mention the package to Mr Brown, that is the assistant foreman on site, so when we stopped for lunch I 'ad a word and drew it to 'is attention that there was a parcel of something abandoned downstairs."

"Were you there when the item was disturbed? When it was unwrapped?"

"Nossir. It wasn't 'till about three quarters of an hour later that I 'eard about what they found."

Where Weldbore was gaunt, George Brigden was plump. A few years ago the Gurner & Son labourer would have been strong and fit. Now he was running to seed. He peered nervously at Holmes as he was questioned. Perhaps his previous interrogators had been less subtle?

"It was Mr Cheque what sent me down there," he explained. "Mr Cheque is foreman bricklayer. Mr Brown 'ad told Mr Cheque what old Weldbore 'ad said about there being a side of bacon dumped down in the second basement, so Mr Cheque sends me down with a lamp to 'eave it out and get rid of it."

"This was around 1.20 in the afternoon of the 2nd," Holmes checked.

"Yes, if that were the Tuesday. So I went down there to 'ave a look at the job. The parcel was just where I was told, in the far corner next to rubble from the drain excavation."

"Was it dusty?" Holmes enquired urgently. "Was there evidence to show whether the package had been there before the latest debris was piled in the room, or did it lay atop scattered soil from the spill-heap?"

Brigden looked baffled. "I… I can't rightly say, sir. I didn't…"

"Carry on, Mr Brigden," I intervened. Holmes could vent his frustrations on some other victim for not being asked to the crime scene in a timely manner.

The labourer crushed his soft cap in his nervous fingers. "I took a lantern and dragged the parcel out where I could see it, like. It were black cloth, not rough stuff like you'd expect, but more like a lady's dress. There was a sort of lacy pattern to it, like as you might see on a posh curtain. It was bundled up with string, so I got out my pocket-knife and cut that. Then I could unwrap it, and I saw…"

"Go on, man," Holmes urged.

"It were a dead woman. Well, part of one. A body, but no 'ead or arms or legs, cut away just under the belly. No clothes. Bloody, but all dried brown like rust and crusted everywhere. 'Er skin was near black with rot and once 'er wrapping was loose the stench was nightmarish. I tell you, sirs, I 'aven't had a good night's sleep since that moment, and never 'as my Pledge[4] been so sorely tested."

"Was the inside of the fabric package also encrusted?" Holmes wanted to know. "No matter, I shall see for myself. Carry on with what you did, Brigden."

"Well, I was… I didn't rightly know what to do. So I hollers for 'em to get Mr Brown, and down he comes and sees what was there and he sends to fetch Mr Cheque. We all stand there looking at this gory 'orror and at last Mr Cheque gets 'is wits and tells Mr Brown off to go to King Street Police Station. And all the lads got word of what we'd found and wanted to come and see but Mr Cheque sent them about their business and said that nobody was to come in until a policeman was brought."

"From the time you called for help about your discovery there were several of you present at the scene at all times?"

"Well, me and Mr Cheque at least. And later Ernest Edge brought some more light. I thought he was going to faint when 'e saw the lass, but whether from the sight of 'er mangled remains or 'er bare boobies I cannot say."

*　　　*　　　*

Assistant foreman Charles William Brown was a man of careful habits, well able to outline information cogently enough to almost satisfy even Sherlock Holmes.

"We have been working on the Cannon Street site about three months now. The architect is Richard Norman Shore. He was personally selected by Mr Matthews the Home Secretary to design New Scotland Yard. His plans make use of the existing foundations for the projected opera house. The eventual construction will be a Romanesque block of red brick and

---

4   'The Pledge' was a vow first introduced by Joseph Livesy at his Preston Temperance Society in 1833. It became a popular promise to which those seeking to escape alcohol addiction would sign: "We agree to abstain from all liquors of an intoxicating quality whether ale, porter, wine or ardent spirits, except as medicine."

white portland on a base of granite."[5]

"Describe the security arrangements," demanded Holmes.

"As you will have seen on your way in, during construction the site is closed from the road by seven foot hoardings, with entrances on Cannon Row and the Embankment. It would be difficult for anybody who did not labour on the site or have business with the clerk of works to enter unnoticed during the daytime. At night the site is sealed off. Ingress with a heavy package over the Embankment fence or gate would be difficult. Why not simply toss the bundle into the Thames instead? But there was no watchman."

My friend clearly caught some sign of hesitation or evasion to which I was blind. "What concerns you about the provision at night, Mr Brown?" he demanded.

"Ah, well… the fellow who locks up, Edge, has since confessed to police that there was a flaw in our arrangement. It was evidently possible to reach through a gap in the fence and grasp the piece of string which raises the latch and allows admission. Apparently all the workforce knows how to do it."

"So anyone who knew the trick might have got in after work was done, any time after dark," I accused.

"That is so. Nobody had mentioned the flaw to me. The workforce evidently found it convenient."

Holmes waved a hand to dismiss the problem for now. "Describe the events of 2nd October as you experienced them."

The assistant foreman nodded. "It was Weldbore who drew my attention to the package. He mentioned that some old meat might have been dumped there and that it would attract vermin if not attended to. I instructed one of the general labourers, Brigden, to go down and see what was there and to dispose of it. That would be at the end of lunch break, 1.15pm."

"He went alone?"

"Only one man was necessary. Brigden is strong. It was a busy time for us. Everyone was occupied erecting the topping scaffold or finishing the drainage channels. The Embankment site is reclaimed land, still prone to flooding if not properly vented. Brigden must have discovered the corpse around 1.25. He set up a shout for me to come and the message was passed

---

5   Now called the Norman Shaw Buildings, this pair of Grade II and Grade I listed properties constituted New Scotland Yard from 1890-1967 and are now used as parliamentary offices. It is currently the official base of the Leader of the Opposition, the Shadow Prime Minister of the largest minority political party.

that I was required. I attended immediately to see what was wrong."

"Who was present when you arrived?"

"In the vault, only Brigden himself. There were a few other men clustered at the doorway—Lawrence, Edge, Foster—but all were reluctant to enter. A short while after I got there, Mr Cheque also came down."

Holmes sat forward, hands clasped with index fingers pressed together, intent. "What did you see?"

"First I noticed Bridgen's face, pale in the lamplight as if he had seen a ghost. His hand was trembling on the lantern. I had to take the lamp myself to steady it and to train it on the bundle. Then I saw the parcel. Brigden had cut some string that held it fast and had pulled away a black fabric wrapping. Inside was a torso, unmistakably a woman despite significant decay; or rather most of a torso, since it had been severed at the pelvis. The effect was quite macabre."

"Were there any signs of blood apart from where the body lay? Splashes or sprays to suggest that she had died *in situ*?"

"I did not look. I understand that a thorough search by police officers later discovered no such marks."

"Stick with what *you* saw and did, Mr Brown. What next?"

"I held converse with Mr Cheque. We determined that I would summon assistance whilst he kept vigil over the body. I hastened upstairs and thence to the police station. Upon hearing my statement an Inspector and a uniformed constable were dispatched to take charge."

Holmes snorted his derision of how such charge had been taken, but remained intent on Mr Brown. "You are intimately familiar with the worksite. How easy would it have been to access the vault in darkness?"

"Without a lamp? Well nigh impossible for a stranger. I have navigated those cellars myself without a light, but only because I know them well. There are, as you can see, areas where the floors are not finished and holes where drainage trenches are being lined. The chamber where we found the corpse was one such room. Safe entry required balancing over several planks. A stranger without illumination would have toppled into the exposed hole beneath, especially if that stranger shouldered a weight."

"There had been excavation. When was the room last worked in?"

"I can attest with certainty that the parcel was not present on the Friday afternoon before. That was when Mr Franklin, our surveyor, was in the chamber taking measurements. I was present, along with our clerk of works Mr Ereult and several other men. Had the body been there at that time it would have been obvious, even in the corner where Weldbore discovered it."

Holmes allowed himself a moment's satisfaction. The window of time during which the unfortunate lady's remains had been abandoned was now narrowed between Friday evening and Monday morning. The site had been deserted from mid-afternoon Saturday until half past five *ante meridian* on Monday.

There was another aspect to the case which had not yet come up in our former interviews. "The second discovery, yesterday," Holmes ventured. "Were you present when the reporters Waring and Angle inspected this chamber?"

Mr Brown stiffened with disapproval at the journalists' intrusion. "They had acquired a note of hand from young Mr Gurner securing permission to enter the site," the deputy foreman told us, referring to his company's director. "We have had several such intrusions from thrill-seekers and publicity-hounds since the tragedy of the 2nd." He did not go so far as to accuse Holmes and I of being ranked in that number, but I could see that even England's premiere detective was not quite proper enough for the particular works officer.

"Then you were here when they made their search with their Spitz terrier?"

"Only at the first. I have many duties. I left them in the care of Earnest Edge, whose role now extends to keeping watch upon the site on occasion. He had orders to remain with them at all times. You would be shocked what minor items sensationalist souvenir-hunters have attempted to purloin from the site as keep-sakes."

"How did you learn of the dog's discovery?"

"Edge sent word with one of the apprentices. I came down, saw what had been unearthed, and sent again to King Street police station."

"Describe what you saw upon entering the chamber."

Brown considered his reply, assembling his description with his customary precision. "The terrier, which I understand was owned by the reporter Tilbury, had dug a hole into one of the debris mounds in the furthest left corner of the room, on the far side from the alcove where the torso had been discovered."

"These piles had been present all along, since the first find?" my friend clarified.

"There were four such spoil heaps, piles of dirt and clay taken up in cutting the drainage trenches, retained close by for backfilling the holes when the pipes have been sealed. I had been given to understand that they had been searched before by the constables who disrupted our work the day after the former discovery. Certainly the officers made sufficient mess

"These piles had been present all along, since the first find?"

for me to believe the piles had been thoroughly sifted. However, it now appears that the men may not have been as diligent as their inspectors might have wished."

"They had missed something," I summarised.

"Indeed they had, Dr Watson. The dog burrowed close to the base of a mound, scraping out a tunnel for himself in the manner of such animals. He was worrying at something, so the journalists convinced Edge to summon other labourers, who should have been engaged elsewhere, to shovel out whatever the terrier had found. They unearthed a very grubby package, a parcel of brown paper tied with string, but the whole blackened with mud and London clay. The reporters opened it without permission—Edge had not the wit to halt them or to send for instruction—and discovered another human part. In this case it was a putrescent and terribly rotted foot. The stench was most unpleasant, sufficient that men working in the cellar on the other side of the corridor complained of it."

"What happened after the discovery?"

"The journalists were very excited, of course, having found themselves what they referred to as 'an exclusive'. There was a good deal of unseemly congratulation and backslapping and a great fuss was made of the terrier, which became uncontrollable and shot around the vault yipping. Eventually order was restored. I insisted that the new parcel be set aside and not interfered with further, so that it might be properly examined by experts at the appropriate time."

Holmes made a guttural noise of approval.

Mr Brown nodded acknowledgement but continued ruefully. "Whilst I was securing the package in my office, Mssrs. Waring and Angle remained in the cellar. They encouraged the men to deepen the hole. By the time I returned with constables and an inspector they had uncovered another packet from the spoil heap. That one proved to have a quantity of human thigh enclosed within."

"The police cannot be happy to have missed two significant discoveries only to have gentlemen of the press unearth the evidence," I considered.

"I cannot speak to that," Mr Brown replied. "When the policemen came, all further searches were halted until an inspector from the Detective Branch appeared. Thereafter a more careful and planned search was made of each spoil heap, and subsequently of all other mounds in the other chambers, but no further discovery was made."

"You saw all three packages, Mr Brown," said Holmes. "Two were wrapped in paper, one in cloth, all knotted with strings. Did you note whether the packaging was consistent? Were they all neat, all knotted in a particular way, all folded alike?"

"I did observe something of the kind," the assistant foreman owned. "The parcels were well wrapped, as if for mailing. The string was twisted along both axis of the packages, properly secured and tied off with what were probably square knots. Extraneous loose ends had been trimmed short. The wrappers were common brown paper and seemed identical. There was no marking upon them save for the staining from their burial. There was no dried blood on the interior of the paper parcels, although some very unpleasant seeping of putrescence. In short, I would say all of the packages were sealed in a workmanlike manner."

"When were the piles of dirt first heaped in the cellar?"

"That would be at the commencement of the laying of the deep drain, on the 15th *ult*. Or rather that would be the first of them, which was where the dog unearthed the parcels. The others were added as required between then and the 18th." A clatter from somewhere above and a sharp crude oath drew the foreman's attention. "I have been absent from my work for some time. Is there more you wish from me?"

Holmes was satisfied. He even ventured a small thanks to the assistant foreman for his testimony.

— — —

Ernest Edge was not a man who inspired my confidence. The site labourer had been given the duty of securing the premises after each work-day; I would not have trusted him to look after a shovel. Under Holmes' careful consideration he sweated and squirmed like a schoolboy caught in the pantry.

"You have already sold your testimony," Holmes began.

"What? No. Oh no, sirs, I wouldn't do that."

"Your boots are new. So is your hat. You have recently partaken of a dinner of oysters, the remains of which are evident upon your lapel. You have come into a small amount of money but it seems large compared to your usual expectations."

Edge paled. "But…"

"I am less concerned that you have sold information to the press than that you give information to me now, Mr Edge. I presume it was you who tipped off the newspapers as to the original discovery so that they flocked here so soon after Bridgens's find?"

"I don't know nothing about that."

I lost patience. "Oh come, man! This is Sherlock Holmes to whom you speak. He has already read every guilty secret you conceal. Cease this pointless subterfuge and tell us what you know!"

The labourer squirmed more. Holmes directed him with a question. "You are responsible for securing these works at locking up time. Does that include walking the premises? Would you come down here?"

"Of course. 'Course I would. We've 'ad tramps in before now, and they make an awful mess even without the thieving and the setting of fires."

"So you checked each evening before you sealed the premises?"

"Oh yes. I goes to each room, every one."

"And yet you did not notice the discarded bundle that contained a torso. We have testimony that it was present at least on Monday night."

Edge cringed. "Well, it so 'appens that on Monday night I was in a bit of a hurry. It was race night at the dog track, so I was... well I made a quick job of it. They lock that room anyhow so I knew it would be secure."

"You didn't check in there on Monday," I verified.

"I didn't see no need. I didn't see no 'arm. I looked everywhere else."

Holmes pressed on. "You were not present on the Sunday. The site was unmanned. Did you check the room in question on Saturday the twenty-ninth?"

"I did sir." He clearly saw the scepticism on our faces because he protested more, "No, I did! See, one of my duties at the weekend is to check the fence round the site to make sure all the boards are secure. There were a couple coming loose that needed nailing back. I needed an 'ammer, see? And I knows that Fred Weldbore hides 'is kit down there, and I 'ad the spare key for the padlock on my ring, so I nipped down there and borrowed 'is tools to fix up the loose planks. I put all 'is stuff back. Old Fred would've made a right fuss if any of his kit went missing."

"So you went into the room. Did you see the bundle?"

Edge shook his head. "It wasn't there, sirs. I swear to it. I 'ad to grope around a bit, not 'aving a lamp but only lucifers as light, and Fred liking to hide 'is toolbag. As I lit my match I must 'ave stood in the very spot where that package was later on."

"You secured the room again after you?" Holmes checked.

"Nice and tight, sirs. You can't pin any of this on me!"

"Describe security when the site is empty. What happens after you nail up the fence and go home?"

Edge swallowed nervously. Clearly he'd been interviewed harshly on this topic before. "Well, there wasn't a night watchman then. There is now, o' course. Management didn't want the expense, and there were seven-foot hoardings all round the place. But we started getting vagrants climbing them, and one time they broke into the works office, so we nailed strings of that new barbed wire on the top to stop 'em. You could probably still get over, but not without getting scratched up something cruel."

"There are two gates," I remembered.

"Yessir. But at night they're bolted and padlocked from the inside, except for a small let-in gate on Cannon Row. That 'as a lever latch on it so a fellow outside can open it with a key."

"And apparently without one," Holmes noted, recalling the evidence of Mr Brown.

Edge winced again. "Yeah, well, not everyone what needs a key gets one. If one of the lads is first in come morning, he don't want to be waiting round in the cold for some foreman to turn up. So there's this little arrangement—well there was. You slip one of the boards aside and you can get your hand on a bit of string joined to the lever of the latch. Pull that and it opens the lock. It was just convenience, sirs, and secret if you didn't know about it."

"All the workforce knew, though?" I checked.

"Well, most of 'em," Edge agreed. He tried a confidential wink. "A few of the apprentices found it convenient come a Saturday night sometimes, I don't doubt, if they needed a place for a bit of a cuddle with their best girl."

"And did a coin find its way into your pocket to leave such a convenience in place?" I wondered.

"No. No of course not. I'd never do anything like that, sirs!"

Holmes tapped out his pipe and refilled it, perhaps to give himself time to think. "Is there any way known to you, Mr Edge, that a bundle the size of a ham might be brought on site during normal daytime operations without it being noted?"

"What, get past Fussy Brown? I shouldn't think so. Why he..."

"At night, by what routes might such a parcel be carried onto the premises? Remember that the thing was bulky and weighing about four or five stone."

Edge evidently hadn't been asked this before. He paused and frowned before answering. "Well, it would've been 'ard to come over the fence. A bundle like that might've caught on the wire. Only gate in would be Cannon Row. No way to open the rest from outside. I'd say it 'as to be that way, unless you're talking about a lot of men and a wagon to stand on or something."

I noted that the watchman had a criminal turn of mind.

Holmes moved on to the more recent incident of the dog's discoveries. "You were the man detailed to accompany the reporters Waring and Tilbury around the site yesterday."

"I was. Mr Brown, he set me on it, on account of he has no time for 'impertinent questions and sensationalist buffoonery' as he puts it. I've 'ad to show a dozen or more parties round the premises by now."

And had received a useful tip for his services from the thrill-seekers, I did not doubt.

"Did the journalists indicate to you why they had elected to turn up some two weeks after the discovery, bringing a scent-hound?" Holmes wondered.

"Dunno, sir. That fellow from the *Globe*, Angle that'd be, he was givin' the orders, like. Waring was just a correspondent for central news, but 'e owned the dog, see? They'd got themselves a pass from one of the bosses, so Fussy, 'e couldn't do aught but nod 'em past and let 'em get on with it."

"Did they examine any other spaces except the room where the torso was found?"

"Nah. Besides, yesterday was when they were putting in the timberworks for the wainscoting. It was a right racket, all that 'ammering. When we got to the vault we 'ad to shut the door to 'ear ourselves think."

"What happened then? Did they loose the dog generally or direct him to a particular area."

"Waring just loosed the pup's collar and said 'Sniff 'em out, boy,' or the like. The little fellow starts snuffling round, nose to the mud, all over the room. 'Ad a good old smell at that archway where the gruesome 'orrible remains was found, but they pulled 'im off that and set him scenting again. It must 'ave been upwards of 'alf an 'our before he found the fatal mound."

Edge had a tendency to speak like a Penny Dreadful. I suspect he'd been supplementing his income, certainly his free drinks intake, with accounts of his adventures.

He caught Holmes' disapproving frown and went on with his account more directly. "The dog starts to burrow 'is way into the soil, spraying it all over. You know 'ow terriers are going down a rabbit 'ole! Then he backs out, worrying something in his jaws what 'e couldn't pull loose. Took Waring a moment or two to calm 'im down enough to get 'im out of the 'ole. Then I called in a few of the lads to bring spades to 'ave whatever-it-was out of the pile."

"How did the reporters react to the discovery?"

"Surprised, I reckon. But 'appy. We all hop… thought it might be another bit of lady. And it was!"

"What about the second find? Mr Brown was off securing the severed foot from journalistic enthusiasm. You remained in the vaulted cellar with Angle and Waring?"

"I 'ad me orders to stick with 'em whatever. It'd be just like a reporter to go fall 'imself into the deep well and get drowned, and then the company would be liable."

"How did they come to search further? What did they say?"

Edge rubbed his chin. "Well, they were chatting, right animated. Pleased as punch. 'There'll be a nice tip in this for me,' I was thinking. Then Angle says, 'But what if that's not all? Might there be more?' and his mate says, 'The dog's game to go again. Shall we 'ave 'im back in there?' So they show the dog the rabbit, so to speak, and in the little chap goes as if 'ed spied a ferret. 'There's another one,' Waring says, and Angle agrees with 'im. So the boys go in with their shovels again and, lo and behold, another gory bundle! Mr Brown and them police inspectors were proper put out, I reckon."

"Did the reporters open the second find before the police arrived?" I wondered.

"Nah. They were thinking of chancing it but then everyone turned up. Then they was made to stand in a corner and wait while that sour old fellow from Scotland Yard poles up."

"You mean Inspector Gregson?"

"Tow-topped beanpole? Face like a lemon? I never did get his name."

The description was, alas, sufficient to identify one of Scotland Yard's pre-eminent investigators.

"One last point," Holmes told Edge. "When the original incident happened two weeks ago you summoned the press. How did you know whom to call?"

"Ah. Well, that was a bit of luck, see? It so 'appens that I was talking to a bloke in the pub and 'e was buying a round because 'e'd got half a guinea for tipping off the *Telegraph* about this coach accident on Farringdon Road. So I remembered that, and when everyone was milling about giving orders and Fussy Brown was off to the police I thought to myself, 'Ernest, old lad, now's a chance to make a bit of something'. There was no 'arm in it. None at all. I didn't do nothing wrong."

"How long before the gristly discovery was it that you encountered the fortunate reveller in a public house?" my friend enquired.

Edge calculated. "Let's see. They found the lass on the Tuesday, right? So it'd be Saturday night in the Brown Cow. Three days before, Mr 'Olmes. 'Ow's that for a spot of luck?"

We examined the site. It was a vaulted cellar, the middle of three chambers formed by foundation arches. Gregson stood off to one side, arms folded, leaning against a wall as if to dissociate himself from our explorations.

Holmes insisted that the gloomy room be properly lit. He conscripted a half dozen labourers to port lanterns into the chamber. The lights were set on stands to illuminate the space. Then my friend ruined his trousers by crawling over the muddy floor, inspecting it with eyes and fingers, ignoring us and the world.

"We have already done this," Inspector Gregson objected. "Twice."

"That much is evident, from the procession of constabulary boot-marks marring any possibility of clues," Holmes jibed. He carried on.

"The first police search evidently missed two body parts," I reminded the Scotland Yard man.

"I did not conduct the first search," he replied with dignity.

"We must allow Holmes the opportunity to employ his methods," I reminded him as I had before. "A carelessly emptied pipe, a discarded coin, may mean nothing to us but everything to him."

"He has some lucky guesses, I admit," Gregson allowed.

"Inviting Holmes here was not your idea," I surmised.

"We can get along very handily usually without the need for... outside help," the policeman edited himself. Although Gregson had sometimes admitted relief at Holmes' attendance he naturally felt that the Detective Branch should be able to function without one genius' constant supervision and interference.

"You must get that bunion on your left heel attended to, Gregson," Holmes called out as he examined tracks. "You may wish to consult Dr Watson if your gherkin and vinegar plaster is not effective."

The Inspector scowled at me. "He only does that to annoy."

"Holmes has his methods."

"And have those methods found anything that the best of Scotland Yard has failed to discover?" Gregson sneered.

Holmes sneered back. "After two weeks of police bumbling and public visits? There is very little left to learn, save for the lack of foresight from men who should now be better versed in the protocols of forensic investigation. A few trifles, perhaps. You noticed the faint scratches upon the door padlock indicative of it being picked?"

That was significant. "So the intruder did not posses a key," I deduced.

"*An* intruder at the time of the crimes or otherwise was familiar with burglary tools and locksmithing. You will observe that the scrapes are fresh but not shiny, indicating that they were made earlier than yesterday but certainly in the last month or so. A useful indicator, Watson; but more significant is the location of the finds themselves."

"You mean this is an odd place for them to be hidden?" I understood.

"On a building site that contains open drainage ditches, a crude deep well, and countless spoil heaps where the remains might have been concealed forever, and right beside the convenient River Thames, our quarry instead elected to traverse a dangerous and complicated route to one of the least accessible rooms, to place a bundle that must inevitably be eventually found."

"So you think the murderer is a workman here," Gregson decided. "I knew some of them were shifty characters. That Brigden, for example, and the caretaker Edge..."

"Kindly refrain from accusing random staff until I am further along in my investigation," Holmes snapped. "I am certain there will be time for your usual ham-fistedness later on. For now I need to record some observations, and reserve my opinions so that you do not run around terrorising witnesses."

The great detective inspected the walls with a magnifying lens then returned to the print-churned floor with its muddy whorls. "Men, woman, and at least two dogs," he muttered sourly.

I distracted Gregson. "You clearly didn't wish to bring us into this, Inspector. Why then are we here?"

"As you have heard, there is considerable pressure for some resolution," the Scotland Yard man sniffed. "It was felt by my superiors, men who have not had to work with Mr Sherlock Holmes, that he might expedite a solution."

"The Home Secretary is said to have taken an interest."

"I wouldn't know about that. 'Bring Holmes in', I'm told, so here I am putting up with it."

"And so graciously, Mr Gregson," Holmes called from behind the pile of now-scattered debris that had concealed the swathed torso. "Now a question for you. This site has been repeatedly trampled. It has been inspected by many hands, competent and otherwise. Who has examined the scene?"

Gregson shrugged. "Who hasn't? Thomas Hawkings, the inspector from King Street station, was first man on the spot. I suppose he looked around. He gave testimony at the coroner's inquest. Detective Inspector Marshall was next in, with a pair of constables to make immediate enquiries. Then Chief Superintendent Dunlap and Chief Inspector Wren."[6]

"There was a reporter from the *Daily Telegraph* newspaper searching the scene within half an hour of the discovery," Holmes chided. He had done his homework, of course.[7]

"I wasn't in charge of the scene," Gregson grumped. "Scotland Yard wasn't called until later on. Before that Dr Bond was summoned to view the body *in situ*."

I knew Bond, the police's divisional-surgeon. He was a good fellow, both competent and diligent.[8] "Bond would take good notes, Holmes. He may have noticed something before the curious erased all traces."

"There was also Troutbeck, the district coroner. He gave orders to abstract the remains to Milbank-street mortuary. After it was removed there were a number of other searches of the chamber, authorised and unofficial."

"When did you make your investigation, Gregson?" Holmes wondered. Despite his habitual abruptness with the inspector, I have heard Holmes refer to him as 'the smartest of the Scotland Yarders'.[9]

"My first proper search was only yesterday. I regret now not insisting on rechecking the work of colleagues from King Street, but so many of them had been here poking around that I never thought they could all…" Gregson broke off, unwilling to criticise fellow detectives to outsid-

---

6   The main ranks of the British police force have changed little since their institution in 1829. In ascending order they are: Constable, Sergeant, Inspector, Chief Inspector, Superintendent, Chief Superintendent, Assistant Chief Constable, Deputy Chief Constable, Chief Constable, Deputy Commissioner, Commissioner. Investigative officers prefix the title "Detective', as in Detective Constable (DC), Detective Sergeant (DS), Detective Inspector (DI), Detective Chief Inspector (DCI), Detective Superintendant (*not* DS) etc. Women police constables, first appointed in the early 20th century, are referred to as WPCs in the same way as male constables are PCs, but no other title differences exist for female officers.

UK Inspectors roughly equate to US Lieutenants and UK Chief Inspectors to US Captains.

7   The *Daily Telegraph* report to which Holmes alludes was published on 3rd October 1888 and is reproduced at https://en.wikisource.org/wiki/The_Whitehall_Murder

8   Surgeon Dr Thomas Bond FRCS, MB BS (1841–1901) is often cited as the first offender profiler. He is best remembered now for his investigation of the Jack the Ripper murders.

9   Watson reports Holmes' comment to this effect in *A Study in Scarlet*, although Holmes then added, "He and Lestrade are the pick of a bad lot."

ers. "When I was summoned after the second and third discoveries I took charge of the scene. I had a police bloodhound brought in. I personally supervised the sifting of the spoil piles again, in the chamber and elsewhere. I had men empty the well anew and sound the bottom. We even dredged the middens. There are no other remains to be uncovered here."

Holmes stood, brushing the dirt off his hands onto his trousers. "To the mortuary, then," he determined. "Let us see what the dead woman can tell us."

— — —

Dr Bond welcomed us to the mortuary with the air of a man who has been receiving daily telegrams from his superiors about his lack of progress. I shook hands and renewed our acquaintance and he then led us down to the cold-room where the remains were preserved.

"They are considerably decayed now," he warned us. "I've suspended them in a solution of oil to retard further atrophy."

"You conducted the post mortem," I verified.

"With the assistance of Mr Charles Hebburn,[10] the appointed coroner," the Divisional-Surgeon agreed. "The examination took place on the morning of Wednesday the third."

Holmes peered at the large jar in which a blackened shape now hung suspended in solution. The silhouette was that of a woman's torso, though unusually clipped off below the belly. It was in an advanced state of decay. "What did you find, Dr Bond?" he asked as he inspected the remains.

"The trunk is of a woman of considerable stature, aged between twenty-five and forty. It was in an advanced state of putrefaction. The length of the trunk is 17 inches and the circumference of the waist is 35 inches. In life she probably stood at around five feet eight inches. I estimate death to have been approximately twenty days before discovery."

"On or about the twelfth of September," I calculated. At that time, Holmes, his brother, Gregson, and I had been deeply absorbed by the murky events around Mr Melas, Mr and Miss Kratides, and the unpleasant Latimer.[11]

10   It seems as through newspapers misspelling names is not a new phenomena. Various different versions of names associated with the case are offered from differing sources. Coroner Hebburn is also described as 'Charles Alfred Herbert', but must not be confused with his senior, district coroner Troutbeck. Mr Weldbore is also referred to as Mr Wilboe. There are various versions of 'Bugden'. Different accounts have different police officers attending the scene. Our present narrative uses whichever names struck the author as being most likely or most euphonious.

11   "The Adventure of the Greek Interpreter"

Holmes peered at the large jar...

Bond did not need to refer to his notes to report his findings. "The head was severed from the trunk through the sixth cervical vertebra, which has been sawn through. Limbs and pelvis had been removed. Arms were removed at the shoulder joints by several downward cuts over the body. The neck was divided by several incisions and then sawn through."

I tried to make observations through the glass jar. "This skin discolouration, is that some effect of the preservative?" I checked.

"Noticed that, did you?" Bond approved. "No, that was there when she came in. More than rot, that. She's been painted with some kind of solution to keep the stink down, perhaps Condy's Fluid or something like it."

Condy's crystals are permanganate of potash,[12] an oxidising agent and disinfectant used in water treatment, as a basic cure for canker sores, dermatitis, and fungal skin infections, and as an illicit abortion treatment. Some doctors prescribe Condy's Fluid for Scarlet Fever. Mixed in water it produces a pinkish-purple solution. When dried out, it leaves a dark purple crystal crust such as that which contributed to the blackened look of the torso in the jar.

"You have images of the torso as it was when you first had it?" Holmes asked.

Dr Bond produced a number of photographic exposures. "See there? The stuff was already on her, mixed with some crusted post-mortem fluid seepage."

Holmes' fingers traced the images. "Those are clearly defined marks of where the string had been tied. The parcel was wrapped up in a skilful manner to prevent odours and fluids escaping. You have the garment and the string?"

"Those have been taken elsewhere. You would need to refer to one of the inspectors on the case."

Holmes frowned.

"Internal organs?" I enquired of the pathologist.

"There was no fluid in the lungs to suggest drowning, or any indication of suffocation. In life this woman suffered severe pleurisy. From the condition of the breasts this woman has never birthed a child. She may well have been unmarried. There may have been surgery done at some time to

---

12   Nowadays called potassium permanganate, $KMnO_4$, the substance is often included in survival kits since it can be used to purify water, for creating distress signals in snow, and when mixed with antifreeze is a useful fire starter. It is often employed in film and TV production to make props appear aged. In Dr Watson's time, Condy's Fluid was used as an early photographer's flash powder, and as an abortifacient before medical science demonstrated how harmful it was to the woman upon whom it was used.

the left breast, or it may simply be an artefact of advanced decomposition."

"No sign or cause of death?"

"Certainly no force trauma or insult to this part of her body," Bond reported. "The heart was pale and unclotted, suggesting she had lost a lot of blood whilst it was still pumping. The criss-cross marks of the cords had sunk deeply into the skin, as Holmes observed, but otherwise there were no appearances of wounds except where the rough edges indicate the brutal, bungling manner in which the head, limbs, and lower part of the body were dissevered."

Holmes turned his inspection to the smaller preservation jars, where a woman's left foot and a portion of upper leg waited to tell their tale.

"The sole is free from bunions, corns, and blisters," the detective observed. "The nails are neatly trimmed. There are none of the calluses I would have expected from cheaper boots or from clogs, or from going barefoot. The foot was separated from the ankle in the same manner as the cuts to the torso."

"Are you saying that these parts come from the body of a gentlewoman?" I checked. "Surely such a lady's absence would be noted and reported?"

"I can think offhand of a half dozen scenarios to avert that, Watson. The woman may be reported as confined for sickness, or to be travelling. She may have been recorded as deceased, either before or after her death."

"Her murder, you mean?"

"There is no conclusive proof of that," Dr Bond cautioned. "She may yet have died by accident or natural causes. We have no diagnosis of death. Not even with the other..." He glanced uncertainly at Holmes.

"Not even adding in the evidence from the other piece that has so far been discovered," the detective added, completing the uncertain surgeon's sentence.

My brows rose. "What? What other piece? Holmes, do you mean to say that the search turned up more limbs, or a head? Why has nobody mentioned it?"

"Nothing more was discovered on the Scotland Yard site," Dr Bond told me. "They even emptied out the well and sent men down into its muddy bottom. And yet..." He gestured to the shelf where other grisly remains floated in their bell jars.

"There has been another find recently," Holmes informed me. "The so-called 'Pimlico Mystery'..."

"You caught that link, eh?" Bond approved. "Yes, I had the remains sent over here on a hunch. It proved correct."

I confessed that I had not been following the newspapers as assiduously in the last month. I had been distracted.

Holmes supplied me with the information. "There was a gristly find near the Grosvenor Railway Bridge."

Dr Bond indicated one of his gruesome specimens. "This arm was brought up from the Thames mudflats on the 11th of last month. A fellow called Moore was at his place of work, a deal wharf in Grosvenor Road, when loungers on the Embankment noticed a limb lying at the water's edge. Moore waded out and retrieved it to pass on to the police."

Holmes moved to examine the remains. Bond continued my education. "It was mentioned in the more sensationalist papers, but there was no inquest, of course. The law demands enough of a body to prove certain death before an inquest is convened. A limb is insufficient. Until the torso discovery there was no grounds for a full public enquiry."

I also checked the dismembered arm. It was that of a plump female with well-kept nails and had been severed at the shoulder. A piece of blackened string was looped around the upper bicep.

"It is a fit," Bond admitted. "The piece adjoins perfectly."

Holmes turned his magnifier on the older find. "A well-nourished woman who was not accustomed to manual labour," was his immediate analysis. "The nails are well kept and the hand is free of calluses betraying regular work. This is a left arm but the third finger bears no evidence of wearing a ring." He turned to Dr Bond. "This part was found soon after it was severed, soon after death."

"If it is another part of the murdered lady from Scotland Yard then the timing matches that of Dr Bond's estimate," I contributed.

"This evidence has not been presented at the coroner's inquest," Holmes noted. Coroner Troutbeck had opened the hearing some ten days before. It was still ongoing.

"At the time I gave evidence I had not yet received the limb for inspection," the Divisional-Surgeon explained. "I expect to be recalled before the summing-up."

"I suppose records have been consulted for any other unclaimed body parts in recent days?" I checked.

"I have made a thorough search," Bond assured us, although I knew that Holmes would make verification of his own. "I have even examined the literature on the subject. The Harriet Lane murder and the Kate Webster case…"

Holmes' encyclopaedic knowledge of crime supplied me with the details. "In 1874, bankrupt brush manufacturer Henry Wainwright murdered Harriet Lane, his mistress of four years on whom he had fathered two children. He faked evidence of her departure to Brighton and her intention to move to the Continent with a new lover. In fact Wainwright concealed the corpse under the floor of his warehouse. A year later when bailiffs intended to seize the property, the murderer and his brother disinterred the rotting corpse, cut it up, and recruited former employees to help shift the bundled packages, each sealed similarly to those of our present case. One of the porters became suspicious of the shape and weight of his load and peeked inside his parcel, discovering Miss Lane's severed head and arm. He followed the Wainwrights' cab on foot and summoned a constable to apprehend the villains. Thomas Wainwright got seven years. Henry Wainwright hanged at Newgate."[13]

"Their crime might have been a template for this one," asserted Dr Bond.

"Except that the Wainwrights did not elect to place portions of their victim for discovery around London," Holmes pointed out.

"And the other case?" I asked, interested and horrified in equal parts.

"A worse business still, Watson. Kate Webster was thirty years old in 1879 when she took service in Richmond with the wealthy Mrs Julia Thomas. Her employer knew nothing of Webster's long list of convictions for theft and prostitution, nor of her drinking habits. The lady dismissed her maid after a month, but when Mrs Thomas returned from church she found Webster waiting for her with an axe. She was beaten to death, dismembered, and then her parts boiled down in a soup kettle. Webster sold her gold teeth and attempted to sell jars of 'best dripping' rendered from the corpse. Over the ensuing weeks she auctioned off the deceased's furniture and possessions, and disposed of the crated body parts with the aid of unwitting accomplices."

---

13   This real-life case promoted several of the "murder ballads" popular amongst the lower classes at the time. For example:

> "He had to suffer for this deed,
> And Justice she has held the sway,
> By murdering poor Harriet Lane,
> His life, the forfeit had to pay."

and

> "A most fearful murder has been brought to light,
> I'll describe it to you in the verses I write,
> A poor woman's body cut up has been found,
> Causing dismay Whitechapel around."

The late 19th century British nautical expression for canned meat was "Harriet Lane" after this notorious murder case. Further details of the murder are available online at http://murderpedia.org/male.W/w/wainwright-henry.htm

"Monstrous," I muttered.

"Her crimes were discovered when a neighbour became suspicious of furniture being removed from Mrs Thomas' house and summoned a policeman. Webster fled to her native Ireland but was arrested there. She denied all charges during her trial but made full confession to the chaplain before her hanging."[14]

Dr Bond took up the description. "The point of reference is that a box of body parts that Miss Webster and an accomplice threw from Richmond Bridge one night was discovered by a coal man the following morning. As Mrs Thomas had not then been reported missing the remains were unidentified, the affair referred to in the press as 'The Barnes Mystery'."

"You are suggesting that some undiscovered outrage of a similar nature has occurred again," I recognised.

"There is one significant difference," Holmes insisted. "In the Wainwright case the disjoining of the corpse was entirely as a mechanism of avoiding detection, a handy way to transport an otherwise inconvenient body. In the Webster case the murderess sought revenge for her dismissal and slights and sought to profit from the dissection. But in both instances the objective of the separation of parts was to conceal the crime."

"But not here?" Dr Bond asked.

"Consider the evidence, doctors," Holmes appealed to us. "The first limb is found discarded on a Thames mudflat, sufficiently high above the tideline that a man can walk out and retrieve it. It is left where it cannot help but be noticed, beside a railway bridge and the gathering place of riverside loungers."

---

14   The case promoted another "murder ballad", set to the tune of "Driven from Home":

The terrible crime at Richmond at last,
On Catherine Webster now has been cast,
Tried and found guilty she is sentenced to die.
From the strong hand of justice she cannot fly.
She has tried all excuses but of no avail,
About this and murder she's told many tales,
She has tried to throw blame on others as well,
But with all her cunning at last she has fell.

Mrs Thomas' skull was not recovered until 2010, when a pub associated with the case was acquired by naturalist and TV presenter David Attenborough. The skull was discovered during renovations. A coroner's inquest identified the remains and returned a verdict of unlawful killing, superseding the 1879 inquest's open verdict and closing the Barnes mystery 121 years after it had begun.

Details of this case and a collection of useful articles are available at http://murderpedia.org/female.W/w/webster-catherine.htm

"The torso was hidden away, though," I objected.

"Hidden where it was not immediately discovered, yes. But where its discovery at some time was inevitable."

"Do you imply that the killer wants to be caught?" wondered Bond. "That he is placing the body parts to draw attention?"

"I draw no conclusion as to his motive yet," Sherlock Holmes insisted. "I merely emphasise that whoever placed these dismembered parts did so in ways guaranteed to gain notice. One could scarcely choose a spot more likely to gain public interest or official intervention than the site of the future home of London's Detective Branch."[15]

"The other pieces were concealed," I reminded my friend. "They were found only by pure chance."

"Indeed, Watson? How fortunate that two struggling journalists took it upon themselves to have another look at the vault, eh? And how lucky Mr Edge was before that to have encountered a helpful fellow in his local who happened to mention a useful contact at a national newspaper that might pay for stories."

Dr Bond frowned. "Are those journalists complicit in the crime?"

"I shall interview them, of course, but I suspect they are rather tools being put to use than conspirators playing a conscious role. Someone is eager for the case to gain notoriety. That is the person whose identity must be discovered."

꤬ ꤬ ꤬

We interviewed a succession of journalists. The *Daily Telegraph* man who had received Edge's original tip-off was disappointed that his meeting must be off-the-record but offered useful collaborating detail about the original scene of the crime. It was from him that we learned that the dress used as wrapping for the lady's torso was of black mohair or something very similar, and that a tornure was wrapped with the body.

Being ignorant of women's fashion, I confess that I was then unfamiliar with the innovation now generally called a dress improver. This tornure is a development of the bustle, consisting of something like a full-length under-pinafore worn from the waist behind rather than in front. Designed to extend out the skirts to the rear, these items are constructed

---

15   Much of the factual information and the speculation on association with older crimes covered in this meeting with Dr Bond comes from an 8th October 1888 article in the *St James Gazette*, now preserved at https://en.wikisource.org/wiki/The_Whitehall_Discovery_Inquest_Today

of cane or metal wire, covered with fabric such as French crinoline, usually decorated with frills and flounces; or so Mary explained to me after our happy alliance when it was proper for us to discuss such matters.

The reporter testified that such an improver was bundled into the package with the torso, perhaps as extra padding to disguise the body's prominent bosom and make the parcel more regular in shape.

Questioned about Edge's contacting him with information about the discovery, he owned that a runner boy had come from the labourer bearing news and that he had hastened to the scene and bluffed his way in during the chaos. He had not previously encountered Ernest Edge but had indeed offered rewards before for information received, as Edge had heard. He viewed Edge as unreliable and greedy. He was aware of several parties who had since tipped the man for covert access to the site to thrillseek or in hopes of making fresh discoveries.

Jasper Waring, the correspondent for central news at Tilbury, confirmed that it was Edge who had arranged for them to access the site yesterday. Since the watchman had been warned by his supervisors about allowing more idlers into the cellars, Edge had recommended that permission be sought by note of authorisation from one of the company's owners. Waring and his partner-in-investigation W.H. Angle had tracked down the son of Mssrs Gurner & Son and had used the glamour of the press to convince him to grant access. Ernest Edge had received five shillings for his assistance.

Waring introduced us to his dog, Bertie, a lively terrier mongrel who was evidently a devil of a ratter. The little chap was a charmer, friendly and eager. I was well able to believe that his general character as much as his nose made him an excellent hunter.

It was Angle's idea to take another look at the scene. He had sought out Waring because he knew that Bertie was capable of following a scent. They had previously tried without success to use the fellow on other crime scenes. They had chosen to take another go at the cellar because Angle's editor was growing indifferent to more accounts of the daily doings of the inquest. Another line of investigation was required to fill the column inches.

Waring's account of Bertie's discoveries required stripping of journalistic hyperbole but otherwise accorded quite well with the testimony of Edge and of the diggers who had been called to open the mound. As with his other interview on this topic, Holmes was keen to know how deeply the parcels had been buried.

"Not too far," Waring judged. "Bertie only got as deep as his hind legs before he began to worry something. I'd say the first parcel was perhaps a foot inside the spoil heap, near to the base. The second was deeper, but nowhere near to the middle."

Angle proved harder to track, but Holmes brought him to heel at a seedy drinking hole in Shoreditch. Whether the reporter was on a story or enjoying his leisure I never determined. He did not welcome our intrusion and was a generally truculent witness.

"Anything I have to tell will be in the *Globe*," he boasted. "Buy a copy."

"There are elements of this case you would not wish to appear in your newspaper," Holmes advised him, "nor to come to the attention of your editor."

"What's that supposed to mean?" the fellow demanded.

"Your fortuitous idea to revisit the site yesterday; where did that come from?"

Under a degree of badgering and after a dose of the great detective's caustic diagnosis, Angle admitted that he had been inspired by a conversation in a public house. Some chap he did not know and had never seen before had struck up a conversation and the discussion had covered the Scotland Yard Murder. "He mentioned that if he had a bloodhound he would find occasion to go back to the scene and loose it to see what it might find," the journalist reported. "I thought it a rather good idea, so I got hold of a stringer I know who has a dog with a good nose. And what a story we found!"

Holmes extracted a description of the tavern stranger. He was a well-spoken man with an Oxford accent, wearing slightly shabby tweeds and button-up boots. He was aged somewhere between thirty and forty, was clean-shaven, and had unremarkable brown hair. It was hardly an appearance to make further identification easy.

"We now have two people associated with the case being helped along by a friendly stranger in a public bar," Holmes noted when we had left the unpleasant Angle to his skulking.

"You believe this to be the same man, playing some game?"

"It is likely, though by no means proven, that he is the same man. Whether he is gaming or is in deadly earnest is yet to be revealed."

—– —– —–

"Surgeons," I suggested. "The lady's lungs had evidence of pleurisy. She may have endured an operation upon her left breast. Could we not enquire of the medical men and institutions where such a procedure might have been carried out to discover her identity?"

"My dear Watson, if some stranger turned up at your practice wishing to know details of your patients' medical conditions would you oblige him?" Holmes challenged me.

I owned that I would not. "Still, given that the patient in question was then murdered and cut to pieces…"

"Assuming what Dr Bond thought *may* have been signs of surgery was indeed more than the effects of putrefaction, how difficult an operation might it have been? How many men in the country might competently perform it?"

"A fair number," I had to admit. "Hundreds, if not thousands. In many hospitals and clinics across the land." I saw then the difficulties in my suggestion.

"The detail of the lesion was mentioned at the inquest. It has been widely reported in the papers. If any surgeon or attendant recognised the patient from it and was willing to come forward then I might have expected him to make himself known by now."

I knew it to be true. "The solution used to preserve the body, then," I persisted. "Such great quantities as are required to wash a whole body…"

"Are nothing compared to the volume by which Condy's Fluid is purchased in bulk by many institutions," Holmes cautioned. "Even by the hospitals which might have performed an operation upon the departed. Nor may we hope that the smell of decay was detected by some passer-by or neighbour, for given the publicity attendant on this case any such information would have already reached the police. Indeed, I am aware that Gregson has been distracted into making necessary follow-ups to such claims from the imaginative and from attention-seekers. I am afraid that we would have to be very short of options to pursue those unlikely avenues, doctor."

"Then what courses remain, Holmes? All of London, all of England is suspect of the killing. The body offers no vital clue. The circumstances of its various discovery are obscure. Without the identity of the lady, or knowledge of the means of her death, or even explanation of how and why her severed parts appeared as they did…"

Holmes broke in to assure me. "There is still the material evidence to consider. The black dress of subtle pattern. The wire tornure. The knotted string and 'standard' brown wrapping paper. All of these can tell a story. From the fabric we may identify the manufacturer of the linen and thence perhaps the dressmaker, and so the client."

I was well aware what wonders the wizard of Baker Street was capable of performing with the most meagre of material. "The dress might be the key to breaking the case, then."

Holmes sucked on his pipe and tapped the bole reflectively. "It will be most instructive, Watson."

━ ━ ━

Gregson broke the news to Holmes the next morning when we arrived at Scotland Yard. We were then in the old Yard, of course, the cluttered back-end of Whitehall Place, crowded into the cubicle-like box that the inspector used as a workspace.

"It's gone," he told us.

We had arrived to inspect the physical evidence from the building site: the black dress that had wrapped the torso, along with the 'dress improver' that had pressed marks into the victim's dead flesh; the brown paper that had enclosed the other two body parts; and the 'black string' with its square knots that had held the parcels tight. It was not to be.

"Gone?" Holmes repeated, his lips drawing back into an angry snarl.

"I don't know how," Gregson admitted. "Too many cooks, I expect. The original evidence went from Dr Bond to Troutbeck at the Coroner's Office. Tommy Hawkings from King Street looked at the old mohair dress. He remembers there was a faint pattern on it. Then it was sent to D.I. Marshall's office to be examined. He had some idea about tracking the garment's manufacturer, so he cut off snippets and sent them to various textile mills in the North. The evidence was present on the first day of the coroner's inquest, then returned first to King Street at Chief Inspector When's request and then here under Chief Superintendent Dunlap's authority when the case was handed over to Scotland Yard."

"When would that have been?" I asked.

"On or about the 11th. It was placed in storage until needed. It was only when I sent for it yesterday that I was told there was a problem locating it. I went down there myself this morning and sorted through the clutter to confirm the materials were misplaced."

"What about the new evidence?" Holmes enquired his voice tight with fury.

"Now that's a puzzler. That came straight here, to me, and I had it on this very desk only yesterday at five pee-hem." Gregson had undoubtedly been examining it to try and get ahead of Holmes before our inspection today. "Afterwards I had Robson, our records keeper; shelve it away in the

"It's gone," Gregson told us.

store."

"With the other?" I enquired.

"No. Material there is filed by date of logging in until it is placed in more permanent storage. Practical, see? Newest is nearest the door."

"Who has access to this area filled with vital items pertinent to your criminal investigations?" Holmes demanded.

"Any officer here," Gregson admitted. "The room is locked, of course, but there's a key on the general bunch. Any of us might need to go there after hours to check on something, and no time to fetch Robson or one of his secretaries."

"So in short," my friend fumed, "through poor security and poorer record-keeping, essential evidence in addressing this case has vanished from the very archive of Scotland Yard!"

The inspector raised his hands in a calming gesture. "I didn't say vanished. I said misplaced. It's probably an administrative error. There's so much interest in this case, so many detectives wanting to make a name for themselves since the Home Office is watching…"

"I hope the Ministry sees how bungled things have been!"

"It is a mis-step, I own, but…"

"It is possibly the most dangerous part of the investigation!" Holmes shouted. I have seldom seen him so unhappy with the police. "Consider, Gregson, what the disappearance of evidence from your own sealed store means. If this is not mere incompetence then someone amongst you has committed a criminal act. One of your own is working against you, for the prevention of solving this crime!" He snorted and turned to me. "Now we must waste valuable time interviewing every person who works in this place, establishing movements and alibis to…"

"Now hold on!" Gregson protested. "That's just not going to happen, Mr Sherlock Holmes. You don't 'ave *carte blanche* to go rummaging around Scotland Yard, poking your nose into our doings. If there's been something amiss then I'll find it. I don't care how high up word to bring you in came from, you stay out of this!"

Holmes perked up, like Bertie catching a scent. "So you *do* know at whose instruction I was invited to the case!"

"Yes, I know," Gregson admitted through grinding teeth. "Word came down through the Chief Constable from the office of one of the Undersecretaries for State at the Home Department."

"Which one?"

"I believe it was Sir Durham Carrick," the inspector supplied sullenly.

"Then I shall take my complaint to him," announced the irate detective.

I knew Holmes well. "Were you really that infuriated at the loss of the dress and the rest?" I checked as our cab rattled across Whitehall.

"What makes you believe otherwise, doctor?" Holmes tested me.

"I was speculating that perhaps you might have exaggerated your frustration, might have played upon Gregson's knowledge of your character and eccentricities, in order to learn from whence the order to invite you had originated."

My friend snorted. "Every time I believe I have fathomed you, Watson, you reveal some new aspect of your shrewdness. Yes, I needed the name of the man who set this puzzle before me."

"Why so?"

"Because there are two main possibilities about the crimes as we know them. The first is that there is a murderer who deliberately flaunts his kills, for perverse pleasure in the publicity it gleans or in secret self-loathing and hopes of capture, or from some other obscure motive. If so then he will be difficult to identify unless he makes some error in deploying the remaining parts of his victim. The second possibility is the more intriguing: that it is not the murderer who is seeking attention by distributing the corpse."

"Someone else may be revealing the parts? Why might someone do that?"

"For revenge, perhaps, to make a murderer squirm at fear of detection? As a means of reinforcing blackmail? There are many other options, of course. But the method is suggestive."

My mind raced. "There seems to be some public bar-visiting fellow encouraging discovery. If your theory about the body being distributed by someone other than the killer is correct, then that man may be the one putting pressure on a murderer."

Holmes shrugged. "It seems as though Sir Durham Carrick's office issued the fiat that I be consulted. Was that merely political expediency to resolve a well-publicised case that was embarrassing the Home Secretary and government? Did someone hope that my involvement might turn up the pressure on the lady's killer? Or was it even more Byzantine than that?" He shook his head. "I am theorising well ahead of my data and must rein my speculation in. Let us talk to the honourable undersecretary and then draw some conclusions. See, here we are at the Palace of Westminster."

Sir Durham Carrick's staff tried hard to shield him from us, but the character and name of Mr Sherlock Holmes were sufficient to penetrate the bureaucratic cocoon protecting him. "If you do not produce the underminister," I heard Holmes threaten a private secretary at one point, "then I shall go direct to my brother Mycroft for an appointment with the Home Secretary instead."

Sir Durham was a bluff northerner, Member of Parliament for one of the Yorkshire constituencies. He was relatively new to his post, come in with the Marquis of Salisbury's new boys after Gladstone lost the Government of Ireland Bill.[16] He did not seem pleased to welcome us to his office.

"I am a busy man. Speak your piece quickly."

"Why did you instruct that I be consulted on the Embankment torso case?" Holmes asked to the point.

"The matter is of public interest and must be resolved quickly. Confidence in law and order must be maintained in these difficult times."

"Why now, when the enquiry has run so long and the inquest almost over?"

"It became to clear to me that the police were not making headway."

"Why did you order the evidence to be extracted from King Street Police Station?"

Sir Durham's face shifted a little, in surprise. "I did not!"

Holmes smiled thinly. "You did not, Sir Durham. Alas, your reactions betray you. Had I asked about their removal from Scotland Yard, you were prepared to tell a lie: a politician's gift. In shifting my assertion I caught you unawares. Why remove the evidence, Sir Durham?"

"You cannot imagine I would go to the Detective Branch and abstract..."

"There are ambitious officers who wish to advance," Holmes cut him off. "Some at least who would be pleased to be owed a favour from a senior Home Office member. The mechanism is irrelevant for now. I am interested in the reason."

"You are talking bunkum, sir! If you have nothing sensible to discuss, I must bid you good day!"

Holmes turned to me. "Do you know what I shall do next, Watson?"

I considered it. "I imagine you will now turn your abilities to investi-

16   Liberal leader William Ewart Gladstone failed to enact this important legislation and stepped down on 17th June 1886, a little over two years before the present case. Conservative leader Robert Arthur Talbot Gascoyne-Cecil, 3rd Marquess of Salisbury, formed the next government, holding almost continuous office and power until 1900 and becoming the last Prime Minister to run his administration from the House of Lords.

gating Sir Durham Carrick, Holmes. You will look to see if there is any lady in his life, perhaps one with whom he is not publicly associated. You will check whether she has been seen since the early days of last month. You will inspect Sir Durham's business affairs and bank accounts to see whether large transactions have recently taken place, perhaps evidence of blackmail. Then you will concentrate upon the detail of his life, his servants, his family, his work for the Minister…"

Sir Durham was white as a ghost. "You devils…" he breathed.

"You are largely correct, Watson," my companion assured me. "Given my suspicions that it was the undersecretary who arranged for the removal of essential evidence, I am willing to advance a little more of my hypothesis. The most pertinent feature of the torso was that the bottom of it was missing. The body had been severed not at the thighs, which would have been easier and is much more common, but at the hips."

I saw the significance now Holmes drew me to it. "Dr Bond believed the young woman to be unmarried based upon the ring finger, and not to have had children based upon the breasts having never been swollen with milk. But the uterus and womb were missing with the lowest portion of the torso, so although the lady may never have come to full term there is no way of knowing if she had ever quickened."

"A secret affair and an unfortunate pregnancy," Holmes mused. "It has been a reason for murder before."

"That is not so," Sir Durham insisted. "I would never…" He bit his reply short.

"It need not be murder, of course," Holmes went on. "It might as well be a bungled operation of an illicit nature."

"Abortion," I recognised. "There are some back-street butchers out there. All too many such procedures have gone very wrong."

Sir Durham was staring from one of us to the other as we spoke, looking like a man in a nightmare. "How…? But…"

"At this stage your only option is to be candid with us," I advised him. "Sir Durham, who is the lady? What has happened?"

The undersecretary fumbled in a drawer and produced a flask or ardent spirits, from which he took a long sip before answering. "When I brought you into the case I did not expect you to find me," he confessed to Sherlock Holmes. "I had thought that your name and your presence might cow the man who has been perpetrating these horrors, that they might deter him from his work."

"I have been underestimated before, Sir Durham. Now the story!"

"There was a lady, an unmarried lady who lives—lived—in Town. I met her shortly after I took my seat in Parliament and was appointed to my post in the Home Office. I had to spend far more time in the capital than I had been accustomed to before, away from home and family. Grace was… comforting. Affectionate. You know how it is?"

"She became your mistress," Holmes surmised coolly.

"I never kept her," Sir Durham protested. "She was a lady of independent means. She lived at her brother's house here in London."

"This brother made no objection to your liaison?" I wondered.

"He was glad to see her happy—or so I thought. And then, though we took precautions, she fell pregnant."

"There was no question of her keeping the child?"

Sir Durham shook his head. "None of us wanted that, to bring a bastard into the world. Not her, not me, and not her brother. It was he who arranged the operation. Some seedy quack turned up at her house with quivering hands and rum on his breath. It only took him a few moments to botch the job fatally. Grace bled out within the quarter of an hour."

"The abortionist fled," Holmes supposed.

"As soon as he could grab his fee," Sir Durham spat. "Nicholson and I—that's the brother, Faber Nicholson—we were left with a dead woman bearing the signs of an illegal operation. I was terrified. I knew what it would mean to my career and marriage if word got out."

"The end of both," I knew.

"Absolutely. So Nicholson agreed to dispose of Grace's remains privately, a secret burial. To protect us both from charges of murder he proposed that we each prepare and exchange accounts of the physician's visit to verify that it was he, not we, who caused the death. And so we did. Then I hastened back to Yorkshire and left him to put his departed sister to rest."

"Except that he did not," noted Holmes. "Instead he chose to squeeze you, holding as he did sworn testimony in your hand admitting by implication your relationship with the late Grace Nicholson and your complicity in arranging her child's termination. You resisted his pressure; after all, signatures can be forged. So then he arranged for Grace's severed arm to turn up on the Thames embankment."

Sir Durham buried his face in his hands.

"What did he ask?" Holmes said.

The undersecretary's answer was almost inaudible. "Not money. Secrets. He wanted access to information held in confidence by this office on British policy. Police watch lists of possible troublemakers. Confidential reports on the Irish question. Some files we keep on senior men who have been less diligent in their personal lives than might be hoped."

I blew out my cheeks. "Prime blackmail material indeed!"

"So I thought," admitted Sir Durham. "The more I considered it, the more I realised how he might know to ask for these things. I had been indiscreet in my conversations with Grace. Indeed, she had directed my conversations, sometimes at the most intimate of occasions."

"She was drawing information from you in the bedroom," Holmes surmised. "In short, she was a spy."

"I am unhappily forced to consider it," the politician shuddered. "Her association with me began shortly after I was appointed to this position. In retrospect I have been unwise in what I told her in our cloistered moments. But I could not, would not in good conscience, give Nicholson the information he required for his silence."

"Hence the second warning to pressure you, a woman's torso discovered at the very site that will be home to the Detective Branch. By this time the corpse was in an advanced state of decay and had been treated with permanganate of potash to inhibit its putrescence. When even that discovery proved insufficient to overcome your scruples, additional gristly remains were added to the cellar by one of the gawkers who bribed their way onto the site, and another pair of reporters were set on to new revelation."

"That is so," Sir Durham confirmed. "At that time I knew I had to make one last cast of the die, and so I instructed that Scotland Yard should call upon you, Mr Holmes. I hoped that Nicholson might be frightened off and leave me be."

"But that is not the case?" I could tell from the frightened man's voice.

"No. He has my confession. He still has Grace's head. He has the public's attention as the inquest moves to a close. He can send my letter and his sister's head—if sister she indeed is—to the coroner or the press and destroy me utterly. And so he will, if I do not yield up the files that he requires—tonight!"

As directed, the Right Honourable Sir Durham Carrick MP arrived at the silent New Scotland Yard building works as the city's clocks tolled eleven p.m. Sonorous booms from nearby Big Ben[17] stirred the ground

---

17 'Big Ben' is a nickname for the Great Bell in the well-recognised tower of the Palace of Westminster, the British Houses of Parliament. Once the largest bell in the British Isles, its distinctive tone is due in part to damage it sustained in 1859 which caused a crack that remains unrepaired even today. The tower and its clock were designer Augustus Pugin's last work before he descended into madness and death.

fog that had crept in off the Thames. The pea-souper had mounted the Embankment wall, blurring yellow coronas around the new public gas lamps. The October night turned bitter cold.

Bribes had changed hands. Once again the unreliable Edge had accepted money and made arrangements for the new night-watchman to be absent from his post. The day-constable who guarded the small let-gate at Cannon Road had gone home. The entrance was unlocked, allowing the frightened undersecretary free access to the site.

There was a pause. Sir Durham must have been fumbling with matches to light one of the workman's lanterns that hung from a rail beside the site office. At last he found his way to the main building's unfinished door and scoffolded interior. He stumbled once, swearing as his feet caught on some untidied brick or discarded tool. His steps echoed through the deserted building as he followed instructions towards the cellar steps.

The half-completed chambers above might have been deserted but the vaults to which the politician descended were not quite so empty. Holmes, Gregson, and I squatted in absolute darkness behind the very heap of spoils where Miss Nicholson's torso had been found. We also awaited Sir Durham's blackmailer.

"It's a gruesome twist, Holmes," I had complained earlier when the undersecretary had received a letter via one of the countless anonymous London runner-boys. The unsigned paper brought a final demand and final threat, insisting that Sir Durham bring the confidential files the blackmailer required or face utter disgrace and prison. The meeting place was that same cellar where the lady's torso, thigh, and foot had been unearthed.

"It is good strategy, Watson," Holmes had adjudged. "It is a site known to the villain, well hidden from witnesses, with but one easily watched access point. Not only is it an ideal venue for an exchange, but if the man Nicholson intends to silence his victim too then it is a fine spot for a murder."

"You believe the rogue might do Sir Durham harm? Can we then in conscience send him to the meeting?"

"I suspect that Nicholson is more than he seems. He and his putative sister seem to have targeted Sir Durham with ruthless skill. He was able to pick the padlock to the cellar. It suggests training, resources, information. Sir Durham might have been targeted by a foreign power, or by... a more ingenious planner here at home. Keeping the minister from his appointment would not save him. Sending him to a rendezvous where we can be in attendance may."

"One entrance," Tobias Gregson had reminded us. "Easily watched. He'll know if we go in there."

Such a detail was no inconvenience to Sherlock Holmes. Each of us had entered towards the end of the work day, overcoated as labourers. We had been met by Mr Brown and the punctilious assistant foreman had concealed us until the site closed. Once Edge had made his dilatory checks and handed over to his corrupt night-watchman ally we were at liberty to make our way to the vaulted undercroft and lay in wait.

Sir Durham found the middle cellar and moved inside. His face, dimly lit by his flickering lantern, was etched with fear and horror. The light trembled in his left hand. His right fist clutched the document box that he had abstracted at Nicholson's command.

As we had instructed, the politician made no sign that we were concealed in the alcove shadows.

Time passed. In the near-darkness it seemed as though hours must have gone by, although my pocketwatch insisted it was but a quarter of an hour before the door scraped open again. A hooded lantern's focused glare obscured our view of the newcomers but the sounds of their boots betrayed their numbers. Nicholson had not come alone. Four other men accompanied him.

"Durham!" Nicholson called out as pleasantly as if encountering his friend on a visit to his sister. "How good of you to come. You have brought me what I wanted?" His Oxford tones were light and easy.

The undersecretary tried to keep his voice level. "You have brought what you said? G-grace's head? And that damned paper."

Nicholson set the lamp aside so Sir Durham could see he was holding something in his other hand. He gripped the dead woman's head by the hair, proffering the rotted skull unwrapped towards his prey. "Aren't you going to kiss my sister?"

"You…" Sir Durham began, but could not find an epithet vile enough.

"Here's Grace and your confession. Now give me my documents."

"These men…?"

"Oh them. Merely staff. They are here to secure the guardians whom you have surely brought. Perhaps now you would call forth Mr Sherlock Holmes?"

We had been discovered! Nicholson had known of our visit to Sir Durham's office earlier in the day. He must have considered the possibility of Holmes cracking the case and drawing out the undersecretary's confession. He had turned our trap against us.

"Come out, Holmes, with all your allies. Must I shoot Sir Durham now to make my point?"

Nicholson carried no firearm but each of his supporters did. The brutal men turned their weapons at the trembling politician.

Holmes rose from concealment. "That will not be necessary," he agreed. "Here I am."

"And your friends," he insisted. "Dr Watson? Perhaps one or more Scotland Yard plodders?"

Gregson and I rose from cover and joined Holmes in the open. We slipped our guns into our pockets as we appeared.

"Edwin Nicholson, I am arresting you," Inspector Gregson instructed the blackmailer. To the others he said, "I am an officer of the law. Put down your firearms or you'll swing."

"No," Nicholson denied. "All of you live or die at my... grace." He grinned at the putrescent remains he still held in his grip. "Hand over my box now, Durham, there's a good fellow. Slowly. Lay it on the floor."

The terrified politician placed the wooden document box on the muddy flagstones and backed away to us. He tried to speak but his horror had dragged him past words.

Nicholson lifted up the dead woman's severed head and looked at it. "Grace thanks you for your assistance in our mission—or would if she was able to enjoy this moment. Your efforts, Durham, will immeasurably assist our employer. Not only have you betrayed your nation's invaluable secrets but you have placed into my hands Mr Sherlock Holmes. I will warrant that the information he holds inside that head is as valuable in its own way as the data in this box. That is why, though you and the others will never leave this cellar alive, Mr Holmes will accompany us to a place where every hidden compartment of his brain can be opened and explored."

"If you think yourself a match for Sherlock Holmes then you are a fool as well as a scoundrel!" I told the man.

Nicholson set down Grace's head and flipped the latch on Sir Durham's case. "I *do* think myself a match for the detective," he admitted. "His match and more, for I..."

His boast was interrupted by the flash powder that exploded as the box's lid was lifted. Holmes' trap worked very effectively. The simultaneous actinic flare and deafening boom were immediately followed by a spray of choking dust that clogged eyes and mouth. Had we not been prepared for the eruption, Holmes, Gregson and I would have been as surprised and debilitated as Nicholson, Sir Durham, and the mercenaries.

Holmes sprang forward with a complicated move that dropped one of the gunmen to the ground. I fell upon a second with a roundhouse to his jowls that drubbed the fellow to the ground. Gregson, more practical than either of us, simply drew his revolver and shot the other mercenaries without hesitation.

Nicholson stumbled to his feet, blinded by the lycopodium explosion, groping for his revolver. His sole trod down on Grace's discarded skull and his sister twisted beneath him. He slipped onto his back, winded. I stamped down hard on his gun-hand and heard a satisfying crunch of carpals.

Shocked and disarmed, the other gunmen yielded to Gregson's steady pistol.

Nicholson reached into his coat with his remaining hand. Holmes seized him before he could draw out a black tablet he evidently intended to swallow. I happily clubbed the fellow until he lay quiet.

Sir Durham grovelled on the floor, blinking away the spots in his vision after the brilliant powder-flash. His sight cleared upon the view of Grace Nicholson's rotted face looking up on him.

His scream echoed and re-echoed through the cellars of New Scotland Yard.

Epilogue

Holmes is consulted for his detective abilities and for his discretion. Officially, the Scotland Yard Murder was never solved. It remains a stain upon the record of the Detective Branch to this day, and one of the central features of their Black Museum of criminal horrors.

My own account of the incident is written with posterity in mind but will join that body of Holmes' cases which will be sealed away in a secure place for many years before it can be added to the public record.

Although Nicholson was prevented from swallowing his pill of cyanide salts, the villain never came to trial. He was found dead in his cell of unknown causes less than twelve hours after his arrest. Dr Bond's autopsy was unable to find a cause of death and an inquest returned an open verdict. Gregson harboured dark suspicions that the Nicholsons were actually agents of the Iron Duke Bismarck, set on our empire for the advantage of the German League. Holmes considered possibilities of criminal co-ordination closer to home but had not yet assembled a body of evidence sufficient to confirm his ideas. With Nicholson's demise the trail ran cold.

Sir Durham's end was abrupt and tragic. Only four days after his last encounter with Grace Nicholson in that cursed dark cellar, the under-secretary fell under a hackney carriage and was killed. Since no cause of suicide was offered and no proof of foul play could be found the matter was ascribed to accident. Scandal was averted and the Carrick name was unstained.

Holmes and I received an invitation to the grand opening of New Scotland Yard in 1890 but we declined to attend.

The End

The Ghost of Scotland Yard

A reflection on fictional & real-life Victorian crime-fighting.

Of course Scotland Yard is haunted. Its 'Black Museum', a collection of gruesome artefacts associated with cases dating as far back as 1874, has long been said to be visited by a veiled lady swathed in black. Often assumed at first to be a visitor, she is only revealed as a phantom when she is close enough for the observer to realise that beneath her veil she has no head.

Yes, the ghost of New Scotland Yard is reputedly the unnamed woman whose torso was discovered in that same cellar during the time the site was being fitted out. This spectre is claimed to have made the transition with the contents of the Black Museum to the concrete office block of new New Scotland Yard, where she has troubled late-night constables and sleepy administrators since the 1960s. There is no word yet on whether she will make the transition to new new New Scotland Yard when the Metropolitan force transfers to its latest location. Meanwhile, the headless ghost is still occasionally reported at her original venue, now the offices of the honourable Leader of Her Majesty's Government's Loyal Opposition.

The Black Museum was so dubbed by an *Observer* reporter who was denied access in 1877. It is now known by the more politically correct title of the Crime Museum. It was first unofficially assembled by Inspector Neame from items confiscated under the 1869 Prisoners Property Act. Within a year Neame and a constable had been permanently appointed to maintain the collection as a source of training and instruction for members of the Criminal Investigation Division. Although closed to the public and press, the site had many prominent visitors and was open to any police officer.

Although the museum may seem like a grisly trophy collection, it is actually an illustration of the development of policing in its formative years. In little more than half a century from the first appointment of a

Detective Branch at rooms backing onto Scotland Yard, the Metropolitan Police force developed into an agency that became the pattern for law enforcement across the world.

Those years saw the development of forensic and detection techniques which are now commonplace, such as fingerprinting, chemical analysis, profiling, and databases of known criminals. The whole apparatus of modern crimefighting was invented by trial and error as the wheels of justice slowly turned towards professionalism. Assembling old cases and artefacts to study, learn, and remember in a Black Museum was an early step in the journey.

Paralleling the real-life evolution of police work was the development of crime fiction. From its earliest roots in Poe's *Murder in the Rue Morgue* and Collins' *The Moonstone*, the public had become fascinated with the depiction of crime-solving. Doyle's publication of the Sherlock Holmes cases came at exactly the right moment to capitalise on the public's appetite. Those accounts rode the early wave of genre popularity and reflect the progression of the story-form. In many ways, Doyle's accounts became exemplar templates of the range of stories that could be told.

The Canon Holmes tales come in several flavours, each of which has now matured into a sub-genre of its own.

First there is the Fair Play Mystery, in which the reader is given all the clues that the detective has and can race the investigator to the solution. This artform probably reached its zenith under the pens of Agatha Christie and Dorothy L. Sayers, but Holmes has his fair share of these puzzles too. "The Red-Headed League" in *The Adventures of Sherlock Holmes* is a good example.

Then there is the Odd Occurrence tale, in which some difficult or improbable event requires explanation. Although these can be fair play whodunits they might also be more of an adventure of discovery, in which readers and detective alike come across solutions for a seemingly insolvable circumstance. Cases such as *The Sign of Four* come into this classification.

Next there are the Catch the Villain stories, in which a known and identified felon must be hunted. Holmes' trap for Colonel Moran in "The Adventure of the Empty House" in *The Return of Sherlock Holmes* is one such episode.

Action Adventure yarns are rarer in the Canon but do occur, wherein Holmes and Watson respond in a more physical, reactive way to present dangers. The emphasis is not on detection but upon resolving an urgent threat. Holmes' ultimate confrontation with Professor Moriarty in "The Final Problem" from *The Memoirs of Sherlock Holmes* focuses not upon the genius of the two clashing intellects but upon the chase as the Napoleon of Crime hunts his nemesis across Europe.

Cases may be made for many other categories of Holmes story, but for now it is sufficient to illustrate that narratives in styles which would later become more developed and distinct forms were present in Doyle's collections during the formative years of detective fiction.

In adding to the world's sum total of Sherlock Holmes stories I have tried my hand at each kind of tale mentioned above. My first contribution, "The Problem of the Western Mail" in *Consulting Detective volume 1* is a Fair Play Mystery. "The Lucky Leprechaun" in *Consulting Detective volume 3* is certainly an Odd Occurrence. "The Affair of the Norwegian Sigerson" in *Consulting Detective volume 10* is at least in part devoted to Catching the Villain. "The Adventure of the Failing Light" in *Consulting Detective volume 9* is certainly from the Action Adventure school.

One of the joys of having a century of hindsight to draw upon and access to the modern corpus of detective literature and forms is that an author can now bring those styles and techniques to bear on a Sherlock Holmes enigma. There are sub-genres that have appeared since Doyle's time that well fit Holmes' style.

Perhaps chief amongst them is the development of forensic detectives, as evidenced by the plethora of CSI-style material now available on television and in books. Holmes was an early forensic detective but his stories seldom describe the processes of his chemical analysis or follow him step by step through his scientific endeavours. Dr Watson may make reference to some monograph in which Holmes has established his expertise; the story may even hinge upon the great detective's ability to identify cigar ash; but in the seven or eight thousand words of a typical Doyle offering there is rarely time for detailed description of the process.

The Procedural is the most popular televised form of detective story these days, wherein the viewer follows the investigator through a series of steps that lead towards a solution. The format is well-suited for hour-long episodes and is utilised in everything from *Columbo* to *The X-Files*. These procedurals trace their origins to the short pulp stories of a pre-television age, with talented detectives going through their paces patiently racking up plot pointed through observation, interview, and analysis.

All of them owe a debt to Holmes, who did it before them. However, just as Scotland Yard's techniques were accreting in real life, so Holmes'

Canon stories generally feature a work-in-progress form of the Procedural.

Hence "The Scotland Yard Murder", in which a true crime story meets Sherlock Holmes in a proper by-the-book procedural investigation, heavy on evidence and interpretation. We discover the truth alongside Holmes. As with most real-life casework, Fair Play early solution is not possible. The detective's genius comes in making that extra leap at the story's end. We would expect Holmes to be the pioneer of modern detective methods; here he demonstrates it.

The guest appearance of Dr Bond, who was involved in the actual case and was a real-life pioneer of forensic policing, is by way of tribute. Undoubtedly he and Holmes would have insights to share.

Doyle wrote many kinds of Holmes story and left the way open for others yet. I hope the present case finds favour with the present reader.

If not, there is still an unidentified ghost in Scotland Yard's Black Museum, searching for her head.

⌐ ⌐ ⌐

I.A. WATSON - went to his first ever convention in 2015 and was surprised that some people had heard of him. He has authored a number of novels, most recently *Vinnie De Soth, Jobbing Occultist* and *Holmes and Houdini* and *Blackthorn: Spires of Mars*, and quite a lot of novellas and short stories. The full list is at http://www.chillwater.org.uk/writing/iawatsonhome.htm

As of "The Scotland Yard Mystery", I.A. Watson has written more words about Sherlock Holmes than any other character, with the detective finally catching up with Robin Hood in four volumes beginning with *Robin Hood: King of Sherwood*. He has also received more award nominations, shortlistings, and trophies for his Holmes work than any other endeavour. The author is pleased at the chance to have worked with two of the three great literary archetypes of British adventure fiction. The third, King Arthur, is overdue his attention.

Watson now lives a hermitic existence in a rambling, crumbling, ancient house in an obscure part of Yorkshire and is ever more becoming of a Warning To Others.

Sherlock Holmes

in

"The Adventure of the Artful Forger"

By

Lee Houston Jr.

From my customary seat at my writing desk after that morning's meal, I turned to see Sherlock Holmes lost in deep thought at his work table. My friend was conducting another of his detailed specimen examinations, although of what I did not know, when a familiar sounding knock came upon the outer chamber door. Uncertain if Holmes even noticed the intrusion on our privacy, I rose from my chair to see what Mrs. Hudson required.

As I opened the door to the outer hallway, I observed our landlady with a taller man, who stood ramrod straight with hands at his side. He was stern of face with graying temples, which offset his brown hair. Even without my long friendship to and tutelage under the consulting detective, I could tell the man was ex-military like myself, yet was unable to say offhand whether or not the poor fellow had ever seen actual combat.

His neatly pressed, three piece suit was not quite the high quality that a true gentleman would wear, but was far superior to what I have observed to be the average uniform of a gentleman's gentleman.

The new arrival remained silent as Mrs. Hudson said, "I'm sorry to disturb you and Mister Holmes when you had asked me not to, but this... gentleman was quite insistent that you are needed on a most urgent matter."

"Quite all right Mrs. Hudson," I said, reassuring her as I stepped out into the hallway, while partially closing the door behind me. I turned to our visitor and promptly requested his name and business.

"Jonathan Bryce, head of household staff to his Lordship, Reginald Van Horton," the man said proudly.

I nodded my head in acknowledgment of recognizing the family name. The Van Hortons were a minor, yet well established noble family who could trace their lineage back to at least the late 1600s in the United Kingdom, if not earlier elsewhere within European society. While I could not attest to the origin of their fortunes, it was respectable old money, with the Van Hortons' current income masterminded and maintained through shrewd investments in a multitude of London based businesses.

"Sir, my employer requests the presence of Mister Holmes at his estate immediately," said Bryce.

"Did your employer inform you why he wishes to see Sherlock Holmes?" I inquired.

"No. I was only told that the matter requiring Mister Holmes' attention was most urgent. I have a carriage waiting for us outside," added Bryce, as if our traveling with him was a foregone conclusion.

"If the matter is as important as you say, should not Scotland Yard be summoned also, if not instead of us?" I asked, curious as to what Bryce's response would be.

"That is a question I am unable to answer, as I know not if the Yard has indeed been contacted. His Lordship has tasked me with the assignment of bringing you gentlemen to him, and I have never failed to carry out my duties," Bryce stated proudly.

While no outright threat was actually spoken, the slow motion of Bryce's right hand toward the small of his back was not lost on me.

I was uncertain whether I could defeat Bryce in a struggle, but my efforts and the small confines of the corridor would at least allow me ample opportunity to detain the man long enough for Mrs. Hudson to safely escape, provided he had no confederates lurking about outside.

However, such action on my part proved unnecessary.

While I never heard him approach, Sherlock Holmes was suddenly out the door, past me, and confronting our visitor himself. Holmes swiftly restrained Bryce's right hand as he moved forward to discover what the manservant was reaching for. Concurrently, I had placed myself between them and Mrs. Hudson to make sure no harm came to her.

We both obviously had feared the man in possession of a weapon. Yet Holmes was just as surprised as I to discover Bryce's concealed objective was a thick envelope full of one hundred pound notes!

Holmes politely released Bryce, but demanded an explanation instead of apologizing to him.

"Please forgive me gentlemen if I am out of line and not following whatever the proper protocol is for obtaining your services," said Bryce, while massaging his right wrist. While better known for his great intellect, Holmes does have a strong grip when needed.

"I was instructed that if you did not come for the intrigue of my Lordship's situation, then I was to offer you his monetary incentive," Bryce explained. "There is five thousand pounds within that envelope, with Lord Van Horton's personal assurance of another five thousand for your assistance upon the resolution of his dilemma."

"I see," replied Holmes, as he took a closer look at the currency. "And his Lordship shared no details as to what this 'urgent situation' is?" he asked Bryce, while giving me a slight nod, indicating that there was indeed five thousand pounds within the thick envelope.

"No sir. I was only charged with obtaining your services, but…" and then Bryce hesitated and eyed Mrs. Hudson uneasily, for one should never publicly discuss the private affairs of our superiors.

"I understand." Holmes reached inside the envelope and extracted a single, one hundred pound note. "This is for your troubles and inconvenience Mrs. Hudson, courtesy of Lord Reginald Van Horton," he said, handing the currency to our landlady.

The woman was beside herself. While Holmes and I had not always been the most ideal of tenants, there was also no denying that we were both very fond of the dear woman, and would move Heaven and Earth to help her if she was ever in trouble.

Mrs. Hudson clutched the note in her hand, smiled at Holmes and myself, and then excused herself before retiring to her personal chambers.

With that, Holmes led Bryce into our receiving room. I followed, closing the door behind us.

"Now, what is this about?" Holmes demanded once we were alone, while staring intently at our visitor.

"Well sir," began Bryce, "the day started as usual. Nothing was amiss, or at least, no one was aware of anything being wrong until after his Lordship entered his private study."

"Alone?" asked Holmes.

"Yes sir," replied Bryce. "Except for the future Lady of the House," and I could not help noting that while he did try to hide it, there was a slight hint of disdain in the manservant's voice at saying that phrase, "no one is allowed in there unless you are either a summoned servant or a visitor granted permission. Despite my position as head of household staff, I personally can still count on one hand the total number of occasions I have been within that room, and our employer never has the same maid clean it twice in a row."

While I personally found the arrangements peculiar, Holmes expressed no outward sign of an opinion as he requested Bryce to continue.

"Lord Van Horton entered the study, closing the door behind him. A few moments later, I heard my employer shout."

"Of what nature was the noise?" Holmes inquired.

"Sir?" asked Bryce, not understanding the question.

"Was it a yell of dread? A cry of shock? A shriek of surprise?" Holmes, as always, wanted as much precise information as could be acquired.

"I would say shock, sir," Bryce replied, after pausing to consider the question. "Being still outside the study in the main foyer at the time, because I was giving the rest of the staff their assignments for the day, I rushed to see if his Lordship was well. However, Lord Van Horton was already coming back out of the study before even the guard stationed outside that room could knock on the door."

"How did he appear then, compared to when you last saw him?" asked Holmes, ignoring the comment about the guard for the moment.

Bryce paused, for saying more would betray a confidence. Then, realizing what he knew may actually be important, answered. "A bit pale, and starting to perspire. Something I have never seen his Lordship do in all my years of service to him. It was as if he had yet to fully recover from whatever happened. Otherwise, his Lordship seemed fine, physically."

"Then what happened?"

"Lord Van Horton ordered the guard posted outside the study door to resume his post. All he said to me was to summon his personal carriage and have the driver prepare for a trip into London," Bryce answered. "I did so and, upon my return to inform him when it would be ready; his Lordship was waiting for me in the foyer. He handed me that envelope, with the instructions I have faithfully obeyed. I saw my employer return to his study, and I departed when the carriage arrived. The rest you are already aware of," Bryce added.

"And what of the guard you mentioned?" Holmes queried.

Bryce hesitated, but answered the question. "He only enters the manor upon being summoned, since His Lordship keeps his own schedule. The guard's duties are defined by event, not to the hour, however. The guard usually accompanies His Lordship to the front of the study door, then stays positioned outside until either dismissed for the day or assigned another task."

"What does this guard do when not on duty?" I asked.

"Other than the fact that he and the rest of those charged with maintaining Lord Van Horton's security live in the servants quarters on the estate grounds with the rest of the household staff, I have absolutely no idea how he spends his free time," Bryce replied.

"I see," Holmes said, growing silent as that familiar look of deep contemplation came upon him. When he reached whatever conclusions he could at the time, he handed the remainder of the envelope back to Bryce. "While my fee is at a fixed rate, it is based upon my availability and the exact nature of whatever dilemma Lord Van Horton finds himself in."

Bryce was about to say something, when Holmes added, "It just so happens that I am free this morning. Care to join us Watson?"

"Just let me get our coats," I replied, thinking that I should also bring my service revolver along as well.

— — —

It was a rather pleasant spring morning as we rode with Bryce in his Lordship's personal carriage back to the Van Horton estate outside of London.

The main house was a sprawling two story manor in the center of a clearing at the end of a cobblestone lane, surrounded in the rear by a rising hill. There was no immediate indication of how far Van Horton's property actually extended, but the placement of support buildings and a paddock currently occupied by six additional horses showed that his Lordship definitely owned a very large parcel of land.

As we came to a halt parallel to the front porch of the manor, we were promptly greeted by a footman who assisted our departure from the coach. Stepping out, Holmes and I could not help noticing the presence of a guard stationed directly next to the front door of the Van Horton residence. A discrete glance also revealed a sentry stationed at each corner of the building.

"Thank you, Jenkins. This way, gentlemen," said Bryce. Those were the first words spoken by any of us since leaving Baker Street. Holmes preferred to remain silent during our journey, presumably lost in thought, and I followed suit. Whether out of respect for us or not knowing what to say, Bryce never tried to strike up a conversation.

As the manservant opened the door and escorted us inside, we immediately saw another guard positioned at the interior of the entrance way. None of these sentries were mentioned in Bryce's account of that morning. I am sure the same questions were on Holmes' mind that currently occupied my own. Why did Van Horton feel the need for such security measures? Had the additional guards always been present and just failed to prevent whatever happened, or did recent events require their presence now?

Not knowing how long we would be there, Holmes and I only unbuttoned our coats and removed our hats, while Bryce ushered us across a large marble foyer. Our footsteps echoed in the open space as we were led to an ornately decorated oak door in the far corner. A third sentry was positioned in front of it, but he did not challenge our presence, presumably because of Bryce accompanying us and knowing we had been sent for.

The manservant knocked once on the door, to which a strong, deep voice inside asked, "Is he here?"

"Yes, sir," replied Bryce.

"Good work. Please send him in, then resume whatever you were originally scheduled to do today."

"Very good, sir," replied the manservant, before stepping aside to allow us entry into the private study of Reginald Van Horton.

Holmes reached out with one hand to turn the decorative knob, found the door unlocked, and opened it to step inside.

As I was about to follow, Bryce stopped me just long enough to hand me back the envelope from earlier. "You can explain it to him better than I could sir," was all he said, before turning to leave.

I simply nodded, placed the envelope within my hat, and entered.

There were no guards inside the study itself, indicating Van Horton's preference for privacy. Holmes was standing in the middle of the open floor space between the lone door and his Lordship's large, finely polished desk at the far end of the rectangular shaped room. I did not know if my friend noticed the lush Oriental rug he was standing on, for his eyes were taking in the shelved books that lined most of the walls. My own quick look at some of the spine titles revealed the collection covered a vast range of subjects and that many of the volumes were quite valuable.

I personally could not help noticing all the curios and other antique bric-a-brac that sat amongst those shelves, along with the fine art that adorned the rest of the available wall space. Most of the works I recognized immediately, although there was one painting of a young lad fishing, my view of it partially blocked by the open door, that I could not identify. As I turned to close the door behind me, I immediately took note of the reason for our summons, but waited until Van Horton addressed the situation to speak on the matter myself.

"Gentlemen," said his Lordship, rising from behind his desk to greet us. About my height, Reginald Van Horton had to be somewhere between his late forties and early fifties, but that estimate was only based upon the few creases present around his mouth and eyes. Otherwise, our potential new client appeared to be quite fit, with no slouch in either his posture or stride as he approached.

After the formal introductions were made, our host said, "Thank you for coming on such short notice. If this was not such a dire emergency..."

"So your representative said," replied Holmes, "although Mister Bryce was not well informed as to the details of the situation," he added, while holding out his hand. I reached into my hat and retrieved the envelope. "Your... retainer, sir," said Holmes politely, handing his Lordship back the money, "minus a small compensation for inconvenience. My fee is an established rate, but dependent upon whether or not I take your case," he explained.

"Quite right. My apologies Mister Holmes," said Van Horton, taking the envelope from Holmes and placing it within a pocket of his well pressed velvet smoking jacket, without even bothering to discover the amount it was short by. "If not for how valuable what was stolen is to me..."

"You refer to the missing painting," observed Holmes, nodding slightly at the empty wall space to the left of the study entrance that I had noticed earlier. "From observing the section of wallpaper that has been protected from years of light exposure, compared to the surrounding area, one can tell a fairly large painting hung in that spot until quite recently. Present circumstances leads one to accurately surmise it was stolen. However, considering the many other fine works on display within this room, exactly what piece of art was stolen?"

"It was a portrait of my late wife, Delores," replied Van Horton, with a note of sadness briefly creeping into his voice. Regardless of how long ago she departed this world, it was obvious the man still missed her dearly. Yet, I could not help thinking about Bryce's unspoken opinion concerning "the future Lady of the House."

"Please tell me everything, and leave no detail out, no matter how small or trivial you think it might be," requested Holmes, as I hastily moved to find my notebook and pencil.

"Her portrait still hung there proudly when I retired about nine last night," began his Lordship, as he led us back toward where the painting hung. "I had it placed in that particular spot so I could always see it from my desk, even if the study door was open."

As I observed earlier, an open portal would obscure the painting of the boy fishing when in use, leaving the opposing space in clear view.

"Was nine your usual hour to retire?" inquired Holmes.

"No. There is no set schedule. Unless I have an appointment the next day, I always stay until my work is completed, so the time of my departures and returns to this room vary regularly," replied Van Horton. "This morning, the first thing I noticed upon entering the study was that the window by my desk was slightly ajar. There was a light breeze coming in from the hillside, so the curtain was billowing somewhat and some of my papers were lying on the floor. Unaware at that moment whether it was my own carelessness or something else that led to the state of things, I moved to close the window when I noticed my dear Delores was missing."

I could see Holmes nod, thinking that must have been when Bryce heard his Lordship shout.

"Other than picking up the fallen papers and placing them back on the desk under a paperweight, I left everything else alone as I made preparations to have you gentlemen summoned at once," Van Horton added.

"And why not Scotland Yard?" inquired my friend.

"The Yard is a fine establishment and serves its purpose, but I prefer to have Delores returned to me as soon as humanly possible," was his Lordship's answer.

"I see," said Holmes, while taking another look at the study walls. "Was anything else stolen? Curios? Documents?"

"While it appeared untouched, I have already examined the contents of my safe, along with the rest of this room. Delores' portrait is the only thing stolen, although I was in the midst of inventorying my desk to be absolutely certain when you arrived," explained his Lordship.

"What did the stolen painting look like?" I asked.

"Delores was fair of skin. Fiery red hair the exact opposite of her actual temperament, and deeply rich emerald eyes that a man could get lost in and never want to return from," replied Van Horton, speaking like someone still in love.

"While I have made some deductions and estimations based upon my observation of the empty wall space, would you happen to know the exact size and weight of the portrait?" wondered Holmes.

"Alas, no," admitted his Lordship, "but the painting was within the best mahogany hardwood frame I could acquire at the time."

"Very well," said Holmes, turning to face his Lordship again. "I shall begin by examining the window while someone brings us a ladder and a measuring rule. Otherwise, I will do what I can to retrieve your missing painting."

I watched as Van Horton reached for the bell pull near the door and rang for a servant. When Bryce arrived, his Lordship asked him to bring the requested items. I joined Holmes by the casement window.

It was a somewhat bow-shaped fixture, stretching almost from floor to ceiling, occupying what would be the right side of the wall behind Van Horton's oak desk when seated. On the other side of the desk was a brick and mortar fireplace, taking up most of the corner space.

Bordered by thick wooden shutters of equal size that matched the interior décor of the study, the window was all glass panes within trimmed wood, arranged to form two huge rectangular panels that opened inward on hinges and were secured by a small locking mechanism.

The view not obscured by Holmes' presence was of a small garden that we would later discover spanned the back of the house and received plenty of morning sun. While official access to properly view the flowers and shrubs could only be obtained from either another room or outside the manor itself, the space created by the panels unfastened and fully open proved to be ample enough for a man of average girth to enter and leave the study.

As I approached, Holmes said, "Note the pry marks Watson," while pointing to the scratched metal of the latch and handle. Sherlock kept his voice low so Van Horton wouldn't overhear us while he waited for the ladder and measure. "Someone forced a small tool into the framework and opened the window from the outside."

"Damaging the window frame somewhat in the process, hence being unable to properly close it upon leaving," I observed in a similar low voice.

Holmes nodded, indicating that my deduction was correct. "An unconventional method of passage, but effective nonetheless."

"Any clues as to the identity of the culprits?" I asked.

"Alas, not inside," Holmes replied. "Any footprints exist only in either the garden proper or beyond. After examining the surrounding floor space, I have not found even a speck of dirt. When his Lordship said he picked up the papers before discovering the portrait stolen, he might have walked over and inadvertently destroyed any potential evidence."

I looked down. While quite large, the Oriental rug did not stretch to our present location. We were on a very clean but bare section of wooden floor. Besides Van Horton's apparent preoccupations with privacy and security, the room was well kept. There were no physical indications of foot traffic between our position and where the theft was actually committed.

"Our thieves were either smart or had been instructed to remove their shoes before proceeding into and out of the study, to reduce the risk of making any noise that would attract unwanted attention. Observe this lone gray thread I found, caught on the outer edge of the window framework," Holmes added, holding up the evidence between his thumb and forefinger for me to see. "Since the material is worsted wool, plainer than what one would expect even commonplace outer clothing to be made from, it proves the culprits wore only hosiery upon entry."

"The material is worsted wool, proving the culprits wore only hosiery upon entry."

"Then would that not also prove they were experienced criminals?" I inquired.

"If not them, then whoever else was involved," agreed Holmes, as he secured the minute thread within his handkerchief, before folding it up and placing it back within his jacket pocket. He leaned out the window as far as he safely could. "Observe the bare edging against the house," he requested, as I positioned myself to have a better view. "The border is quite firm, thus not as yielding to footprints as softer soil would be. Yet this patch of ground directly below the window appears even more compacted than the surrounding dirt, thus indicating where the thieves stood."

I concurred, and then Holmes pointed out a rectangular impression in the soil alongside the edge of some nearby shrubbery.

"That is from a container for the purloined painting; presumably a wooden crate. The fact that it was assembled prior to the crime shows events here were planned well in advance. Everything else, from forcing the window open to replacing their shoes before leaving, occurred in that spot before you. They likely waited until they were away from the house before resealing it."

All I could do was nod in silent agreement as Holmes continued, still keeping his voice low. "Based upon what little evidence is visible before us, including the dimensions of the casement window at its widest point of openness and my current estimate as to the stolen portrait's size, our art thieves are two men of average height and build."

"Yes. It would require at least two men to safely carry a large painting out of the study," I replied, softly. "But could they have carried it between them all the way up that hill?" I was hoping to surprise Holmes with my own deduction. The hillside behind the Van Horton estate, while taller than the main house at its peak, possessed a gentle slope and looked no more difficult to ascend than a pleasant stroll across the public rights of way through Kensington Gardens.

"You are correct in your presumption that the thieves would take the most direct and unseen route to and from the manor," agreed Holmes, "but not of the means of transport. Whatever his Lordship's past or present security arrangements might be, obviously no one thought of this window as a possible access point."

Holmes glanced up the hill. "Last night the moon was waxing gibbous, almost full. With tree growth in this area somewhat scattered, there was enough nocturnal light to preclude needing a hooded lantern until they fell within the shadow of the house itself. We shall make a through inspection of the grounds before leaving. Yet what puzzles me most about the matter is, with so many far more valuable paintings and other items on display for a thief to choose from, why was only the portrait of Van Horton's late wife stolen?"

"For money?" I asked in return, stating the obvious reason.

Holmes was about to respond to my query when Van Horton announced that our requested items had arrived.

We turned from the casement window and saw Bryce and another servant enter the study, carrying a small ladder between them. They set it up in front of where the missing painting should be. The other servant then handed me a cloth measuring tape spooled inside an ornate case that looked like it belonged to a woman, before both men left the room.

Holmes climbed the ladder and when high enough to reach, asked me for the measure. He proceeded to document the size of the less aged areas of the now visible wall space. By comparing them to the rest of the wallpaper's subtle color gradings and shade tones, he was able to calculate the actual dimensions of the missing art as I dutifully recorded each fact. Then Holmes handed me the measuring tape before descending. Not knowing what else to do with it, I set it on one of the ladder rungs once Sherlock was down.

Back on solid footing again, he said, "Even crated, I doubt the portrait weighed more than a couple of stones at most." Then my friend leaned closer and whispered, "Yet I have discovered something else that makes this mystery more complex."

Before I could inquire as to what that was, Holmes turned back to his Lordship and asked, "Other than finding the portrait missing this morning, were there any other unusual occurrences overnight? A stranger spotted on the grounds perhaps?"

"Nothing. The groundskeeper and the security personnel on duty would have addressed such matters immediately, before bringing them to my attention," replied Van Horton, thus revealing that his security measures were already in place at the time of the theft and that the culprits took advantage of some weakness in the arrangements.

"I see," replied Holmes. "We will need to know all you can tell us concerning the creation of your late wife's portrait."

"Yes, of course," agreed his Lordship, as he walked back to his desk long enough to retrieve something from within a drawer and return to us with it.

"The image does not do Delores justice; but other than the portrait and my memories, it is all I have left of her," Van Horton said sadly, as he handed us a photograph.

Holmes and I studied a gray toned image of the lady, as Van Horton walked over to a finely polished oak cabinet across from the wall of bookshelves. He opened its hinged front doors and then proceeded to pour himself a snifter of something from a fine crystal decanter. Holmes and I both declined a libation when offered, however we did agree that the woman was lovely as Sherlock gave our new client back her photograph, which he set upon the top of the cabinet for the moment. Considering how wide open the cabinet doors were, we also could not help noticing the small assortment of beverages His Lordship had access to, including what appeared to be an expensive bottle of vintage cognac.

"On the eve of our tenth wedding anniversary, Delores took ill, forcing us to cancel a romantic stay in Paris," began Van Horton, before taking a short sip of his drink. "Of course I immediately sent for our family doctor, but his initial prognosis was not promising. After further tests, he announced that my wife only had about another year of life remaining to her at most, and there was nothing medical science could do to prevent my tragic loss. You can imagine how devastated I was to hear that the love of my life was on the verge of being taken from me. It was then I made the decision and ordered the doctor not to tell Delores, determined to make her last days as happy as I could," confessed his Lordship, still standing in front of the open liquor cabinet.

Neither Holmes nor I said a word as Van Horton continued his story. "I wanted some way to memorialize Delores, to always have her with me even long after the inevitable happened. That was when the thought of having her portrait painted crossed my mind. After a couple of weeks of frantic interviews and having private agencies screen potential artists, as there was no guarantee of exactly how long my wife had left, I finally selected a promising young talent. After some carefully staged and well chaperoned sittings so Delores did not discover the real reason I commissioned the art work, I had the finished painting hung proudly in this room about five months before she passed away. It has been there for over a decade since, until its theft."

Holmes and I then observed the subtle hand gesture Van Horton used to brush away the tears and realized that the grief over the loss of his wife was still as painful to him now as the day she died.

Sherlock then inquired as to the identity of the painter and where we might find him.

"Robert Donaldson," replied Van Horton after refilling his snifter, despite the fact it was not even half empty, "although I do not know his current address. Perhaps Benjamin Anderson, my solicitor, does. He executed the contract for Donaldson's services. Before your departure today, I shall provide you with written instructions for him to fully cooperate with your investigation," he promised.

As Holmes thanked his Lordship, there was a knock at the study door.

Before Van Horton could respond, it opened and two women walked in. The first was very pleasing to the eye and appeared to be near thirty. Barely my height, she had long ebony hair secured in a bun and piercing blue eyes that seemed to take in everything as she entered the room.

A family resemblance could be seen between her and the other woman. The second lady was much older, her hair fully gray. Yet while possessing the same alert blue eyes, she had a much sterner countenance.

"I apologize for the interruption, but you asked me to remind you that we need to be at the caterer's by twelve," the first lady said to Van Horton.

"Quite right. Thank you, Dear. Our business will be finished soon," he told her. A quick glance at my pocket watch revealed it was now almost eleven.

With that the lady smiled and turned to leave, but stopped when she saw the empty wall space before the second woman started to move. The first lady stared at it for a moment, then her smile grew even larger as she turned to face his Lordship again. "Oh darling, I know how you feel about her, but thank you," she said, forgetting our presence and hugging him.

That earned a disapproving frown from her companion, but otherwise the elder lady remained silent.

His Lordship hesitated a moment before saying, "Well, I promised you I would."

Before Holmes or I could speak, Van Horton said, "Gentlemen, my fiancée Miss Annabelle Thompson, along with her aunt Miss Harriet Thompson. We plan to marry this fall."

We started to exchange polite pleasantries, but our new client stopped us from properly introducing ourselves. "These gentlemen are here to make the final arrangements for the storage of Delores' portrait, since we lack the proper facilities to do so ourselves," he told her, not mentioning the real purpose of our visit.

I could see a scowl forming on Holmes' face. As a gentleman, it was impolite to lie to a woman, regardless of the circumstances.

"Storage? I see," said Miss Thompson, sounding a little disappointed. "What about the *other* matter we discussed?"

"Arrangements have been made to have your portrait painted and hung in Delores' place after we return from our honeymoon," replied his Lordship.

Holmes had put his hat back on, preparing to leave. Neither of us knew why his Lordship said the things he did, but Van Horton's words went against traditional social morals.

For a moment, I thought I saw a look of mixed emotions upon the woman's face, but her reaction indicated I might have been mistaken. "You wonderful man," said Thompson, giving him another smile. "I will leave you to your business then. Gentlemen," she acknowledged us with a polite inclination of her head before departing, her aunt following close behind.

The moment the study door was closed again, Holmes said, "If the requirement of our services is based on falsehoods…"

"No sir, I assure you it is not," Van Horton insisted. "Delores' portrait was stolen sometime between last night and this morning. While Miss Thompson and I have had previous discussions on the subject, I will admit to being hesitant about selecting a storage agency. It would be like… It would be like saying goodbye to Delores all over again," he confessed.

I was pondering another matter. Other than the fact that there would soon be a new Lady of the House, I failed to see what it could be about Miss Thompson that had at least Bryce, if not some of His Lordship's other employees, unhappy about the impending marriage. Could their loyalty to the late Mrs. Van Horton still be just as strong as their employer's persistent grief?

Then his Lordship looked deeply into his snifter, before asking in a low voice, "Can you gentlemen keep a confidence?"

Holmes and I simply nodded affirmatively.

"My affection for Miss Thompson, I mean… Annabelle, is quite different from how I felt about my first wife, but is still genuine. We met about five years ago at a social function. She comes from a good and proper family and in many ways, fills the void in my life and makes me feel whole again. Yet I also cannot deny that there shall always be a part of me that longs for Delores' return, no matter how impossible that is."

With that, there followed an awkward silence. I could not help wondering if any thought of Irene Adler might have crossed Holmes' mind, while pleasant memories of Mary entered mine.

As Van Horton wrote our letter of reference to his solicitor, I noticed that for some reason, Sherlock Holmes took advantage of his Lordship's distraction to examine the chairs within the study. There were three. Two in front of the man's desk and Van Horton's behind it.

The guest chairs were given a passing glance and then quickly ignored. When his Lordship stood to present us the letter, I accepted it to give Holmes a chance to discretely examine Van Horton's chair behind the man's back. At this point I now believed I knew what he was searching for, but the look upon Holmes' face revealed it was not there either.

With that, the three of us walked back out into the foyer. Van Horton summoned Bryce and arranged our transportation back to London when we concluded our initial investigation, then told the guard in front of the study door he needed to see Smith.

The guard briefly stepped outside the house for a moment, then returned with another man. Van Horton introduced us to Mister Smith, in charge of the estate's security personnel and arrangements. As Smith offered to personally show us around the grounds, his Lordship left to prepare for his appointment with the caterer.

Smith escorted Holmes and myself through the manor house's main hall to a pair of thick glass doors, the formal access point for the garden. Outside and past the double doors, we immediately turned right and went to the window of Van Horton's study to start our search.

After a brief explanation from Holmes as to what we were looking for, Smith offered to help. We walked from the window through the garden in as straight a line as we could toward the edge of the hillside, with Holmes in the lead and one of us on either side of him, but a few paces behind.

During our search, I made a passing comment in regards to the natural beauty surrounding us.

"The groundskeeper and his staff have been maintaining the garden since the passing of Lord Van Horton's late wife," replied Smith. "She was the one who initiated the project."

I simply nodded and could see that while Holmes was still concentrating upon the search, he was also listening to our conversation in case it yielded any new information. "I would imagine the previous Lady of the House was well liked?"

"So I have heard, but I was not working for his Lordship before her passing," Smith answered.

A partial footprint on the edge of one flower bed proved that we were on the right trail. Alas, nothing of relevance was discovered during our search of the garden. With that, we started up the hillside.

Beyond the rear property line of the Van Horton estate, the grass was unkempt and growing freely. The distinctive path of uncut verdure having been trodden upon was relatively clear, leading from the garden upward.

"The ground is a bit softer here," observed Holmes, staring downward as we ascended.

Upon reaching the first small grouping of Fraxinus Excelsior, more commonly known as an Ash Tree, Holmes announced, "Two men milled about here for some time," while walking a perimeter around the bare ground of one specific tree. "One has a clear view of the manor house from here," he added, looking back the way we came. "Since his Lordship revealed he has no set schedule for retiring each night, the thieves waited here until they felt it safe to proceed. Unfortunately, there is no indication as to how much time might have passed before they continued their mission, but this proves my theory about them waiting until a distance away from the house before sealing their crate," Holmes added, while picking up a common carpenter's nail. "Tell me Smith, which window belongs to his Lordship's bed chamber?"

"Having never been on the second level, I cannot say," was Smith's reply. "However, I am grateful to you for exposing the faults within our present security arrangements. I can assure you that they will be addressed immediately, for I would be a failure in my position if someone managed to get that far inside again," he declared, while looking back at the house.

"Quite," was Holmes' only reply, as he looked upward. "This tree is in an ideal position. From here, they could observe the manor below and see their confederate at the top of the hill too," Sherlock continued, while pointing in that direction.

From our vantage point, I observed that our destination appeared relatively flat, indicating a well traveled path awaited us at the top.

Then Holmes looked back down at the ground and shared his further deductions. "There were two men, both of average height and build. However, one of them did recently have his left shoe resoled. See how one footprint is smoother, compared to the others? A clear indication that sole is newer than the rest, with less wear and tear. Yet the man without the resoled shoe was stronger than the other."

"How..?" Smith began, when Sherlock provided the answer before he could finish.

"See how the set of footprints without the resoled shoe, in the rear of the trail before they disappear back into the grass heading upward, are a bit deeper than the other set? While we have yet to learn the actual weight of the crated painting, these tracks indicate the latter man bore the greater amount of the mass during their ascent."

Smith stared at my friend with a dumbfounded expression. It never ceased to amaze me how much other people were impressed the first time they witnessed Sherlock Holmes' logic for themselves.

"So he was the stronger of the two?" Smith finally asked, bending momentarily to examine the footprints more closely while Sherlock studied our escort, or more specifically, the weapon hidden upon his person that was briefly revealed when Smith bent and his unbuttoned jacket opened. It appeared similar to my service revolver, but of more recent manufacturing.

"Yes," replied Holmes. "Otherwise, there is no indication of a limp or other distinguishing characteristics," he added, sounding a bit disappointed. "They carried the stolen painting the rest of the way after sealing their crate, for there are no wheel tracks from a cart or wagon present, though from this distance any noise such a device might make would be negligible."

With that, Holmes resumed climbing the hill and we followed.

At the top of the hill was a well traveled country road. With any tracks obscured by the wheels of many other conveyances since the crime was committed, we were uncertain exactly what type of horse drawn vehicle was waiting for the art thieves, before it left via whatever route they chose.

We walked up and down the dirt road for about twenty feet in either direction, yet found no further evidence to aid our investigation. Clueless, we returned to our arrival point.

"I suspect London as their most likely destination, and since a meeting with his Lordship's solicitor is our next order of business anyway, that shall be ours as well," announced Holmes, before he proceeded back down the hill.

On the return trip to the manor, I took the liberty of trying to satisfy our personal curiosity in discovering why Reginald Van Horton had more security than we first thought, but failed.

While polite, Smith's only response to my inquiry was, "Gentlemen, while I am a great admirer of your reported exploits between the *London Times* and *The Strand*; I cannot betray the confidence of my employer."

"I understand," replied Holmes. "However, there is one question germane to the investigation that I must ask. Was there a guard stationed outside the study door last night?"

"Since we believed the grounds to have been secured, no," was Smith's answer. "Should there have been?"

"That will depend upon the results of our investigation," was all Holmes would say.

⸺ ⸺ ⸺

Other than being transported in a different carriage and without Bryce, the journey back to London was akin to our ride to the Van Horton estate. Holmes sat silently, staring at nothing in particular; yet I could tell that he was considering every aspect of the problem before us.

Before we left the study, I knew he was probably searching for signs of how the thieves were able to take the portrait off the wall unaided. There was no indication that they had brought their own ladder, and nothing within the study itself was used as a makeshift step, so unless one man was momentarily perched upon the shoulders of the other...

⸺ ⸺ ⸺

After showing him our letter of reference, the senior partner of Anderson and Myers eagerly answered all our questions.

"For a young and unestablished artist, Robert Donaldson was paid a rather tidy sum for creating the portrait of the late Mrs. Van Horton," said Benjamin Anderson, as the attorney searched and secured from his files a copy of the contract between his Lordship and the painter.

I confessed that my limited knowledge of the art world did not include him, while Holmes remained silent and read over the document.

"In truth, I would be surprised if anyone did at that point in his career," replied Anderson, whose framed credentials on the wall behind his desk stated he officially became a solicitor almost twenty years ago. "Although the man does possess some talent with a brush, he was still quite young compared to his contemporaries and his works have yet to become as highly sought after as theirs. Donaldson was barely in his twenties when he received the Van Horton commission over a decade ago, but that situation was more a case of being in the right place at the right time, in my humble opinion."

"Oh?" said Holmes inquisitively, before handing me the contract to read. The document had the full details of the event, from the date of hire to the date of completion. I took some satisfaction in noting that the recorded dimensions of the art work and Holmes' calculations were practically identical, off only by the merest of fractions.

"Considering that time was working against Van Horton in regards to the fate of his late wife, my client did choose what was then the best man readily available," Anderson assured us. "As a patron of the arts myself, I privately believe that there were more talented artists to consider, but none of them were in a position to undertake a new commission with such short notice and tight schedule. However, having seen the finished work myself, I will say the missing portrait is a rather remarkable likeness."

"What is Donaldson's reputation as an artist today?" inquired Holmes.

"A promising talent who has done a few works of note since the Van Horton commission, but has yet to produce anything that would establish himself as a true master," was Anderson's reply.

Holmes then requested a current address for Robert Donaldson as I returned the contract to the solicitor's desk.

The request made the solicitor pause, but whatever might have been on his mind at that moment remained unknown. "I never had one concerning a private residence. I can give you that of his studio at the time, but his Lordship has had no dealings with the artist since the conclusion of their original transaction. The information I have shared with you concerning Donaldson's career was obtained through my various connections within the art world," explained Anderson, before he searched his files again.

After the solicitor carefully wrote out the address in his backhanded script, we parted company.

— — —

Having dismissed Van Horton's driver after reaching the solicitor's office, Holmes hired a hansom cab to take us to our next destination. Doing so allowed Holmes the chance to talk freely about the case in route.

"I have yet to ascertain a motive for this robbery," he said. "The portrait of Van Horton's late wife would have a higher sentimental value than being an actual financial asset. Also, if money was the reason for its theft, his Lordship is wealthy enough that any reasonable ransom demand could be met within a business day."

"Could the theft be a personal matter then?" I wondered.

"What is Donaldson's reputation as an artist today?"

"Perhaps; yet our client seems under the impression he is nothing more than the unfortunate victim of thieves," observed Holmes. "However, until seeing so many armed men on the property in his employ, I was under the impression that Reginald Van Horton was not one of the more prominent peers in London, let alone in British finances. While the relevance of that fact to the problem at hand remains to be seen, it is a curiosity that might make me reassess my knowledge of him."

"Could the culprits have been capable enough to commit the robbery, but mistakenly stole the wrong painting?"

"That is one possibility," agreed Holmes. "If so, then they are uneducated in matters of art. Yet there is enough evidence present to indicate that at least two other people were involved. Someone to drive their transport vehicle and someone with personal knowledge of the Van Horton estate, or at least the study, provided our unidentified suspects are not the same person. No indication of our culprits being in possession of their own ladder when committing the crime suggests the possibility that someone within the estate might have provided one. Yet the logistics involved, considering his Lordship has no set work schedule, forces me to discard that theory. Any prolonged absence by an accomplice in Van Horton's employ would have been noticed."

"What if the thieves did not need a ladder?" I asked, before sharing my personal theory of one momentarily being perched upon the shoulders of the other.

"That does give further credence to the evidence showing one man being stronger than the other, for I can think of several experienced criminals who have acted in tandem that way before. With enough practice, any capable duo could perform that feat at least once without making any unwanted sounds, especially since there was no guard outside the study door when everyone was asleep. Yet this does not rule out the possibility of someone within the manor possibly being behind the crime either," Holmes pointed out. "We have met one person who obviously dislikes all the attention paid to the late Delores Van Horton's portrait, but jealously alone does not a criminal make. There are more direct, let alone discrete, methods available to rid oneself of an unwanted painting than outright theft. There is also the matter of the crate itself, unless..."

Then Holmes steepled his fingers and grew silent again, lost in thought until we reached our destination.

The address we were given for Robert Donaldson's studio was a loft in a rather nondescript building within a less than favorable area. After settling our fare and sending the driver on his way, since we could not say how long our business would be and the man was unwilling to wait for us, we entered the building. It came as no surprise to discover that the studio was also Donaldson's private residence as well, to save on personal expenses. However, the presence of a bobby standing guard in the hallway outside the entrance to the loft was.

"Mister Holmes. Doctor Watson," said the constable in friendly greeting. "I was unaware that he had summoned you, but please, go right on in," he added, holding the door open for us.

Puzzled, we entered the premises.

The loft consisted of much wide open space, with a few areas curtained off by old blankets draped across ropes tied to support beams to create some sense of room division and privacy. An artist's easel near a bank of large windows displayed a small scene of the Thames in the process of creation. Canvases of various sizes, completely blank or finished, were stacked everywhere; a strong indication that painting occupied the majority of Donaldson's life.

However, the body on the floor in the middle of the room, being examined by a man with which we were well familiar, posed the question of whether or not Donaldson's passion for art also contributed to his death as well.

"Since you are present, Inspector Lestrade, then I fear those are the mortal remains of Robert Donaldson you are kneeling next to," said Holmes. While we held our positions upon entering, he was a few steps closer to the Scotland Yard officer than I.

Although the man never bothered to turn and face us properly, I was certain Lestrade's dark eyes narrowed at hearing Holmes' voice. "Doctor Watson. What brings you gentlemen here?" he asked, displaying his occasional impatience with Holmes by directing the question to me.

"We came as part of an investigation on behalf of a client and were hoping to speak with Robert Donaldson, not expecting to find him deceased," answered my friend.

"Hmmm..." was Lestrade's only response, as he stood up and faced us properly. I could now see the handle of some small tool, used as the murder weapon, was sticking out of the dead man's chest. However, I could not tell from this distance whether the man died from the stab wound or the resulting loss of blood. "No known motive so far, although I personally have not ruled out one possible suspect," reported the Inspector.

"Oh?" asked Holmes. While nothing appeared to be in the state of disarray one would expect to find after a fight had occurred, the loft did support Anderson's statement concerning the deceased's minor status in the art world, as well as Donaldson's lack of housekeeping skills.

"According to the building's other tenants, no one heard or saw anything that might help with our investigation," continued Lestrade.

"If the rest of this building's tenants are also artists or other creative types, then I would be surprised to discover otherwise, for all were likely busy with their own endeavors," observed Holmes.

"Well, everyone was at home and a few complained about being rudely awakened when we questioned them," Lestrade revealed. "They all claim Robert Donaldson did not have any known enemies and very few friends. In fact, no one could recall the last time someone other than the landlord might have paid the victim a visit."

"Given your tone of voice, I presume it is he you suspect of the crime," said Holmes.

"Unofficially," admitted the Inspector. "Donaldson was overdue on paying his rent, so the landlord let himself in. Personally, I don't trust the man, so whether his intention was to legitimately attempt collection of the outstanding debt or the private hope of being able to nick something remains to be answered," said Lestrade, as he wrote furiously in his own notebook. "Either way, he claims to have discovered the body upon entering the loft and summoned us. May I ask what exactly you are investigating?"

"The theft of a painting that Donaldson created," replied Holmes, as he continued observing every detail he could see of our surroundings from his current position. "We were hoping to acquire some background information on the matter from him."

"My men and I have already searched the loft for evidence concerning Mr. Donaldson's demise, but the coroner has yet to arrive for the remains. If you'd care to take a look for yourselves…" Lestrade offered in a rather hopeful tone.

"Thank you," Holmes answered as he approached the deceased, while I hastily retrieved my notebook and pencil once more.

"First, I have observed that while there is at least one better quality suit in his possession for public appearances, as shown by the hint of a well tailored sleeve sticking out from behind that makeshift curtain in the rear," Holmes said, while pointing to the far corner of the loft, "Robert

Donaldson was a man of meager means."

The Inspector simply nodded in agreement, although I suspect it took him a more thorough search of the premise to arrive at the same conclusion than simple deductive reasoning.

Holmes knelt on the floor where Lestrade was earlier. "This is further supported when one notes Donaldson's current attire. For example, this artist smock he wears is faded in color while the sleeves show evidence of much use, as indicated by the cuffs being somewhat threadbare while the stitching is starting to come loose on the right shoulder. It was either his personal favorite or the only one he owned."

"The latter," replied Lestrade. "That curtained off section appears to be what passed for his personal bedchamber. There was very little attire present and even less indication that Donaldson owned anything of value."

"The murder weapon was a common pen knife that belonged to the victim, judging by the amount of old paint splatters on the hilt. That indicates the murder was not preplanned," Holmes postulated.

"The landlord claims he last saw Donaldson at the first of this month to collect the rent. The deceased told him he was still owed for previous work and was supposed to be paid handsomely for it within a fortnight, which ended yesterday," Lestrade reported. "When no rent payment was made by the time he finished his morning meal, the landlord came up here and found the body. So perhaps if Donaldson was paid, had the cash on hand and caught the landlord trying to rob him..."

"I understand what you are suggesting, but I must respectfully disagree," Holmes replied, holding out the artist's stiff right arm for us to look at. "Right handed, and was probably painting just before he was killed, for the most recent paint stains have yet to completely dry, with no attempt to clean his fingers beyond simply wiping them. Probably because of the cost of turpentine," he surmised, while gently lowering the arm. "Whoever entered this loft and killed him was someone Donaldson knew. That visitor must have been here early this morning, for rigor mortis has started to set in," added Holmes, while gently placing the arm back at the deceased's side.

"When I questioned him, the landlord admitted that he didn't come up here until almost twelve, for he previously had a 'late' engagement at the local pub last night," Inspector Lestrade informed us. "Although even if he's telling the truth, the first constable was not summoned until about twenty minutes after the fact. I didn't arrive to begin my investigation until a quarter before one."

At the mention of the time, I checked my pocket watch and saw it was now half past one.

"I see. When the landlord entered the loft, did he actually unlock the door himself or was it simply closed?" wondered Holmes.

"I asked him the same question, but the man inserted his passkey as a matter of course, so he had no answer," the Inspector told us.

"Watson, take a look at Donaldson's feet," my friend requested.

Moving to comply, I was quick to note, "The left shoe has been resoled."

"Is that significant?" Lestrade asked in a bewildered tone.

"Curious, at least," answered Holmes, before bringing the Inspector up to date on our day's activities without betraying our client's rights.

"Well, I understand why you wanted to speak to the man, but even if he was involved somehow, why would Donaldson help steal a painting he was paid to create over ten years ago?" wondered Lestrade, while taking another look at the dead man's feet.

"The answer to that question unfortunately escapes me at the moment," admitted Holmes, as he stood upright again. "There are no signs of a struggle, so Donaldson probably stopped his work to answer a knock at the door and let the new arrival in."

"Then an argument developed between them. Heated and intense enough to result in death," I surmised.

"Yes," Holmes concurred. "The murderer is left handed, judging by the angle of the pen knife leaning toward the right side of the body. I hope this information helps in your investigation, Inspector. Since you have already searched the loft for evidence in this crime, may we hunt for clues to ours?"

━ ━ ━

With Lestrade's permission, Holmes and I began our search. Robert Donaldson being a man of meager means proved to be far more accurate than Holmes first suspected. What little food could be found in the premises was hardly edible. Other than the one good suit, there were very few changes of clothes available for him to wear, with most in need of cleaning if not professional tailoring as well. We were unable to locate any personal possessions beyond those used for basic grooming needs.

"It looks as if Donaldson put every pound and shilling he ever made back into his art," commented Lestrade, while examining some of the finished canvases near him. Until the coroner arrived, the Inspector preferred to remain standing by the deceased while we continued our investigation, so his present review of Donaldson's work was limited. "Not sure I would pay the actual asking price for some of these," he added, staring at a tag tied to the back of one canvas with string, "but I will admit that the man could paint."

Holmes began on the opposite side of the loft, where Donaldson had set up his easel near the windows for a natural light source. I had spied a pile of sketchbooks underneath a table covering, to protect them from stray paint splatters, and began examining their pages. I readily agreed with everyone else that there was no denying Donaldson's artistic talent. Even his rough drawings, which included detailed notes along the margins for colors and shadings, showed signs of brilliance in my humble opinion.

However, within the last volume I found a series of sketches that I felt must be shown to Holmes.

Upon viewing them for himself, Sherlock simply nodded and said, "Good work Watson. Anything else?"

"Not at present. You?"

"Possibly. Can you help me with this?" he requested, indicating a blanket covered painting among a stack of canvases. "It feels framed," announced Holmes, grabbing the top. This added to his suspicions. Besides being somewhat protected, all the completed works within the loft were unframed.

I grabbed the upper edge of the canvas next closest to Holmes and pulled with both hands, for Donaldson's other art in this stack had kept the one Holmes was focused on pinned against the wall. The task turned out not to be as easy as I first thought it would, for it took both hands to hold the mass momentarily away, thus allowing Holmes to pull his objective out of the stack.

We both paused upon hearing the only entrance to the loft open, but it was just the coroner and his assistants arriving to collect the mortal remains of Robert Donaldson.

After we finished extracting the covered object, Sherlock quickly replaced the unfinished scene of the Thames on the artist easel with his discovery. The removal of what appeared to be a brand new blanket from the painting, compared to the others in use around the loft, revealed the missing portrait of the late Delores Van Horton.

Inspector Lestrade would later take the painting as evidence until the case was closed. Yet that was not all we found, as Holmes removed a collection of papers from the lower left hand corner of the art work, wedged between the finished canvas and the frame itself. I stood to one side and watched as he examined them. Each sheet was about the size of and appeared to have belonged in one of Donaldson's sketchbooks, yet none of the ones I searched showed any evidence of being short material.

When I pointed this out to Holmes, his reply was, "Then either our search is incomplete, or else the volume these came from is not on the premises." Each page contained notes and sketch lines in what we now recognized as Donaldson's handwriting, but oddly, not one sheet represented a complete drawing.

Silently, Holmes hurried over to the worktable and removed the remaining sketchbooks, before individually laying out the collection of pages on the now vacant flat surface. However, there was not enough room for him to place them in a singular row, and Holmes seemed unsatisfied with creating an additional line of sheets below the first.

Now free of his immediate responsibility concerning the deceased, Inspector Lestrade came over and joined me as we watched Holmes rearranging the order of the sheets, switching and altering their positions until together, they formed a coherent whole image four pages horizontally by four pages vertically.

"These drawings do not represent multiple projects, but are very detailed sections of one specific canvas," Holmes announced, stepping back to study his work in its entirety. "The notations and attention to detail are commendable, but we have seen this piece of art before Watson," he added, to which I simply nodded in agreement.

With that, Holmes turned to address Lestrade and together, the three of us made plans for that afternoon, which began by interviewing the landlord.

With the sketchbook I showed Holmes and the pages he found in my possession, Lestrade escorted us back to the first floor of the building, and then down the main corridor to a side turn that we missed seeing upon our entry. From there, the much shorter hallway ended at one lone door, with another officer positioned in front of it.

Nodding to his man, the Inspector opened the door and we entered the private living quarters of a man identified to us simply as Johnson. The bobby adjusted his position to stand in the open doorway facing the room as we questioned the landlord. He was an obese and slovenly sort of fellow; heavy set, with uncombed hair and in need of a shave. Even without the noticeable reek of an unwashed body, Johnson's ratty attire appeared to have been worn for many months without change.

Upon our entry, the landlord glanced up at us from his bare wooden chair and demanded, "What now?" before tippling directly from the decorative bottle of vintage cognac in his right hand. How long he had been enjoying his libation was uncertain, yet it was quite obvious that Johnson was not used to the liquor, for he appeared to be inebriated already.

With that, Holmes turned to Lestrade and said, "This man is not the missing accomplice of the art robbery, nor is he your murderer Inspector. However, I can attest that he did steal from the loft of the deceased."

"Here now, what's all this?" asked Johnson, slurring his esses while failing to successfully stand up and challenge Holmes' accusation.

"That is a fine bottle of cognac you have. Too expensive for a common man more used to the taste of beer or gin to acquire honestly. Where did you get it?" Holmes challenged him.

"I found it," was Johnson's curled-lip reply.

"Somewhere in Robert Donaldson's loft, I'd wager," Lestrade said with disgust.

Johnson stared at the Inspector with bleary eyes before saying, "He weren't never goin' ta drink it. Damn shame too. This is good stuff," he added, taking what could only be described as another swig before letting out a ghastly belch. "Found it under his bed, unopened."

"I see," was all Holmes would say, while studying our surroundings. A single, unmade bed sat in the rear of the small space near a coal burning stove and a metal bucket of fuel. Other than a well worn desk next to the creaky chair Johnson occupied and a wooden chest beneath the room's lone window, there was nothing else. Filthy clothing and rubbish was strewn everywhere, attesting to Johnson's lack of housekeeping skills.

"Did Donaldson ever pay you the delinquent rent?" Holmes queried.

"De...what?" asked Johnson in return.

"Delinquent. Late," explained Holmes.

"Oh. No, which is why I went up there to begin with," the landlord replied. "When he never answered me knock, I let myself in," he explained, struggling to pull on a small metal chain attached to the waistband of his pants until a key came out of his pocket. "Wasn't about to touch a dead body, but I did go looking for me due."

"Including this?" Inspector Lestrade wanted to know, while yanking the bottle out of the landlord's hand.

"Hey now. That's mine fair and square," Johnson cried, demanding the cognac back.

"When you found it, was the bottle dirty?" Holmes asked, examining the vintage in the Inspector's hand. The vessel was handcrafted and of the same high quality as one we had already seen that day.

"What? No! I try to stay away from the cheap stuff. That will rot a man's guts out if he ain't careful," Johnson answered.

"No. I meant, was there dust on the bottle when you found it?" Holmes said, clarifying his question.

"Under the bed was dirty, yeah. Donaldson probably never cleaned the place in his life," said the landlord, not noticing the irony of his statement, "but the bottle was clean as a whistle."

With that, Holmes turned to Lestrade and said, "That bottle might have been the 'handsome payment' that Donaldson was expecting, although I am sure he would have preferred cash. I shall leave this room's search and Johnson's arrest for theft in your capable hands Inspector," he added, indicating the cognac.

The landlord attempted to rise in protest again, only to be met by Lestrade's intense glare as he pushed the drunkard back into his chair.

"However, I seriously doubt you shall find any funds from Donaldson's mysterious benefactor here," said Holmes. "Shall we wait for you at our next stop, or meet you at his Lordship's?"

Inspector Lestrade met us just as we were leaving the South London National Gallery with an associate of Holmes'. Within a rented carriage considering the size of our party, the four of us reached the Van Horton estate a little after three. There we found his Lordship and fiancée, along with her chaperone, sitting in his private study. Van Horton and Miss Thompson were presumably discussing further details of their impending marriage as they enjoyed an early tea in the guest chairs before his desk. Thompson's aunt sat off to one side in a chair procured from another room, quietly enjoying her drink as they talked.

Deciding to stand as we conducted our business, instead of waiting for our host to have more chairs brought into the room, Holmes properly introduced ourselves to the ladies and then Van Horton to Lestrade, while recounting an edited version of events since our departure. His Lordship did not look happy to see a representative from Scotland Yard with us, nor did we bother to introduce the other gentleman in our company, who began a quiet examination of the artworks on display within the study.

With that Miss Thompson stood, saying that if we were here on business, she would leave until we were done. I saw her aunt simply nod in agreement as she stood too.

"Normally, I'd appreciate that madam, but our business concerns you as well," announced Lestrade.

"Me?" said Miss Thompson in return, quite shocked to hear that. Her aunt seemed surprised as well, but neither commented on the matter further as they sat back down.

The Inspector began by informing his Lordship that Holmes and I had recovered his late wife's portrait and where it was found.

Van Horton, distracted from noticing the fourth man's presence by the news, demanded its immediate return. I noticed that Miss Thompson appeared unhappy to hear that, while her aunt expressed no opinion whatsoever.

"In due time of course, but it shall have to remain in the Yard's possession until after all the legalities concerning this case are resolved," explained Lestrade.

With that Van Horton seemed to lose some of his bluster, readily agreeing to the arrangements, provided Scotland Yard took good care of the portrait in the duration. Then he demanded to know who took it and when would they see justice.

"That is all part of our investigation," Lestrade reassured him. "Although we have yet to identify the other thief and his employer, the corpse of the primary suspect involved is now in the Yard's custody."

Holmes and I noticed that everyone seemed shocked and surprised at that revelation, as Lestrade finished his explanation.

"But why would the artist who painted Delores' portrait want to steal it after all this time?" wondered his Lordship.

"That is what we were hoping Miss Thompson could tell us," Lestrade said, eying her closely.

"Me?" exclaimed the lady, so startled that her tea cup fell out of her right hand in mid-sip to smash on the floor below.

"Yes," the Inspector answered. "I've been made aware that you are unhappy with all the attention your future husband still shows his late wife through the worship of her portrait."

Miss Thompson was emotionally flustered for a moment, her fair skin blushing red before she answered. "That Reginald still misses his first wife

"Madam...our business concerns you as well."

is no secret, and something he shall probably never be able to completely overcome; but I only want him to stop living in the past and move on with his life. While I am not the first woman to compete against a rival for a man's affections, I certainly am at a disadvantage when I must vie against his treasured memories of one long gone."

"Annabelle, I..." began Van Horton, while Lestrade interrupted him to continue explaining why she was a suspect.

"Secondly, there was an unopened bottle of vintage cognac under the bed in Robert Donaldson's loft, and I am certain a quick survey of his Lordship's wine cellar will reveal it came from here."

Both Miss Thompson and her aunt looked like they were about to say something, but Lestrade never gave them the chance as he continued speaking.

"Third, we found these detailed sketches of you, drawn by the deceased, indicating that the two of you had at least some kind of an acquaintance," he said, before showing the still seated couple the sketchbook I found and had showed Holmes earlier that day.

Holmes appeared disturbed by Lestrade's cavalier treatment of the woman, but before he could say anything, Miss Thompson fell out of her chair and hit the floor in a dead faint.

That was when I stepped in, quickly demanding smelling salts, along with some pillows to place under Miss Thompson's head and to elevate her feet.

As Van Horton rushed to summon a servant Holmes, realizing that Miss Thompson was in good hands, took Lestrade aside for a private chat. The Inspector did not look happy, but was willing to listen, even nodding his head in agreement with Sherlock occasionally. Holmes' friend had paused his work when Miss Thompson fainted, but seeing that she was being taken care of, went back to examining the paintings on display in the study.

After Miss Thompson regained consciousness and was sitting properly in her chair once more, Inspector Lestrade apologized profusely for his earlier crude manners. "I can be fairly single-minded when it comes to seeing justice done. Yet there are still matters that need to be resolved," he added, before showing the lady the sketchbook I found.

"While that is my likeness, and a very good rendering too, I do not see how this is possible," Miss Thompson insisted, staring dumbfounded at the drawings. She looked up earnestly. "I have never met nor posed for this Robert Donaldson person in my life."

"That is true," said Van Horton, coming to the lady's defense. "When we return from our honeymoon excursion, I've commissioned Abraham Knight to paint Annabelle's portrait, since my solicitor said Donaldson was too busy to take on any new assignments."

"Besides, all of these drawings show Annabelle wearing her mother's ivory cameo," said Harriet Thompson, taking a brief look at the sketches for herself before handing the book back to Inspector Lestrade. "She hasn't worn that piece of my late sister's jewelry since Mister Van Horton took Annabelle and I out to dinner about two months ago."

Holmes was about to speak when the fourth member of our party wanted his attention. The two of them stepped aside for a moment after Sherlock excused himself, their voices low. All any of us could observe were a few nods, including one toward a certain picture.

With that, the pair came back toward us. "I should like to introduce Mister Ronald Faversham, art historian of the South London National Gallery," Holmes said.

After a brief round of salutations, Faversham spoke. "You are quite fortunate to own such priceless paintings Your Lordship, like this one by the legendary artiste Pierre Daneil," he said, while pointing to the one across from where the portrait of Van Horton's late wife was displayed. "A very talented artist of his day, but alas Daneil completed very few works before his untimely death during the French Revolution. However, it is my sad duty to inform you that what currently hangs on your study wall is a masterfully detailed copy."

"WHAT?" exclaimed Van Horton, aghast, as everyone rose and went over to take a closer look at the forgery, including the Thompsons. The painting was of a young lad in ragged clothing, attempting to fish with homemade equipment off a footbridge in a very rural area on a sunny afternoon.

"I must say Holmes, for an imitation, the quality is quite superb," I commented, taking a step back to admire the painting once more.

Even Van Horton reluctantly agreed with my opinion. "*Pêche Garçon*, or *Boy Fishing*, has been proudly on display in this room since Delores acquired it for me on our first wedding anniversary. She remembered the stories I told her during our courtship about growing up here on the family estate and fishing with my father on lazy Sunday afternoons after church. However, the original transaction was above reproach. I still have all the documentation and certificates of authenticity in my safe, if you need to see them."

"That will not be necessary," Inspector Lestrade assured him.

"Knowing your reputation in the art world, I do not question your credentials sir," began his Lordship, while addressing Faversham, "but just how certain are you that this is a forgery?"

"Granted, it will require a detailed chemical analysis of the paint to be absolutely certain, but when one views this work at more than a traditional perspective, you will notice that there are some portions of the canvas that exhibit more of a sheen than what an older painting should have," explained Faversham, while tilting his head toward the suspect picture at an awkward angle. "There are certain processes that forgers have developed to disguise the actual age of a copy, so it will visually appear as old as the original work. While few in number, the glossier areas indicate that these techniques were not fully employed to create this duplicate, though I cannot say why this is so. Forgers are usually more careful in their work."

"So if this is a forgery, when was the substitution made? Last night? A year ago? Even if Donaldson is the artist who painted this fake, who stole Delores' portrait and why?" asked Van Horton.

Inspector Lestrade had no response to those questions, but Holmes did. "I would say that officially setting a date for your impending marriage forced those behind this charade to alter their schedule, thus not giving Donaldson the time required to properly complete his work."

Then Holmes asked his Lordship the key question that explained everything.

— — —

After hearing Van Horton's response, Holmes elucidated to Lestrade why Miss Thompson was innocent and how circumstances were arranged to make her a suspect. With that, the Inspector wanted to arrest the guilty party immediately, an act Holmes and I readily agreed with and his Lordship demanded be done so at once.

Thankfully we would not have to worry about accommodating Faversham, for Van Horton wished to discuss further art matters with him and guaranteed the art historian's eventual return to the gallery.

Upon reaching our next stop, we were informed by an assistant clerk that the man we wished to see had already retired to his private residence for the day. When asked if there was anything he could do to help, Lestrade insisted that our business was about a most urgent matter and could only be resolved in the presence of his superior. With that, the assistant proved eager to help Scotland Yard and gave the Inspector our quarry's home address.

Our final destination of this adventure was deep in the heart of London. The building was much smaller than the main house of his Lordship's estate, but did appear a bit larger than 221B Baker Street.

As we ascended the short flight of brickwork steps to the front door, Inspector Lestrade's insistent knock was quickly answered by the major-domo of the place. He appeared of average height, but something about the tightness of the jacket sleeves around his upper arms gave me pause.

"We need to see your employer immediately," Lestrade demanded.

"Right this way gentlemen," he said, opening the door to allow us entry.

We entered single file: Lestrade, Holmes, then myself. As we were about to inquire as to the exact location of his employer within the domicile, the major-domo slammed the door shut, while pointing a gun at the three of us.

"I knew there'd be trouble ahead when he saw you today," said the man-servant, as the grip of his right hand tightened on the weapon. "Best to deal with it now in order to make a better escape. But first, your service revolver Doctor Watson," he demanded, obviously aware that Holmes and Lestrade were unarmed.

I claimed not to have it with me. In the small hallway, I was closest to our opponent. Holmes was on my right and the Inspector next to him.

"Don't lie to me," the servant warned, pointing his gun in my direction. "I've read your stories."

"Then you should also know that, depending upon the circumstances, I do not always go forth armed. I did not foresee needing a weapon to locate a missing portrait."

The man squinted speculatively at me, debating whether or not I was telling the truth, then decided it was best not to risk being in error.

With his weapon now aimed at my head, he drew closer as he stretched out his left arm in preparation of searching me for my revolver.

I stared into the barrel of the gun, knowing that if I moved the wrong way I would soon be dead. Lestrade blustered some ineffectual admonishments about threatening honest citizens with bodily harm, but seemed otherwise at a loss for how to defuse the situation without getting me killed in the process. All that managed to do was distract the man briefly as he irritably insisted Lestrade silence himself or he'd see to it personally. It was a momentary wavering in his attention, but it was enough.

Holmes, who had appeared to hang back in dread of either acting or seeing me hurt, unexpectedly lunged out and grabbed the man's right hand and wrist with both of his hands, twisting it upward. That raised the gun higher and away from my head, and I subsequently dropped back, out of the line of fire as Sherlock twisted the weapon around so that it now pointed in the face of its owner.

Inspector Lestrade jumped in to assist Holmes. His intention was to administer a coup de grâce by bodily slamming our assailant into the closest wall. Holmes swung the man around and to the floor at a most inopportune moment as Lestrade alone hit the wall, dislodging a piece of artwork that was on display. A simple painting depicting a vase of sunflowers fell unnoticed as Sherlock continued to wrestle with his opponent for the weapon. The other man's grip was beginning to waver as Holmes continued applying pressure against him in a most determined fashion. I heard a finger bone snap as the man howled, and I could not suppress a shudder.

I took a step back and pulled out my service revolver, ready to use it the moment I had a clear shot, but such action proved unnecessary. Holmes had managed to disarm his opponent in the most cool-headed and graceful manner I have ever seen. Lestrade by then had recovered himself enough to pull our would-be assailant to the ground and pinned the man against the polished wooden floor of the entryway, face downward.

"Strong blighter," observed Lestrade, as he pressed his own body weight against the man's back to keep him in place.

Holmes concurred as he handed me the manservant's weapon. "I would say you have apprehended our other art thief, Inspector." Then Sherlock nodded at me, his silent acknowledgment that we should leave the matter of how the man was disarmed for Lestrade to report as he saw fit, since I was none the worse for the experience. Holmes flexed his long, artistic fingers before he stepped outside to summon additional help.

The arriving constables quickly arrested our assailant. One stayed with the trussed prisoner as the other followed us to assist in searching the premises for his employer.

We found Benjamin Anderson in his study, his wrists tied to the arms of the desk chair he occupied while a handkerchief was crudely stuffed in his mouth as a makeshift gag. Other than being red of face and sweating, he appeared as we last saw him.

Holmes and I took note of the fine art on display, a trait exhibited throughout what we saw of Anderson's residence, as Inspector Lestrade moved to free the man.

"Oh thank Heavens you gentlemen found me," proclaimed Anderson, once he could speak again. "It was all Fredrick's doing," claimed the solicitor, while staring at Holmes. "He was working without my knowledge. Using my connections within the art world for illegal purposes."

The fact that _Pêche Garçon_ was sitting on an easel, undamaged, next to his desk for Anderson to admire was not lost on us.

"Are you willing to write out a sworn statement to that affect, and testify in court when necessary?" Inspector Lestrade asked him.

"Of course," promised Anderson, while rubbing his wrists to restore their circulation. "I shall do so immediately," he stated, pulling paper out of the left hand drawer of his desk before reaching for the pen in its inkwell on the desk's flat surface.

As Anderson began to compose his statement, writing in his backhanded script, Holmes turned to Lestrade and said, "There is your proof that this man murdered Robert Donaldson Inspector."

"What?" said Anderson in a state of shock, looking up at the three of us in disbelief.

"Donaldson's murderer wielded the pen knife that killed the artist in his left hand. The same hand you use to write with," Holmes explained.

Anderson looked at the pen in his left hand and hastily threw it onto the desk as if it was on fire. "There is no crime in being left handed," he said, while trying to compose himself.

"True," agreed Holmes, "but attempting to incriminate an innocent woman for art theft, along with whatever else you had planned, is patently illegal."

"Those are serious allegations. Can you prove your accusations against me?" Anderson demanded to know, acting as if he was now in court arguing points of law.

"Miss Annabelle Thompson's envy of the late Delores Van Horton—who still has much of her widowed husband's devotion—is no secret amongst those who know the parties involved in the matter," Holmes said. "If one could find a way to prevent the impending nuptials between them, then Reginald Van Horton would more than likely expire in due course without an heir; perhaps even sooner if someone planned to hasten his demise before its time."

"This is preposterous!" was Anderson's only reply, but I could see the man had resumed sweating, despite no longer being tied up. "I have known Reginald Van Horton for years. We were just boys when my father handled his family's legal matters. Why suspect me?"

"Because of his Lordship's answer to a question I asked him earlier to-day," Holmes revealed. Anderson had a confused look upon his face as Sherlock explained. "I simply asked Van Horton if he were to pass from this world unmarried and childless, what would happen to his estate? His answer was that, after honoring bequeath requests to various chari-ties and his most faithful servants, the remainder of his fortune would go to you for appropriate disbursement. You sir, he told me, are a man he considers a very close and trustworthy friend, especially since it was you who first introduced him to the woman that would become Delores Van Horton," Holmes said coldly, while staring directly at the guilty solicitor.

"So that is why Anderson had his manservant and Donaldson steal the portrait of Van Horton's late wife," surmised Lestrade. "To discredit the new fiancée. Well, tracking down the coachman and his wagon will be a simple enough matter, and he will likely confess readily to save his miser-able hide. But why create the forgery?"

"Plain greed," answered Holmes. "By his own admission, Anderson is a patron of the art world. The very walls of his residence also attest to that fact. *Pêche Garçon* is a valuable masterpiece, already worth a small fortune and its value will only increase with the passage of time. It would have been years before the solicitor might have legally inherited it, but Van Horton falling in love again and planning to remarry put that pos-sibility at serious risk," Holmes explained. "After all, Miss Thompson did manage to convince her husband-to-be to part with what he considers his most precious piece of artwork. Who is to say she would not grow tired of looking at yet another example of Delores Van Horton's hold on her wid-ower, and have that donated to a museum as well?"

"Quite brilliant, that deduction," Lestrade had to admit. Holmes al-lowed himself a thin, though satisfied smile.

"Making the substitution between the real *Pêche Garçon* and the forg-ery was just simply a matter of convenience when they broke into the Van Horton estate to steal the portrait of his first wife in hopes of driv-ing a wedge between his Lordship and his new fiancée. The couple finally setting a date for their impending nuptials forced Anderson and his accomplices to change their schedule, hence leaving an imperfect forgery in its place. Yet killing Robert Donaldson does not make any sense, since it was his death that led to discovering and foiling the scheme to begin with," Holmes observed.

"I suppose there is no point in trying to proclaim my innocence now," Anderson said quietly, as much an admission of guilt as it was defeat. "Donaldson's death was an accident. We got into an argument very early this morning when I slipped in to pay him for his participation in my scheme, creating the forgery and helping with its substitution for the real painting, before going on to the office for the day."

"Funds with which, in turn, Donaldson promised his landlord to cover his delinquent rent, for it was he who discovered the body of the deceased sooner than you probably hoped it would be found," Holmes surmised. "Not paying him was a wise move, for it laid doubt to the existence of Donaldson's mysterious benefactor and hid the fact you were ever there to begin with."

"You can imagine my shock at hearing my clerk announce you and Doctor Watson wanted to see me this morning," added Anderson. "If Scotland Yard had been involved with the matter from the start, they would have investigated a simple art robbery and gone directly to Donaldson if necessary, without ever contacting me. No matter when his remains were found, I was extremely careful not to be seen entering or leaving his building."

"Quite," said Holmes. "Yet what prompted the disagreement?"

"If the portrait's disappearance was not enough to have Van Horton change his mind in regards to marrying Miss Thompson, the next step would have been to destroy the painting, while arranging things so Van Horton discovered the pieces and blamed his fiancée for its destruction," Anderson answered blandly, revealing the rest of his plan. "I had no idea where Donaldson hid it, for I was not an active participant in the actual theft, but he grew quite enraged when I told him what might happen next. Donaldson demanded to know how I could do that to a work of art, let alone one of his paintings."

"Which resulted in the argument that led to his death," I deduced.

"Well, he can plead his case before the magistrate when he stands trial," said Lestrade, while pulling Anderson to his feet.

"I must know. Did you suspect me from the start Mister Holmes?" wondered Anderson. "I thought I was extremely careful during your visit to my office."

"You were, but the thieves came prepared with their own crate, indicating foreknowledge of their objective."

"The contract," realized the solicitor.

"Precisely," acknowledged Holmes. "Although oriented differently, it was a fortunate coincidence for you that the portrait and *Pêche Garçon* are basically the same size. That explains everything except when did Donaldson ever have the opportunity to sketch Miss Thompson without the lady's knowledge or permission?" inquired Holmes.

"As his friend, Van Horton would occasionally chat with me about his social plans. I looked for any opportunity, but the only time I could ever arrange things properly was once when he treated his fiancée and her aunt to dinner. We sat where Donaldson could observe the lady unnoticed and make sketches of her."

"Because the accusation of an unmarried woman allegedly spending hours alone with a man well beneath her social station would have been enough of a potential scandal for Van Horton to cancel his wedding plans," realized Holmes.

"Correct, but even if I could have figured out a plausible way to present the sketches to his Lordship, Donaldson refused to turn over the drawings," Anderson complained.

"Meaning?" asked the Inspector, not understanding the implication of what the solicitor had said.

Holmes answered the question. "He means that Robert Donaldson, having observed the subject in all her innocent joy, developed a latent conscience."

Inspector Lestrade's response to that comment was lost as I said, "Out of curiosity, was the cognac yours, or did you steal it from Van Horton's wine cellar?"

"Mine," Anderson replied. "Ironically, Van Horton gave it to me last year as a Christmas gift, and I had it with me when I went to visit Donaldson this morning. Originally I was going to give it to him as a bonus for his expertise in reproducing the Daneil; but after his death, I hid it in the loft to further incriminate Miss Thompson," he admitted. "Besides, since the office was my next stop, I did not want to bring it with me."

As Lestrade prepared to leave with the constables and their prisoners, Holmes stopped them.

"Just one moment more, please," Sherlock requested, as he bent down over Anderson's desk to write a note. Then Holmes walked over to Lestrade and said, "Even if he came by all of them honestly, Benjamin

Anderson has several paintings of note in his collection, a few of which are quite valuable. This is the contact information for Mister Faversham at the gallery. He can assist with ascertaining their true ownership and disposition."

"Thank you," said Lestrade drily, taking the note from Holmes with a sigh of resignation.

Our carriage ride back to Baker Street was quiet and uneventful.

When we returned to 221B, Mrs. Hudson greeted us at the door.

"I know it's late gentlemen," she said, referring to the fact it was now well after six that evening, "but you have another visitor. This one I'm sure you'll want to see, so I let him into your rooms."

"Thank you Mrs. Hudson, I've been expecting him," Holmes replied cryptically, as we ascended the stairs.

Curious as to who it might be, I followed Sherlock as we entered the main room of our quarters and discovered Mycroft Holmes perched rather uncomfortably in one of our chairs, his stout frame making any thoughts of relaxation a bit difficult.

"Your presence answers any further questions I still had about Reginald Van Horton," declared Sherlock, before moving forward to greet his older brother.

"Oh?" Mycroft said, while setting down the cup of tea Mrs. Hudson must have served him.

"Yes. The guards at an otherwise quiet estate, armed with weapons that only the British military could have issued. I presume that his Lordship must perform some service to the Crown that warrants such protection," observed Sherlock.

"Reginald Van Horton *might* be a trusted financial adviser in some key government matters, or one brother could simply be paying a friendly social visit to another," was Mycroft's only response.

"I see. And Miss Annabelle Thompson's role in Van Horton's life?" Sherlock prodded.

"Truthfully? Pure coincidence, though the lady obviously passed a thorough background check. The rest is strictly a private matter between them," Mycroft replied. "Now, unless you gentlemen have other plans this evening, I have made late dinner reservations for us at a fine restaurant in town. Can you join me Sherlock? I should like to hear all about your outing, for it sounds like you and Doctor Watson had a rather interesting adventure," he said, finally acknowledging my presence with a quick glance and a nod.

— — —

The next day we received word from Faversham that his Lordship was donating Delores' portrait to the gallery once Scotland Yard no longer needed it as evidence.

Two days later we received confirmation by private courier that the sum of ten thousand pounds, the amount previously promised us by his Lordship, had been deposited into Holmes' bank account.

With that report also came a personal invitation to the upcoming wedding of Reginald Van Horton to Miss Annabelle Thompson. Considering some of Sherlock's opinions in regard to the fairer sex and marriage, we would send them a nice gift along with our regrets that we could not attend.

The End

Mysteries in the London Fog

og shrouded cobblestone streets, the sound of a horse drawn conveyance fading in the distance as a constable blows his whistle upon discovering some foul deed having been committed within the lonely night far from the closest gaslight. Those are just some of the images one thinks of upon hearing the names Sherlock Holmes, Doctor John Watson, and Sir Arthur Conan Doyle.

My earliest memories of Victorian England's famous consulting detective are of Saturday matinees on television featuring Basil Rathbone and Nigel Bruce as Holmes and his closest friend, which led me to the Doyle canon.

Between four novels and fifty-six short stories, Holmes investigated and solved mysteries with just his intelligence in an age without computers, genetic evidence testing, and other modern conveniences. While I have no intention of ever giving up such things like my cellphone and computer, it is always a great joy to read a fantastic Sherlock Holmes adventure, whether it was written by his creator or one of the many talented people who have carried on the legacy since.

— — —

Lee Houston Jr.—is the writer/creator of the HUGH MONN, PRIVATE DETECTIVE and the ALPHA superhero novels published by Pro Se Press. He is also the Editor-In-Chief of The Free Choice E-zine at www.thefreechoice.info , maintains a professional blog at http://leehoustonjr.blogspot.com , and is an avid reader in what he laughing calls his "spare" time.

For Airship 27 he has already contributed stories to *Ghost Boy Volume 2*, *Sinbad-The New Voyages Volume 5* and *Tales of the Hanging Monkey Volume 2*.

Sherlock Holmes

in

"The Adventure of the Manhunting Marshal"

By
Peter Basile

*I*t should not be presumed that, in the wake of Professor Moriarty's demise, no one else made any attempt to rise to the level of eminence he had attained in London's criminal underworld. What *is* true is that there were none who were able to combine Moriarty's unique blend of intellectual prowess, ruthlessness, leadership skill, strategic and tactical brilliance, and sheer single-minded determination to succeed. And few who could match him for cruelty, calculated malice, or the pure delight he took in evil.

Those in his organization with the talent to have made a credible, if still inferior, substitute, such as his chief of staff, Colonel Sebastian Moran, or his most successful operative, John Clay (the architect of the Red-Headed League plot), had either been placed behind bars or hung, and his apparatus of trusted associates, what Holmes occasionally referred to as his "curia," had long since been dismantled. The one professional criminal at large in London who might have had the intelligence to undertake such a succession, Charles Augustus Milverton, was, in the first place, a specialist in a particular type of crime rather than a general practitioner like the Professor, and, in the second, had neither the temperament to work within an organization, nor the desire to lead one.

Still, nature abhors a vacuum, and Moriarty's absence created one. A vacuum which many were anxious to fill, and which some did for a short time, only to be quickly deposed by subordinates who, in their own turn, were also quickly deposed.

However, eventually, and perhaps inevitably, one figure did rise. One who, if he was not quite the equal of Moriarty, nevertheless displayed extraordinary talents and skills that served not only to put him at the top of London's criminal pyramid, but, for an unexpectedly lengthy period of time, to keep him there.

The paths of Holmes and I crossed his when, on a spring day in 1896, we received a visit, and a request for assistance, from a man who, in a former life, had been a trusted colleague of my old friend.

As we relaxed in the sitting room of our lodgings at Baker Street that afternoon, we heard Mrs. Hudson's opening the door below to allow someone entry. Heavy footsteps followed her lighter ones up the stairs.

"We're about to receive a visitor, Watson," said Holmes.

"A visitor or a client?" I responded.

"Perhaps both. I should think it likely that our caller will be an American, in his 30's, though looking perhaps five or ten years older than his actual age because he is an outdoorsman, his features weathered by frequent exposure to the elements. He will be tall, even taller than I, broad-shouldered, with a lean, muscular build. He will walk with the gait of one accustomed to spending a great deal of time on horseback, and will, I think, be wearing boots designed for riding. He will also be wearing a black waistcoat and trousers, and a black frock coat. His hat will be high-crowned and wide-brimmed. He will be armed with a .45 caliber Colt's Single Action Army revolver, the so-called 'Peacemaker.' Specifically, an Artillery model, with a five and half inch barrel, two inches shorter than the better-known Cavalry model. He will be carrying it in a cross-draw holster just off his left hip, under his coat. He may have a metallic star or shield pinned over the left breast of his outermost garment, signifying an official position he holds."

At first I was puzzled that, even with his great deductive genius, he could glean so much information having not even seen our caller, but then it occurred to me how he must have drawn his conclusions.

"I imagine he is someone you know, then," I said, "whose footsteps you recognize, even after the passage of some time. His attire must be his usual mode of dress, at least when he is in town. Though, since he is habitually an outdoorsman, the occasions on which he finds himself in town are, perhaps, relatively infrequent, which is why his dress at such times is so predictable. And from the rest of your description, I would infer that he is a member of a frontier constabulary of one sort or another, charged with the maintenance of law and order in some part of the American West."

Holmes chuckled. "You have spent enough time with me to have picked up some of my methods, Watson. Your attempts to apply them are not always correct, but, with time and practice, you have gotten much better, and are now accurate more often than not. My congratulations."

The door opened, and Mrs. Hudson announced Mr. Cordrell Vance. He was, as Holmes had predicted, a tall, lean, mustachioed man, with rugged, weathered, yet not unhandsome features. His attire was just what Holmes had foretold. I discerned a bulge under the coat which I concluded must be the pistol Holmes said he habitually carried. Over the left breast pocket of the coat was pinned a silver-colored, encircled five-point star.

Holmes smiled broadly as the gentleman entered. He had a great fondness for Americans, and for the United States, and believed that the rift that had led our respective nations to fight two wars in the comparatively recent past would, in time, be mended, and that, like family members who had quarreled, our two peoples would find the ties of blood, culture, and history too strong to resist, and, in consequence, be happily reconciled. In the year 1896, that reconciliation was already well-advanced.

"How may I help you, Mr. Vance?" he asked, giving no indication of a past relationship.

"Mr. Holmes," said Vance, "I'm a Deputy United States Marshal, normally commissioned in the Indian and Oklahoma Territories. Just now, I'm attached to the US Embassy here in London. I'm here to ask for your assistance on a missing persons case."

"And who is missing?"

"The best partner I ever had. A deputy marshal named Mike Croft. He showed up at the Federal Courthouse in Fort Smith, Arkansas, early in 1893. Claimed to have had some experience in detective work, and showed us a letter of reference from a Lieutenant Wilson Hargreaves of the New York Police Department. He was able to display some considerable skill at deduction by telling the presiding judge, Isaac Parker, things about himself, things no one else knew, just by looking at him. The judge said that anyone who was that observant would probably be a fine tracker and recommended that Marshal McAllister deputize him on the spot. Once he was sworn in, I was told to take him under m'wing, break him in, and teach him the ropes. He learned fast, damned fast, and, in a matter of months, the two of us made an outlaw-hunting team that rivaled the Three Guardsmen."

Even here in England, the frontier jurist whose court held virtually total criminal authority over the Indian Territory, was well-known. He would, in later years, come to be known as the "Hanging Judge" because of the number of people he had sentenced to the ultimate penalty. Bill Tilghman, Heck Thomas, and Chris Madsen, the three legendary peace officers who formed the law enforcement triumvirate known as "The Three Guardsmen of Oklahoma," were not as widely known in England as the court they rode for, though I was aware of them due to Holmes's constant perusal of crime and police news from all over the world.

"I see," said Holmes. "And what happened to end this marvelous partnership?"

"One day, late in November, while we were both back at Fort Smith, testifying in court cases that we'd been involved in, and preparing for our next trip down the owl hoot trail, I was called into Judge Parker's office. He told me that he'd received a piece of mail containing Mike's star and a letter of resignation from Mike saying that, while he was very proud of his service as a deputy, circumstances in his private life were such that he was forced to resign with immediate effect. No other explanation was given."

"And you believe this Croft might be here in London."

"I'm as certain of it as I am that I'm standing here looking at you."

The marshal had not greeted Holmes as a former acquaintance, despite Holmes's averral that my deduction of their already knowing each other was correct. That, along with the name of the missing deputy, "Mike Croft," and the name of his New York Police reference, Wilson Hargreaves, were certainly strong clues to the missing man's actual identity, as were his skill at deduction, and his nearly immediate mastery of the rudiments of fighting crime in an untamed and unfamiliar environment. And the marshal's response to Holmes's question suggested that he, too, might have had an inkling as to Mike Croft's true self.

"If I may interrupt, Marshal," I said, "may I ask why you have come to consult Holmes? As a policeman yourself, wouldn't it be more appropriate to seek the aid of Scotland Yard or the British Home Office prior to securing the assistance of a private consultant?"

"Am I, by any chance, addressing Dr. John Watson?" asked the marshal.

I bowed.

"A genuine honor, sir," he said. "And more'n an honor. A genuine pleasure. I'm a great admirer of yours. Own of all four of the books you've written about your work with Mr. Holmes, here. Don't have 'em with me at the moment, but sometime before I'm sent home, I'm hoping I can persuade you to sign 'em all for me."

"I'd be happy to, Marshal. But regarding the question I asked?"

"Yeah, well, without going into details, let's just say I reckon Mr. Holmes here is right well acquainted with ol' Mike. Probably better acquainted than any other person on the planet."

Holmes had been keeping both his own counsel and a poker face, but this declaration was too much for him. He started laughing uproariously.

"I felt," he said when he recovered himself, "that, of all those with whom I had spent any considerable time during what Watson has called my 'Great Hiatus,' it would be you, Vance, who would be able to make the connection between whatever identity I had adopted and my real self."

Vance joined in the laughter, and walked towards Holmes, offering his hand. Holmes stood up and gripped it with enthusiasm.

"I had my suspicions even when we were riding together," said Vance. "But the doc here was so definite that you were dead, that I was inclined to discount 'em. Still, your body was never found, and it occurred to me that, if you'd actually gotten the better of Moriarty, which, all things considered, didn't seem that unlikely, it might be prudent to fake your death 'til the remnants of Moriarty's command staff were all accounted for. When you suddenly disappeared from Arkansas, and, within a few months Sherlock Holmes was reported alive and well in London, I was reasonably sure my suspicions were right. And when I saw you sitting there, I was absolutely certain. A beard and a mustache don't disguise as much as most people think. Nor do spectacles that anyone could see were plain glass rather than cut to a prescription."

Holmes turned to me and, seeing what must have been a puzzled look on my face, said, "Are you so surprised, Watson, that I should turn out to be our visitor's long-lost colleague."

"Not really," I answered. "You had already made it clear to me that there was a prior acquaintance even before he entered. And your adventures in Asia and Africa while you were supposedly in your watery grave make a trip to the Americas a circumstance of your absence hardly likely to strain my credulity. Further, the pseudonym you chose for the occasion, 'Mike Croft,' was an obvious enough clue, even without the description of your abilities at the art of detection. Since the marshal, who, judging from his extravagant praise for my poor efforts as your chronicler, is probably familiar with 'The Greek Interpreter' and certainly with 'The Final Problem,' he might also have been struck by the phonetic similarity between the name you chose for your American alter ego and the Christian name of your brother. The letter of introduction from Lieutenant Hargreaves was also telling, though I don't believe I have mentioned him in any of the accounts of our adventures published to date, so Marshal Vance might be unaware that he has long been a friend and colleague of yours."

"Bravo, Watson," said Holmes. "Well reasoned. To what, then, may I attribute your look of puzzlement?"

"Notwithstanding my reasoning, I am utterly astonished that, even under a false name, you would be willing to become an officer of a lawfully authorized police agency. Given your oft-stated contempt for the organizational strictures under which so many of our official colleagues have to labor, to say nothing of your own stubborn independence, it is not an occupation I would expect you to choose."

"It does seem surprising, put in that light," Holmes admitted. "But Judge Parker, though careful about preserving the smallest niceties of due process, is a man more concerned with getting the job done, than in satisfying pettifogging bureaucrats, comfortably seated behind desks, who needlessly burden those charged with performing the dangerous duty of enforcing the law in the field with onerous and pointless regulations. Moreover, Vance was almost as agreeable a comrade as you."

He turned to Vance and said, "I've heard the judge is sickly."

"He is. Can't see how he'll last out the year. When he was all the law there was in Indian Territory, he was like to work himself to death. Now that some of the load's been taken off, with the opening of courts in Kansas and Texas, and the splitting of the jurisdiction into two territories, Indian and Oklahoma, he still hasn't let up on himself. Laboring harder'n ever, as if he knows he hasn't much time left to complete his work. Also, he's been talking to his wife about converting to her religion, which, to me, means he sees the end coming."

"Why is that?" I asked.

"Judge is Methodist. His missus is Catholic. Very devoted to her faith. A bit more, I think, than the Judge is to his, though he's very much a God-fearing man. When you see the end coming, and there are some eighty men who've had their necks stretched on your say-so waiting for you on the other side, well, maybe you might get to thinking that you need a little stronger backing to meet your Maker than the Reverend Mr. John Wesley can provide."

"Parker's a fine man, whatever his faith," said Holmes. "A man of duty and commitment. I hope he finds the comfort he seeks."

Turning to Vance, he pointed to a chair, and, when the marshal was comfortably settled, said, "Since your missing persons case is solved, is there any other way I might assist you?"

"There most certainly is," he said. "You remember Sailor Ned?"

"The man who shot Martin Thomas. I do indeed. He's never been caught?"

"No he hasn't. And I believe he's here in London. I mean to find him, arrest him, and get him extradited back into Judge Parker's court while His Honor's still alive to preside at Ned's trial. And I need the help of a man who's as familiar with the criminal byways of this town as I am with the owl hoot in the Territories."

"Perhaps you could give Watson a quick summary of the case," said Holmes.

"Nothing easier," replied the frontier law officer. "It starts with a group of bandits called the Bolton Gang, led by three brothers, Rob, Matt, and Elliot, who were distantly related, by marriage, to Frank and Jesse James. They formed their gang around 1889, just about the time the western half of Indian Territory got opened up for settlement to become Oklahoma Territory. Their specialty was robbing trains, but they held up banks pretty frequently, too. And, while they spent most of their time in the Territories, they covered the whole West, from New Mexico, to California, to Colorado. There was a fourth brother, Will, who lived in California, and rode with the gang on the only robbery they committed in that state, the hold-up of a Southern Pacific train. Technically, I suppose, he was a member of the gang, too, but that was the only time he was ever an active participant. I mention him, 'cause he becomes important later.

"By 1892, they'd probably stolen more in three or four years than the Jameses and Youngers did in more'n fifteen. The combined totals on the rewards for their capture offered by the railroads, express companies, and banks amounted to more than $25,000, more'n twice what was offered for Frank and Jesse. Course, there were three Boltons, four if you count Will, and only two Jameses.

"They'd gathered a pretty sizable gang to back 'em on their raids. Jeff 'Muddy Waters' Newsome, a fellah named Chuck Price about whom not a whole lot's known, a Texan named Cal 'Powder Burn' Byrnes, Rick Brood, Phil Abel, and a fellah they all called 'Sailor Ned.'

"This fellah Ned, spoke with an English accent. Refined, but with just a touch of rough, working class cadence under the educated varnish. Claimed he'd been born in the States, but that his father was an Englishman, a sailor in the Royal Navy who'd married his mother while his ship was docked in New York. After Ned was born, his mother joined his father in England, and that's where Ned grew up. When Ned was about twelve or thirteen, he followed in his father's footsteps, and joined the Royal Navy, only he was on the track to a commission. Enrolled in the Royal Navy's training school at—you're a military man, Doc. Where'd that be?"

"Perhaps you're thinking of the Royal Naval Academy at Dartmouth."

"That's it. Anyway, he claimed to have graduated with honors, and that he moved up the ranks pretty damned fast, considering there was no war. Said he made commander before he was thirty. For a time he was an instructor in mathematics, which he had a particular knack for, at Dartmouth. But, being the son of a common sailor, he was never respected by his brother officers, and was eventually cashiered out of the Navy on trumped-up charges.

"Being American on his mother's side, he returned to the land of his birth, and sought a new life out west. Believe it or not, a sailor's skills can come in right handy on the frontier. The Great Plains are a lot like an ocean, 'cept you can walk on 'em. A fellah can go miles and miles without seeing a familiar landmark. And someone who knows how to steer by the stars can be mighty useful. On top of which, being a former military man, he was reliable in a fight.

"You see what I'm getting at, Doc? Here's a man, a former military officer, cashiered out of the service, gifted at math, with experience teaching at the university level. A fellah who combines some of the talents of Moriarty, the mathematics genius and university professor, and Moran, the ruthless former soldier. And with all the hands-on experience he was getting in armed robbery, he was developing the same kinds of practical skills at crime as that Clay fellah.

"Now in the Fall of 1892, Rob Bolton got the idea of robbing a town near where they grew up, Coffeeboro, Kansas. Small town, but big enough that it had two banks. He got the notion of robbing both banks simultaneously in broad daylight. It'd be a crime that required split-second timing and careful planning. The story is that Sailor Ned talked against it, thought it was biting off more'n they could chew, and strongly advised 'em not to try it. But Rob was dead set on doing something that even the Jameses weren't able to bring off. Figured if they could succeed at this robbery, they'd be one up on their shirt-tail cousins who failed miserably when they tried a similar raid in Northfield, Minnesota."

Holmes broke in at that point, "What Vance leaves out, Watson, is that the Boltons felt pressured to make the raid because Vance was only a step or two behind them. They hoped one big robbery would net them enough that they would be able to leave the area and lay low until the pressure Vance was putting on them died down."

"Well, that's the opinion of some folks," said Vance. "I make no such claim. Anyway, the three brothers, along with Brood and Abel, rode into town on October 5th, 1892. Newsome, Price, Byrnes, and Ned apparently all thought it was too risky. Some accounts say that one or another of 'em rode as far as the outskirts of town, then got cold feet and let the other five ride in without 'im. Some say it was Ned, who spent the whole ride trying

"A fellah who combines some of the talents of Moriarty..."

to talk the others out of the raid, than refused to come in when they hit the outskirts of town.

"Well, the long and the short of it is that the whole thing went wrong. The gang was recognized as soon as they rode into Coffeeboro. Town marshal tried to arrest 'em, got killed for his trouble, but the rest of the folks rose up and immediately formed a kinda makeshift posse. The lead started flying. When the dust settled and the smoke cleared, Rob and Matt Bolton, Brood, and Able were all dead. Elliot Bolton was badly wounded, but survived to stand trial. He was sentenced to life in the Kansas state prison at Lansing.

"Newsome, Price, Byrnes, and Ned were all that was left of the original Bolton gang, unless you count Will Bolton, who was out in California. Ned stepped in and started running things. Will joined 'em a few months later, and, being the last Bolton, regarded himself as the gang's leader, but, if so, he wasn't more'n a figurehead. Ned was the fellah actually running things. And he ran 'em well.

"He added seven new members, and immediately began a crime campaign the likes of which the Territories had never seen before. The newly organized gang robbed trains, banks, stores, post offices; anyplace there was a large supply of ready cash. They amassed more in six months than both the James-Younger Gang and the original Bolton gang did in their whole combined careers. In September, 1893, we ran 'em to ground in an Oklahoma town called Wilder, but we were about as successful apprehending 'em as the Boltons were robbing those two banks in Coffeeboro. Three federal marshals wound up dead. Sailor Ned personally did for one of 'em, Dash Richards. And except for one desperado named 'Arkansas Tim' O'Neal, the whole gang escaped. You were there, Holmes. You remember how it was."

"Indeed," said Holmes. "Too much complicated planning, too many things that could go wrong. And just about everything that could go wrong, did. The notion, Watson, if you can believe it, was to have twenty-seven officers, mostly deputy marshals, some Indian tribal police, and a deputy sheriff from Kansas, enter the town in three covered wagons, supposedly appearing to be freighters or settlers. But we were spotted the night before, and the outlaws were forewarned. As a soldier, you're undoubtedly aware of the maxim that 'forewarned' is, for practical purposes, a synonym for 'forearmed.' They saddled their horses for a quick getaway hours before we rode into town, and were waiting in ambush as we arrived."

"A complete disaster," agreed Vance. "One of the other marshals on the Wilders raid was Deputy Marty Thomas. Decentest man I ever knew. During the gunfight, he managed to get a bead on Sailor Ned, and wounded him pretty bad with his Winchester. We didn't hear anything about Ned for awhile. Some thought he might have died and been buried by the rest of the gang. Will Bolton had apparently taken over the gang. But he wasn't running it as well as Ned had, and little by little, they were all getting whittled down, a bit at a time.

"Turns out, though, that Ned was just wounded, not killed. And he was mighty angry at Marty for injuring him so badly. While his gang was getting cut down to size, Ned was recovering, and planning his revenge on Marty.

"Now Marty Thomas lived in a small house in Salisaw, in the Cherokee Nation of Indian Territory, with his wife and seven kids. Marty was a quarter Cherokee, and his wife a Cherokee full-blood. He was off-duty one night, sitting on his front porch, reading a book. He was right fond of that Dickens fellah. Book he was reading was one of his favorites, *Oliver Twist*. Don't know if that means anything, but it always struck me that he happened to be reading a story about an orphan, since that's what his kids were about to become. As he sat there reading, a rider came up, dismounted and walked toward the front of Marty's house. Marty's wife was hanging clothes in another part of the porch. Four of his seven kids were playing in the front yard of the house. Marty was unarmed, and there was no weapon within his reach. When the rider was about fifteen feet away, Marty looked up. The rider called out to him.

"'I owe you for that rifle ball, Marshal,' He said. And, with that, he drew his pistol and fired all six shots into Marty, every one of 'em belly shots. Hellishly painful, almost always fatal. Eventually. But hardly ever *immediately* fatal. He wanted Marty to suffer before he died. And he wanted Marty's wife and kids to see it.

"He rode off without anyone stopping him. It was a Sunday. No one was armed. No one was on horseback. Twelve witnesses who knew him by sight said it was Sailor Ned. He was never seen again.

"In the meantime, Will Bolton was proving just how important Ned's leadership was. Within months of Marty's death every member of the gang was in jail or dead. Every member except Sailor Ned.

"By this time, Mike Croft had turned in his badge and gone back to whatever life he'd left before pinning it on. A few months after that the Eastern newspapers were reporting that the famous criminal investigator, Sherlock Holmes, long thought to have been killed by Professor James

Moriarty in Switzerland, had turned up alive in London, and had appre-hended Moriarty's second-in-command, Colonel Sebastian Moran. When I read that Holmes was alive, I was sure as I could be, without actually lay-ing eyes on him, that that's who Mike Croft really was. When I finally saw Holmes face-to-face today, I was a hundred per cent sure."

"Fascinating story," I said. "And Sailor Ned remains at large to this day?"

"He does. I asked to be put on his case full-time, and was granted the request. A lawman takes his chances when he pins on a star. Three of us were killed at Wilder, as I said. But shooting it out with an armed officer while resisting arrest is one thing. Gunning down an unarmed man in his own home in front of his family is something else. What happened to Marty Thomas was purely mean and evil and I intend to see that the man who did it gets property punished."

"How did you pick up his trail?" I asked.

"Well, you have to understand, Doc, we federal marshals aren't detec-tives in the true sense of the word. We're fugitive-catchers. Manhunters. It's not our job to identify unknown offenders, or to solve mysteries. We go after people who've already been identified, people we have arrest warrants for. Course, finding a fellah who doesn't want to be found, that might require some investigative skill, but it's not the same as gathering evidence to make a case in court, or drawing conclusions from a crime scene. That said, we're pretty damned good at what we do. I think Holmes here'll bear me out."

"Indeed I shall. At fugitive apprehension, Watson, particularly in a largely unsettled area, there are few who can touch the United States Marshals. Perhaps the Northwest Mounted Police in Canada. Perhaps the Rangers in Texas. Perhaps some of the colonial police forces in Africa, Australia, or India. But, by and large, the Marshals are in a class by them-selves."

"Point I'm making, Doc, is I already knew who I was looking for. Didn't know his true name or history, but I knew who'd killed Marty Thomas. Wasn't a question of figuring out who the guilty party was. Just a question of tracking him down."

I nodded.

"Well, I started with the notion that the rumors about Sailor Ned's past were, at least partly, true. So, with the help of the British Embassy in Washington, I started researching Royal Navy officers who were about the right age, and who'd left the service, or been forced from the service, shortly before Sailor Ned turned up on the frontier.

"Took awhile, culling through all the possibilities, but one possible suspect finally emerged that fit the circumstances better'n anyone else. His name was Edward Dolan. First of all, he was born in New York, though he was a British subject through his father, a petty officer in the Royal Navy. Second, his Christian name was Edward, which 'Ned' is a nickname for. Third, he was a graduate of the Naval College at Devonshire. Wasn't an honor graduate like he claimed, but he did get a prize in mathematics. Fourth, he'd been a mathematics instructor at Devonshire. Fifth, he was forced to leave the service 'cause of allegations involving misappropriated funds. He resigned rather than request a court-martial, which, while jumping to conclusions is never a good idea on a manhunt, is about as close to an admission of guilt as I can imagine short of his actually pleading guilty. Only thing that didn't match, besides not quite being an honor graduate, was he'd never held the rank of commander. Closest he ever got was 'lieutenant in command,' which is what they call lieutenants in the Royal Navy who captain smaller vessels. Got me some official photographs of Dolan, courtesy of the British Admiralty, mixed 'em up with some photographs of other Royal Navy officers who were of an age, and similar description, and showed 'em to all the witnesses who saw Marty getting gutshot. Every one of 'em identified Dolan. Judge Parker upgraded the John Doe murder warrant to one that had Dolan's name written in black and white. Now all I had to do was find 'im and serve it."

"What brought you to England?" I asked.

"Not too much more'n a hunch, Doc," said Vance. "This is his home, the place he grew up. Often, when a man goes to ground, he chooses somewhere that's familiar and comfortable. Of course, when he was actually growing up, it was in places like Portsmouth and Plymouth, where the Navy's prominent. But, if a man's trying to hide, London's the place to go. Further, it occurred to me that, with Moriarty and Moran out of the way, he might see an opportunity."

"An opportunity?" said Holmes.

"The London underworld is currently a ship without a captain. And, after all, Dolan does have experience taking over criminal enterprises that suddenly find themselves without a leader."

"By God!" cried Holmes. "You might have something there, Vance. Watson, do you recall what Lestrade mentioned when he dropped by to visit the other day?"

"Yes, now that you mention it. He said there were rumors that some new figure was successfully taking over what was left of London's various criminal enterprises. Just rumors, though. Nothing confirmed."

"Exactly! And do you recall the name of the person at the center of those rumors."

"He didn't have a name. Just a sort of alias or cognomen that was being spoken of throughout London." I paused as I recalled the conversation in greater detail, then said, "Dear Lord, I see what you're getting at, Holmes!"

"Yes, Watson, it all fits!"

"What does?" asked Vance.

"This mysterious new figure said to have taken over London's criminal underworld is being referred to by the sobriquet 'The Commander.'"

As I mentioned earlier, the state of London's criminal underworld had been in a virtually constant state of fluctuation since Moriarty's departure from this mortal coil, as contenders (not to say "pretenders," since it was not a hereditary position) covetously eyed the post Moriarty had left vacant and started licking their lips. This state of fluctuation that had devolved into outright chaos once Moran was behind bars, and those same contenders for Moriarty's throne vied with each other for position. A few of the most ruthless managed to rise to the top only to be toppled after an embarrassingly short reign. In such a state, the criminal classes did not operate at anywhere near the efficiency that had been displayed during Moriarty's administration.

But, for the last three or four months, the instability had calmed to a degree, and, if thieves and villains had not regained their former level of productivity, they were certainly practicing their trades with greater cooperation than had been the case since the altercation at Reichenbach Falls in 1891.

According to Inspector Lestrade, who occasionally looked in upon us of an evening, just to bring us up to date with what was going on at the Yard, and among London's criminal classes, there were whispers of a new figure wearing Moriarty's crown. Said to be a former military officer, he was referred to only by the title he claimed to have attained during his suddenly curtailed career in the King's Service.

Nothing else was known about him. Not his name, his location, his physical description, nor his history prior to his arrival in the Metropolis.

For that matter, it was not even known with absolute certainty whether or not the so-called Commander actually existed at all, since many insisted he was merely a figure of myth and fantasy.

But the coincidence of his reported rise to prominence in London, coming so closely after Sailor Ned Dolan's apparent departure from the American frontier, seemed significant.

⌁ ⌁ ⌁

"Holmes," said Vance, "since Dolan's personally responsible for the deliberate murder of two federal marshals, is answerable for the deaths of two more, and has led robberies of three different post offices, and four mail cars in train robberies, the Government's offering a reward of three thousand dollars for Dolan, dead or alive. As a federal employee, I'm not eligible to collect that bounty, but I'd back your claim, if you'd lend me your help."

"And what of the railroads, banks, and express companies?" asked Holmes. "Are they not offering a reward?"

"The total amount of private reward money offered for the capture of Dolan, dead or alive, comes to more'n five thousand dollars."

"And this you mean to claim for yourself, should your search be successful?"

"I do."

Holmes would later explain to me that federal marshals were not paid a salary, but rather a set fee for each arrest made, each process served, and each mile traveled with at least one prisoner in custody. That being the case, though barred from rewards offered by the Government, they were permitted to claim rewards offered by private companies or individuals. It was a welcome and, for men with families, often a necessary addition to their income.

"I thought as much," continued Holmes. "And, as you have chased him halfway round the world, you'll have earned every cent. But I rode with you long enough to suspect that, though you have not said so, in this case, if you gain the reward, you mean to turn it over to Marshal Thomas's family."

Vance looked away, embarrassed that his generous intention had been discerned.

"Watson, what say you? If our search for Sailor Ned is successful, and our claim to the US Government's reward upheld, shall we follow our

American colleague's unselfish example? Shall we adhere to precepts so eloquently expressed in the First Letter of St. James?"

"You refer. I collect, to that passage about offering solace 'to the fatherless and widows in their affliction,'" I answered. "I agree whole-heartedly."

And with that, we began to plan.

Tracking down someone who does not want to be found is less a matter of deductive reasoning that it is of legwork and perseverance. But deduction comes into the process when one tries to reason out the most likely place to look.

"Vance, have you copies of the photograph of Dolan?" asked Holmes.

"Sure do. Plenty. The embassy has a photo lab."

"Excellent! You may recall, from Watson's accounts, that I maintain a network of street urchins as informants and semi-professional tails. If we know where to concentrate them, we should be able to find Dolan's location, if he is, in fact, the Commander."

The membership of the Baker Street Irregulars had changed over the years as the original boys grew older and went on to more adult pursuits, while others took their place. The group had entered a period of inactivity following Holmes's supposed death, but had been reorganized upon his return. The one-time leader, Sam Wiggins, now an adult, had gone on to become, of all things, a constable in the Metropolitan Police, and had recently been promoted to a "Winter Patrol," a plainclothes detective in training, at one of the Yard's local divisional stations. At the time of this adventure, the leader of the Holmes's improvised corps of junior sleuths was a young fellow named Bill Fitzgerald.

"Though the professional London criminal regards the entire Metropolis as his rightful hunting ground," continued Holmes, "it is in the East End that he truly feels at home. The majority of the East End's residents are, of course, decent, law-abiding people, but the neighborhood is, nevertheless, quite properly regarded as the abode of London criminality in general. And the hub of the East End is Whitechapel. Hence Whitechapel is where we shall begin."

Results were not long in coming. Three days after receiving the assignment, Fitzgerald reported that the group's surveillance of Whitechapel had yielded two strong possibilities. Both closely resembled the figure in the photographs they had all been issued. Both were seen entering and exiting warehouses in the district. One seemed to actually have lodgings in the warehouse. The other commuted to a nearby residential neighborhood.

"The one what lives there," said Fitzgerald, "seems to take 'is meals and such there, too. But, every day, 'e comes out and takes 'imself a trip in a 'Ansom out 'ere to Westminster. Goes to a Turkish bath what's next door to the Northumberland Arms near Trafalgar Square."

"That's him!" said Vance. "Ned always had a weakness for steam baths. Just before he dropped out of sight completely, I almost caught up with him in Eureka Springs. I'd heard he was spending a few days 'taking the water' there. Probably thought it would be more out of the way than Hot Springs. But the spas at Eureka Springs are almost as popular. I arrived around noon only to find he'd checked out that morning and was in the wind."

Both Holmes and I shared Sailor Ned's fondness for steam baths, and the bath house next door to the Northumberland Arms was familiar to both of us. As was the hotel itself. Shortly before my marriage to my dear, departed Mary, nearly a decade earlier, the Northumberland had figured in cases I have recorded elsewhere as "The Adventure of the Noble Bachelor" and *The Hound of the Baskervilles.*

"Does he arrive at the bath house at a regular time?" asked Holmes.

"Gen'rally, 'e leaves 'is digs 'round two o'clock. Usually 'rives at two thirty or thereabouts," replied Fitzgerald.

"Then we shall start our surveillance tomorrow at two," said Holmes.

The following afternoon found us seated at a table by the front window of a small tea room across the street from the inn and the bath house. From this vantage point, we were able to see all arriving Hansoms and other conveyances and to view all men entering the spa.

Vance, standing out from the crowd both by virtue of his size and by the obviously non-British cut of his clothes, had elected to disguise himself. Since his suit was already black, he simply replaced his string tie with a clerical collar, and his wide-brimmed, western-style Stetson with a

We were able to see all arriving Hansoms and to view all men entering the spa.

more modest shovel hat of the type favored by both Anglican and Roman clergy in England. The circled star that bespoke his status as a law officer employed by the US Government had been removed from his coat and pinned to his waistcoat, out of sight. He had also shaved off his mustache, and added a pair of spectacles. The transformation made by these small adjustments was really quite astonishing.

Holmes and I, being on our own home ground, and dressed in attire typical of London gentlemen, already blended into the surrounding area with relative ease, sans any sort of disguise.

At twenty-five minutes to three, a Hansom cab came to a stop at the entrance to the bath house, and a tall, cadaverously thin, well-dressed man got off and entered the building.

"That's him," said Vance. "Lost a lot of weight recovering from that Winchester round Marty put in him, but it's him. Let's go fetch us a beat cop, then go in and serve my warrant."

The constable on patrol in that neighborhood turned out to be almost painfully youthful, with less than six months experience at his trade, and less than a month's patrolling on his own without an older, more experienced officer looking out for him. To say he was thoroughly nonplussed at a tall parson introducing himself as a federal policeman from the American West, and claiming to have an arrest warrant for the man running London's underworld would be an understatement. But when he learned that said lawman was being assisted by Sherlock Holmes, he was positively dazzled.

"Sherlock Holmes of Baker Street?" he said, his eyes wide as saucers. "Well, of course, if *you* say it's all right, Mr. Holmes."

It was amazing to me how Holmes's relations with the official police had improved over the years since he had first set up his practice as a consulting detective. Though he had always had friends and supporters on the Force, there were, in the early years, many who regarded him with suspicion, and many who looked askance at the irritatingly self-confident young interloper with his odd theories about the science of deduction. Now it seemed that the suspicion had been replaced with a kind of hero worship, and I had no doubt that there were many in the Metropolitan Police who would follow an order given by Sherlock Holmes more readily than one given by Colonel Sir Edward Bradford himself, who, as the

Commissioner of Scotland Yard, was nothing less than the highest-ranking policeman in all the Realm.

It had, by this time, been some ten or fifteen minutes since Dolan had entered the bath house, sufficient time for him to have disrobed and entered one of the steam rooms. The four of us entered and quickly obtained the location of the tall, thin man who had come in a short time earlier. Holmes and I, familiar with the bath house from our own frequenting of it, led the way to the room we were directed to, but when we arrived, Vance insisted on going in first.

"The officer here's in uniform, so it can't be him. And he might know you and Watson from your pictures in the papers. But in this parson's get-up, I can take him by surprise. Anyway, it's *my* arrest. The constable should wait just outside the doorway, and you and the doc hang back just inside and be ready to back me up."

With that he boldly entered. Holmes and I followed him through the doorway, but hung back as he had instructed. The young constable, as directed, stayed out of sight by the entrance, ready to lend a hand when needed.

Dolan, lounging comfortably on one of the benches, opened his eyes languidly, and seeing nothing but a parson and two London gentlemen who'd apparently lost their way trying to find the dressing rooms, closed them again.

Vance walked over to the bench on which Dolan was laying, drawing his Colt as he moved forward. When he was standing over the fugitive, he abruptly pulled him into a sitting position, and sticking the barrel of his pistol under Dolan's chin, said, "Don't make a move, Sailor Ned. You're under arrest."

"Who are you?" said the astonished outlaw.

"If you look close, I think you'll recognize me," replied the marshal. "But all you really need to know is, first, that I'm Law, and, second, that Marty Thomas and Dash Richards were both friends of mine."

"Cord Vance," hissed the bandit king.

"Right the first time."

"You have no authority here, Vance."

"I got me a warrant in my pocket signed by Judge Parker himself and diplomatic status to go with it. And, if that's not enough, I got me a

London law just outside this room. Whatever authority I don't have, he does." Raising his voice he called out, "Constable, come on in. Sailor Ned here needs to see someone with authority."

The constable entered with dispatch and, with all the legal niceties scrupulously observed, Sailor Ned Dolan was taken into custody.

The process of extradition can be a lengthy one under the best of circumstances, and, in this case, the issue was complicated by the fact that the party whose extradition was requested by the United States, though a US citizen according to the American constitution by virtue of his birth in New York, was a British subject according to the legal principle of *jus sanguinis*, since his father had been British. Still the facts of the case against him were fairly clear, and, even if Dolan had not been American by birth, British subjects were extraditable to America for crimes committed there, just as American citizens were extraditable to Britain for crimes committed in our nation.

Nevertheless, Dolan was contesting the request with all his might and main. He was incarcerated in the Newgate Prison, adjacent to the Old Bailey, while one of the justices reviewed the request for extradition to make sure there was a case to answer before submitting the request to the premier, Lord Salisbury, who, in his additional capacity as Foreign Minister, would make the final decision. Dolan was utilizing a virtual regiment of lawyers to delay the final outcome.

In certain respects, this delay worked to Vance's advantage. Enchanted with London, and happy for the chance to renew his friendship with the man he had first known as "Mike Croft," he contracted with Mrs. Hudson for the short-term use of a spare bedroom she had on the first floor of 221 Baker, and, at our invitation, made full use of our apartment's sitting room. He even worked with us on a case, one in which Inspector Lestrade was particularly involved, that came our way while the extradition was slowly working its way through the mills of justice, a case I have recorded separately since, aside from the coincidence of its occurring while the ultimate fate of Dolan was still at issue, it had nothing whatever to do with the account you are now reading.

For myself, I was happy for the chance to become better acquainted with Vance. One evening, after dinner, as the three of us relaxed in our sitting room over pipes and cigars, I asked Vance how he had come to be a federal marshal.

"Well, Doc," he said, "I was born in Missouri during The War." To Americans of his generation, "The War" could only mean the tragic, bloody conflict between the states that had nearly torn the American nation asunder between 1861 and 1865. "Missouri was a border state. Slavery was legal, but the state had elected to stay in the Union. Still, a lot of Missourians were pro-Confederate. Lots of families, including mine, had relatives fighting on both sides. To this day, a lot of the old resentments still smolder. Wasn't a pleasant place to grow up, so, when I was sixteen, I lit out on my own, headed for Texas, and joined the 8th Cavalry. Spent three years fighting Apaches in Texas and New Mexico. Didn't take to military life as well as you did, Doc. Proud of my service, and all that, but I wasn't meant for a lifer, so I came back home to Missouri.

"Kansas City had started its own police force a few years earlier, so I joined up. For two years, I walked a beat in uniform, a lot like your bobbies over here. Now I might not have liked soldiering, but I did like letting a horse do most of my walking for me, so I resigned after two years, and headed back to Texas. Spent some time with the Rangers under Captain George Baylor. Did a little more Indian fighting, but mostly we chased outlaws. After I left the Rangers, I signed up with the Katy—that's the Missouri, Kansas, and Texas Railway, Doc. We call it the 'Katy' for short —as a railroad detective. Since the Katy ran through Indian Territory, a lot of us cinder cops got ourselves deputized by the US Marshal at Fort Smith so we'd have law enforcement authority there. Eventually, I gave up the railroad job and went to work for Judge Parker full-time."

"You've packed a lot of living into a comparatively short time, Vance," I said. "You're not even forty, yet."

"Actually I'm not quite 35, but you're right. There's a lot of mileage on this face of mine. On the other hand, I never fought in Afghanistan. Never chased the Napoleon of Crime into Switzerland. Never carried out a mission at the personal request of the King of England or the Pontiff of Rome. Or the President of the United States, for that matter, which would've been more likely. Never fell in love or married. You've had a fairly eventful life, too, Doc."

"Falling in love can have a bitter side," I said.

"Sorry, Doc. Didn't mean to worry a wound that's still festering. But, after all, would you be happier now if you'd never met her at all?"

"Of course you're right," I answered. "I cherish every moment I was able to spend with Mary."

"I envy you that," he said. "I'd gladly take the pain if it came with the memories.

— — —

Marshal Vance's apparent wistfulness about never having fallen in love, may, if Tennyson is correct, be attributed to its being spring. However, in my own experience, which, as I have noted elsewhere, extends over many nations and three separate continents, it does not have to be spring for a young man's fancy to turn to thoughts of love.

All it takes is meeting the right lady.

For Cordrell Vance, thoroughly American peace officer of the western frontier of the United States, the right lady turned out to be one nobody could ever have predicted. Her name was Naya O'Riley. Like my Mary, she was the daughter of a soldier in the Indian Army who had spent a good portion of her youth in the Bharatan Subcontinent. Like my Mary, she was named for the Savior's mother. And, like my Mary, she was em-ployed as a governess in London. Unlike my Mary, she was the product of an Irish father and an Indian mother, not an uncommon circumstance there, but one that might cause many in London society to look askance at the match. Vance was oblivious to any such criticism. Though misce-genation was illegal in many of the states of his homeland, in the Indian and Oklahoma Territories such mixed-race unions were not at all unusual, and, for him, the qualities that mattered had little to do with her exotic background.

She was sweet-natured, kind, modest, honest to a fault, intelligent, and extraordinarily pretty. Everything Vance could hope for in a life's partner.

It had been, in a sense, one of the children Miss O'Riley cared for who had been the means of bringing the couple together.

Vance had made it a habit, while staying at Baker Street, of trading in what he called his "town suit" for his rough trail clothes two or three times a week, hiring a horse from one of the nearby stables, and riding it through the Regents Park.

"A man who spends as much time in the saddle as I do, Doc, needs to feel a horse under him every now and then."

On one such afternoon, Miss O'Riley was in the park with her charges, the three children of Colonel and Mrs. Wentworth. Five-year-old Peter Wentworth, the only boy among the three youngsters, saw the horse and its rider, a man in a wide-brimmed hat and frontier regalia who, to a young lad, must have looked like the cover of a western penny dreadful come to life. Before his governess could stop him, he ran off for a closer look, putting himself in Vance's path. Vance, however, knew better than to risk bringing his mount to a full gallop in a public park, and had been riding his horse in that frontier version of a canter known as the "lope." Thus, it was fairly easy for him to rein up before lad and horse collided. When he met the young lady into whose care the young fellow had been entrusted, he was rather happy that circumstances had caused the paths of the boy and the mount to cross.

The courtship proceeded quite quickly, since Vance wanted things settled before he had to return to the United States with his prisoner. Her parents had both passed, so there was no need to seek their approval. Her employers chose not to stand in her way. And there was no law in Britain prohibiting it.

The sticking point, surprisingly enough, was Miss O'Riley's religion. She had been baptized a Catholic, like her father (on that occasion she had been christened with a name that had represented a compromise between her parents, since it meant, translating very roughly, "virgin" in Hindi, and thus honored both her mother's heritage and her father's devotion to the Blessed Mother). Her mother, in the course of time, had also eventually converted to the creed of her husband and her daughter. Consequently, Miss O'Riley, faithfully raised in the Roman faith, insisted on getting married in a Catholic Church, and, as Vance was a Baptist (though, as he put it, "I don't work at it that much."), some hurdles had to be cleared before the Church would sanction the marriage.

Accordingly, Vance had to work his way through a lot of Canon Law paperwork, signing agreements promising that any children produced after Miss O'Riley became his wife would be raised Catholic, and that he would never stand in the way of her practicing her religion. Though he, himself, did not agree to convert, he did promise that he "would study on it seriously."

As he said to me one evening at Baker Street, after one of several counseling sessions with a priest the couple attended prior to their nuptials, "After all, Doc, Mrs. Parker's a Catholic, and she's one of the finest women I know. And Naya . . . well, Naya's *the* finest woman I know. Might just be something to this here Catholicism."

Eventually, the ecclesiastical obstacles successfully overcome, the banns were called for three consecutive Sundays, and on a bright, sunny Saturday morning, early in June, at St. James's Church in Spanish Place, the couple was united in the sacred bonds of matrimony. To me, an Indian Army veteran like her father, came the honor of giving the bride away in her father's stead. Holmes stood up with Vance, performing the same office that he had once performed for me and my Mary. Miss O'Riley was attended by one of her Irish cousins. To young Peter Wentworth, the serendipitous matchmaker came the important duty of carrying the bride's train. The youngest Wentworth daughter served as the flower girl, while the two older were junior bridesmaids.

There were, surprisingly, since her parents had both died, a fairly large number of guests on the bride's side, family members from both the Indian and the Irish branches, along with the Wentworth family. On the groom's side of the church, there were only Holmes and myself, some employees of the American embassy, and a few colleagues from the Yard. Lestrade, Gregson, Hopkins, Jones, Bradstreet, and Lanner, along with their various ladies were all present. Patterson, out of town on a case, was forced to miss the festivities. MacDonald, dedicated to his own "Kirk," and retaining more than a vestige of that long-standing antipathy to the Roman Church so common among Scots, declined to attend a service he regarded as "idolatrous."

Following a short celebratory repast arranged by Mrs. Hudson, the couple was off to the North of England for a short honeymoon in the Lakes District.

And it was while the happy bride and groom were enjoying their wedding trip that Sailor Ned escaped from prison.

"It's as though he disappeared into thin air," said Lestrade.

He had arrived at our Baker Street lodgings a few minutes earlier to give us the intimate details regarding Dolan's escape from Newgate.

"It's impossible for anyone to disappear into thin air, Lestrade," said Holmes. "Therefore, that can be safely and immediately eliminated as an explanation for Dolan's escape. The actual solution, however improbable it may turn out to be, must be something within the realm of actual physical reality."

"In principle, Mr. Holmes, I agree with you," replied Lestrade. "But the fact remains that one second he was there, and the next he was gone, and I can't account for that by any means within what you call 'actual physical reality.'"

It had begun with a minor altercation between Dolan and another inmate. Shoving had turned to grappling, which turned to blows being struck. Soon a half-dozen other prisoners were joining the fray, followed by a similar number of guards, rolling around in a huge pile on the floor of the cellblock.

"When they were all pulled apart, separated, and all brought to a standing position," said Lestrade, "the number of prisoners was one fewer than it had been when the fight first broke out, and the one who was missing was Dolan."

"One prisoner less there may have been," said Holmes. "I would be willing to wager, though, that when all the opponents were separated, there was one guard more."

"What do you mean?" asked Lestrade.

"I suggest that the fight was a prearranged ruse to conceal Dolan's flight; that the prison uniform he was wearing had been specially prepared with seams that could be easily pulled apart while the participants in the altercation were piled up on the floor. Underneath that easily shed prison garb, Dolan was wearing a stolen guard's uniform. When peace was restored, and Dolan's absence was noticed, no one observed that there was one more guard than there had been prior to the altercation, and, in the confusion he was able to slip away unnoticed, and exit the prison without detection."

Subsequent investigation would later prove the hypothesis offered by Holmes to have been the correct one. At that point, though, providing the correct explanation was of little use. The immediate problem before us was Dolan's recapture.

"What's being done to track him down, Lestrade?" I asked.

"A close watch is being kept at all exit points on the Thames, at all railroad and underground stations, and on all roads leading out of the Metropolitan area. Was it anyone else, I'd say he'd certainly be apprehended within a short time. But anyone who can escape from the Newgate so cleverly will probably be able to get past those we have observing possible escape routes."

"Then," said Holmes, "it is as well for us that escape is, in all likelihood, not his first priority."

"Well if it's not," said Lestrade, "I'd certainly like to know what is."

"Revenge," Holmes replied.

"Revenge?" I asked, after a moment during which Holmes's dramatic pronouncement sank in. "On Vance?"

"Of course on Vance," said Holmes. "It was Vance who uncovered Sailor

"What do you mean?"

Ned's true identity, Vance who so unrelentingly pursued him across the ocean, Vance who apprehended him, and Vance who, in consequence, has deprived him of his hard-won position at the top of London's Underworld. Dolan will not depart until he has exacted vengeance from his unyielding nemesis."

"You are so certain that evening the score is this important to him?" I said.

"Look at past actions, Watson. After the altercation at Wilder, when he was still known only as 'Sailor Ned,' he was believed to have died of the wounds sustained during that gun battle. No one was looking for him. He could have easily made his way back to England with no one the wiser. Yet he stayed in the immediate area until fully recovered, then, in broad daylight, mercilessly cut down the man who had wounded him, in front of his wife and children, with numerous witnesses looking on. Would he be any less unforgiving of the man who cost him his position as King of London's criminal element? Moreover, given the unspeakably cruel way in which he murdered Marshal Thomas, I would regard it as likely that he will try to contrive his attack on Vance so that the former Miss O'Riley is there to see it."

"Then he'll be heading to the Lake District," suggested Lestrade.

"No need. Why go to so much trouble when he knows Marshal and Mrs. Vance are due to return almost any day? He does not, however, know the precise date they are expected, and we do. This, gentlemen, is the one advantage we have."

Three days after our conference with Lestrade, the day Marshal Vance and his lady were due back, Holmes and I were in our Baker Street lodgings, preparing for the deadly encounter we were expecting.

I was loading the old Adams Mk III revolver that had been my constant companion during my military days. As I slipped the bulky but dependable weapon into my overcoat pocket, I looked up to see Holmes, dressed in the rough clothes of a laborer, strapping a belt and holster rig around his waist. This, I inferred, must have been part of the equipment he had habitually worn during the period he had joined with Vance in bringing law and order to America's western frontier.

It was functional, rather than decorative and fancy, as such pieces of equipment are often depicted on the covers of lurid penny dreadful novels. It was, nevertheless, well-made and well-maintained. There were two holsters, right and left. Cartridge loops held spare rounds. In the left holster was the pistol Holmes had always habitually carried from the very beginning of our association, at least on those occasions when he felt such equipment might become necessary, a Webley No. 5, popularly known as the Royal Irish Constabulary revolver. The weapon in his right holster was one I had never seen before, nickel-plated and ivory-handled.

"It's a Colt Peacemaker," said Holmes, discerning my thoughts as he so often did. "So ubiquitous among the deputy marshals who rode for Parker, it was almost standard issue. The nickel plating and ivory handles were a sort of mark of office adopted by many of the marshals, much like the gold crown embossed on the truncheons once carried by our own Bow Street Runners. The second pistol is not a boast of ambidexterity. It was common for marshals on the scout to carry two. Having a second as a back-up made reloading unnecessary. Most encounters were over before more than twelve shots were fired. If we went to pistols at all, that is."

"Rifles were more common?"

"Indeed," he replied. "In the Territories, It was not Colonel Colt who was king. It was Oliver Winchester. That's not to say that revolvers were never resorted to. Vance in particular was what Lady Catherine de Bourg would call a 'true proficient.'"

No matter how long I had known Holmes, he was always able to surprise me. In all our years together, that was the first time I had ever detected even a hint that Holmes was a devotee of the works of Jane Austen.

"He is quite accurate, then?" I asked.

"Unbelievably accurate and unbelievably swift. I have seen him draw a pistol, uncocked mind you, fire six times, and hit six empty bottles from a distance of twenty-five yards, in less than three seconds, shooting from the hip. He can fire even more quickly if he 'fans' the hammer instead of cocking and squeezing, but what he gains in speed he loses in accuracy."

"Remarkable."

"The talent may stand him in good stead today," said Holmes.

"Let us hope not," I replied.

"On the contrary, let us hope so. The issue must be settled, and the sooner the better. For Vance. For his wife. For Marshal Thomas's widow and children."

He paused a moment, then added, "Besides, if it is not settled today, it means I was mistaken about Dolan's likely plan. And you know how I hate to be mistaken. Now, let us be off, Watson, for the game's afoot!"

Holmes had telegraphed Vance a few days earlier, an expensive telegraph because it had to give details, not only of Dolan's probable intentions, but of Holmes's plans for countering them. Given Holmes's vexing habit of never, if he had any choice, communicating his plans to any other person until the instant of their fulfillment, that meant that Vance probably had more information than I. Still, knowing Holmes, even Vance's knowledge was likely to be less than complete.

That afternoon a train from the Lake District arrived at the Euston Rail Station. I was there to see Vance and his wife exit their compartment and step out on the platform. Mrs. Vance, wearing a wide-brimmed hat, pulled a veil arranged on top of it down over her face.

"Cabs are out this way, Sweetheart," Vance told her, and they made their way to the doorways leading to Cardington Street, a porter carrying their luggage close behind. I followed discreetly. Holmes, I knew, was also nearby, though I hadn't yet spotted him. Nor did I expect to.

Since they had a good deal of baggage, the couple chose one of the four-wheeled "growlers" in the cab line rather than one of the Hansoms. Following Holmes's dictum, Vance chose the third such carriage, oblivious to the protests of the first two drivers. The luggage was loaded in first, then Vance handed his lady in, and put a foot on the floor of the compartment to join her.

"Cord," I heard her say, "we've been sitting so long, and Baker Street isn't that far away. Let's take a walk through the park. It would be so nice if the last thing we did on our honeymoon was to visit the place we first met. We can send the luggage ahead so we don't have to carry it."

Vance asked the driver how much a trip to 221 Baker would cost. The driver named a price. Vance handed over an amount, then added a bit more.

"For your trouble," he said. Then added yet more. "And that's to help the lady at that house get these bags inside. A fair price for all that?"

"More'n fair, guv," replied the driver.

I saw out of the corner of my eye five men who had been standing, apparently waiting, suddenly enter two Hansoms, and give some hurried instructions. The Hansoms took off at a fast trot.

Vance helped his wife out of the four-wheeler, and, at a leisurely pace, they started walking toward the eastern entrance to Regency Park on their way to Baker Street.

I followed at a discreet distance, my hand in my overcoat pocket, tightly clutching the grip of the Adams revolver.

Holmes's instructions were to observe them as they exited the train, then keep them in sight as they walked from the station to Baker Street. He did not tell me the route they were likely to take. All he said was that they would engage a cab to take their luggage, but make their way to their lodgings on foot.

Though he didn't say so, the conclusion that he was trying to give Dolan an opportunity to confront Vance seemed inescapable. I was surprised that the plan involved putting Mrs. Vance in harm's way. Holmes, for all his apparent misogyny, is actually quite chivalrous when it comes to the fair sex. Perhaps he felt that the presence of the lady was necessary to draw our adversary out, given his past history of delivering vengeance in front of his intended target's loved ones.

"Be prepared for anything, Watson," he had told me. "Our opponent is trained in tactics and strategy, and we don't know where on the board his pieces are assembled. On the other hand, he is as ignorant of how we have arranged ours."

The couple entered Regency Park from the east side, and proceeded along one of the many walking paths. I kept behind them and bit to their right, scanning the area for trouble. There was a ragged hunch-backed man off to their left who I did not recognize, but whose identity, after many years with Holmes, I suspected.

The encounter, when it came, was sudden. Four men standing at disparate locations started to move as the couple made their way through the park, suddenly coming together in the path along which Vance and his wife were moving, standing abreast and blocking the way. I didn't get a close enough look at the train station to be sure, but I thought they might be the group of men who suddenly boarded two Hansoms when the Vances told their driver they'd walk through the park.

A fifth man started moving toward the group as the couple came to a stop.

"Would you gents like to make way?" asked Vance, good-humoredly. "If not, I suppose we can walk around you without too much trouble."

At that point the fifth man, reached the other four, and took his place in the middle of the group, two men on either side of him.

It was Sailor Ned. Holmes's plan to draw him out, if that was his plan, had borne fruit.

"Ned," cried Vance, as if he'd met with a long-lost friend. "What a fine surprise! I was hoping our paths would cross once I was back in the Smoke."

Vance's adoption of the affectionate nickname for the Metropolis was a sign of how comfortable he'd become in London. Vance addressed the other four men.

"Don't know the rest o' you fellahs," he said. "But my advice to you is to skedaddle. Judging from who y'all choose to hang with, I imagine the London police might like the chance for a little parley, but, speaking just for myself, y'understand, I've no interest in you. Run along now, before y'get hurt."

"Before *we* get hurt?" roared Ned with laughter. "I'm holding three aces over kings. At best you've got a king and a queen, that is if you count this half-breed toffer y'married as a queen. And I don't expect you went heeled on your honeymoon. You'll lose this hand once I call."

Vance pulled back his jacket to show his ivory-handle Peacemaker resting in a cross-draw holster. "Didn't want to make the same mistake Marty Thomas did," he said. "And I'm not the only one who took precautions."

With that, the feminine figure beside Vance swept off the broad brimmed hat revealing, underneath the veil, the face of Inspector Lestrade, who proceeded to tear off the very feminine dress which turned out to be covering a thoroughly masculine ensemble of a white shirt and dark pants.

"Lestrade of the Yard, mate," he said to Sailor Ned, while reaching toward his lower back. "And you'll note that, under this dress, I'm wearing trousers. And where I have trousers, I've a hip-pocket. And where I have my hip-pocket, I've something in it."

The something, in this, case, as I could see from my vantage point, was the walnut grip of a short-barreled Webley Metropolitan Police revolver. Drawing my own pistol from my coat pocket, I held it at my side and walked over to join Lestrade at his right.

"I believe Marshal Vance now has three aces, Commander," I said to Nolan. "And he still has a hole card."

Holmes has as great a sense of the dramatic as anyone I know, and, with that as his cue, he threw off the overcoat, pulled away the pillow he had been using to simulate a hump back, and standing erect, joined Vance at his left, resplendent in his western-style two-gun rig.

"And now it's four aces, Dolan," said Holmes. "Even without a fifth card, that still beats a full house."

"You mean to make a fight of it, then?" asked Dolan.

"I mean," said Vance, "to see to it that you pay with your life for what you did to Marty Thomas and his family. Whether you take the long drop from Marshal Maledon's gallows on a date Judge Parker sets, or I just settle your hash right here and now's up to you. Which one'll you have?"

"You seem pretty sure of the outcome," Dolan replied, "considering I still have you outnumbered."

"Well, in that case, why don't you fill your hand, you murderin' bastard?"

Though his assertion that he still outnumbered us was mathematically correct, his five to our four, the anonymous hired bullies Dolan had flanking him were not to be relied upon. And I think Dolan must have known this. He had counted on being supported by four armed men while he faced an unarmed Vance accompanied by no one but his wife, whose sole function would have been to bear witness to his murder. And perhaps provide amusement to her husband's killers afterward. Instead he was facing four armed men, all of them with some experience in deadly encounters, and no vulnerable young lady he could horrify or take advantage of. The sensible thing would have been to surrender and take his chances in court.

But now his pride was too inextricably mixed into the situation. To back down would be to lose face with the men he had hired, and worse, to lose face with himself. So instead of doing the sensible thing, he reached for the revolver he had stuck into his waistband.

Even having been told of Vance's swiftness by Holmes, I was not prepared for how quickly he drew, cocked, and fired his Colt. Shooting, from the hip, faster than it can be described, his first round drilled into Dolan's forehead. He paused for the barest moment to bring his weapon up to shoulder height and take more careful aim with his second shot. This one entered the nose of the deposed king of crime.

I had brought my own pistol to bear on the man standing two down from Dolan's left, who had his hand in his jacket, furiously trying to remove a weapon that had become stuck in the fabric.

"Stop," I said, more as a sop to my own conscience than in the hope he would actually withdraw an empty hand from the pocket. I had taken dead aim, and he would have no chance to get off a shot should he manage to pull the gun free.

Lestrade's revolver was out and up once the shooting started. As I assumed he would, he took the man immediately to Dolan's left. That one had less trouble drawing his weapon than my own adversary was having, but Lestrade was ready for him. He fired off four shots as quickly as he could squeeze the trigger, all of them entering the ruffian's chest. Two, we later learned, had penetrated his heart.

My man finally pulled his gun free, but was never able to bring it to bear, let alone get off a shot. As soon as I saw the pistol torn free from the jacket pocket, I fired three times, all of them head shots. He fell into an unceremonious heap.

Vance, meanwhile, had fired two more shots into Dolan, both of these chest shots, and, believing he had quite done for him, turned his attention to the two henchmen standing to Dolan's right.

Holmes had, in true Wild West show style, drawn both his weapons. The Peacemaker in his right hand, and the Webley RIC in his left, he alternated shots, firing the Colt at the gunman directly to Dolan's right, and the Webley at the one on the end, his eyes darting back and forth to keep track of each of his foes. Both had sustained three chest wounds apiece, but were still standing, and still attempting to get at least one shot off, to give at least a tolerably respectable performance in the deadly competition into which they had unexpectedly been thrust.

Vance, with two more rounds left, and Sailor Ned crumbling to the ground, no longer a threat and undoubtedly well on his way to his new home in the fiery regions, turned his attentions to Holmes's two adversaries. He fired his penultimate round into the head of one, and his last into the head of the other, as Holmes was sending a shot apiece into the would-be assassins' torsos.

That finally ended the fight. The elapsed time from the moment Dolan reached for his pistol until the last man went down was less than twenty seconds.

When five men are violently killed in the remote, unexplored regions of America's western frontier, it's one thing. When they are violently killed in one of London's Royal Parks, it's quite something else. So it may be inferred that our actions were thoroughly investigated before being given an official imprimatur, and that this investigation was not completed in a mere hour or two. Vance, having diplomatic status, could have avoided it all, but, in the interests of justice, voluntarily waived the immunity his position as an embassy attaché gave him.

The reader, having, I hope, confidence that our actions were thoroughly justified, will not need a detailed description of the legalistic warrens through which the four of us had to navigate, to know that such navigation necessarily occurred before the powers-that-be made a similar judgment.

Suffice it to say that such judgment was not, all things considered, that long in coming. But it was still longer than comfortable.

As I surmised, each of us was given just enough information to play our parts in the showdown that Holmes was orchestrating.

I knew when Vance and his wife were due to return, and, as Holmes instructed, kept them under surveillance.

Lestrade knew that he was to wait in the third of the four-wheeled "growlers" dressed in a feminine ensemble identical to that worn by Mrs. Vance on the last leg of her train trip from the Lakes to London, and then, when the lady was handed into the cab, to exit and take her place by Vance's side after she loudly expressed a preference for walking through Regency Park from inside the passenger compartment.

Mrs. Vance knew that she was to arrive in London wearing a particular dress and a particular hat, and, once she was in the cab, to make a loud pronouncement about ending their honeymoon by visiting the park where she and Vance had met, then stay quiet while her place was taken by Lestrade, ride home in that same cab with their luggage, and wait safely at Baker Street.

Vance knew almost as much about Holmes's plan as Holmes, but he didn't know, until Lestrade whipped off the ladies' hat and veil, that it was the comparatively small-statured Scotland Yarder who was standing in for his wife.

Holmes, as always, knew everything.

Some weeks later, Holmes, Lestrade, and I were on board a steamship that was scheduled to leave the Plymouth harbor for New York. Marshal and Mrs. Vance were sailing on that ship, and my two companions and I were there to see them off.

We were all enjoying a light repast in the couple's stateroom when the "all ashore" alert sounded.

Mrs. Vance graciously thanked us all for our friendship and promised to write regularly, as she daintily shook our hands.

"I will always keep you all in my prayers," she said, "for so bravely supporting Cord in his dangerous work."

Vance's own grip as he followed the example of his wife was heartier and firmer. To Holmes he said nothing except, "So long, pard." But the look he and Holmes exchanged as they clasped hands was enough to make the depth of feeling clear.

To Lestrade and myself he said, "I've always told folks that Holmes here was the best partner I ever had as a lawman. But I'd have to rate the two of you mighty high as well. Where I come from, one of the highest compliments you can give a man is to say he'd do to ride the river with. Well, Doc, Inspector, either or both of you would do to ride the river with."

Lestrade, visibly moved, merely nodded, and muttered something about a debt of gratitude he owed his American colleague.

For myself, all I could do was say softly, "Thank you, Vance."

With that, the three of us disembarked and stayed on the dock waving goodbye as the ship sailed off.

The Vances kept in touch by letter, but we never again met them face to face.

Judge Parker, as Vance predicted, died shortly after the young newlyweds arrived in Fort Smith. The court he had served so devotedly was effectively disbanded when its jurisdiction was transferred to other districts. As Vance predicted, Parker converted to Catholicism on his deathbed. He was buried from Immaculate Conception Church, where his wife had worshipped for years, the pastor of the Church, Father Lawrence Smyth, who had baptized the judge and given him the Last Rites, presiding.

Vance, who followed the judge's example and eventually converted to Catholicism himself, continued "marshalling" as he called it, for other government courts until 1898, when the Spanish-American War broke out, and he, along with other noted frontier peace officers such as Buckey O'Neill, Chris Madsen, Ben Daniels, and Tom Rynning, enlisted in that famed irregular military regiment, the First United States Volunteer Cavalry, better known to history as the "Rough Riders." Commissioned a lieutenant based on his prior Army experience, he was among those who made the fabled charge up San Juan Hill.

Upon returning to civilian life, he resumed his law enforcement career, serving, at various times, as the Chief Deputy for the Tulsa County Sheriff's Office, as the police chief for the City of Tulsa, and, after the Indian and Oklahoma territories reunited and entered the Federal Union as the State of Oklahoma, as one of several former federal marshals who were appointed by the Governor to serve as special investigators reporting directly to him.

He and his wife were blessed with three children, two sons, Michael (for the name under which Holmes served as a marshal), and Cordrell (for his father), and a daughter, Maria (after the same Blessed Lady for whom Naya was indirectly named).

He finally retired in 1913, and died a year later of complications from a touch of malaria he had contracted during his Cuban service.

Holmes and I, both long retired ourselves, were notified of his death during our investigation of a case we were persuaded to take, recorded elsewhere as "His Last Bow." That particular investigation had made it necessary for Holmes to travel to Chicago and Buffalo, among other places in the United States, and he was able to take a small amount of time to travel to Oklahoma City in time for the Requiem Mass offered for the repose of Vance's soul. There, he and five other former deputy marshals were pressed into service as pallbearers. When he returned to England, he and I reminisced about our old friend at length.

"He had all the attributes needed to make a fine criminal investigator, Watson. Courage, intelligence, an ability to read, and to make correct inferences from physical evidence. But if there was one quality that made him stand out, it was tenacity. He never gave up a chase no matter how small was the likelihood of such a pursuit ending in an arrest and conviction. He was fundamentally incapable of giving up the hunt. For him, the game was *always* afoot. But, more than all of that, he was, like you, my dear Watson, loyal and reliable to a fault."

A fitting epitaph, I thought, for a man so determined to see justice done, that he pursued the killer of a friend halfway across the world on little more than a faint intuition.

The End

Sherlock Holmes and the American West

*H*as it ever struck you that Sherlock Holmes was a contemporary of Marshal Matt Dillon, the Lone Ranger, and Shane?

Oddly, it rarely occurs to people that Britain's Victorian Era, so associated with Sherlock Holmes, coincided almost exactly with America's Western Frontier era. But it did. And one person who was very aware of this was Holmes's creator.

When Arthur Conan Doyle (he wasn't "Sir Arthur" yet) wrote *A Study in Scarlet* in 1886, he did more than introduce to the world the most famous protagonist in detective fiction. By setting the novel's long flashback sequence, "The Country of the Saints," in Utah, and incorporating the saga of the western migration of the Mormon pioneers, and even making frontier legend Brigham Young a character, he wrote what is, arguably, the first mystery/western cross-genre piece.

Conan Doyle's fascination with America's western frontier, and with the settling of untamed frontiers in general, is understandable. A patriotic Briton to his core, and like most Britons of his generation, an imperialist, he saw in America's pioneers who settled and developed the West the same hardy spirit that he saw in those emigrants who developed similar frontiers in Africa, Australia, and Canada. These were people he admiringly described as "the rugged, hard-faced men, the brave and earnest women, who look as if they had known much suffering and hardship—these are the type of pioneers that—go out and develop a state or an empire."

And those American frontiersman who became celebrities, like Buffalo Bill Cody, Kit Carson, or Wild Bill Hickok, whose adventures were fictionalized in scores of lurid "dime novels" here in the States, were equally well-known in the United Kingdom, where those same dime novels were reprinted as "penny dreadfuls" and "shilling shockers," publications with which Conan Doyle, a voracious reader, must have been at least peripherally familiar.

It should be noted, of course, that Conan Doyle's depiction of the Church of Jesus Christ of Latter-Day Saints in *A Study in Scarlet* was not merely unflattering, but inaccurate, or at least highly exaggerated. Years later, he was reported as having privately apologized to members of the LDS Church during a visit to Salt Lake City, and, in 1991, his daughter, Jean, would say in an interview, "You know, Father would be the first to admit that his first Sherlock Holmes novel was full of errors about the Mormons."

Mistakes notwithstanding, Conan Doyle continued to be fascinated with the American West, and would also use it again, this time as the background for the Holmes short story, "The Adventure of the Noble Bachelor," first published in the April 1892 issue of *The Strand Magazine*, and later included in the first collection of Holmes shorts, *The Adventures of Sherlock Holmes*. In "Noble Bachelor," Holmes investigates the disappearance of Hatty Doran, the daughter of a California miner who'd struck it rich years earlier. She mysteriously vanishes right after exchanging marriage vows with the titular English lord. When Holmes solves the case, the explanation involves a flashback sequence that harkens back the western frontier. We learn that Miss Doran was really Mrs. Frank Moulton, the widow, or so she thought, of a prospector who'd been reported killed in Arizona during an Apache attack. When she learned, during the wedding service to His Lordship, that her supposedly dead husband was still alive, she disappeared until she could figure out what to do.

The next Holmes story with some connection to the Old West, "The Problem of Thor Bridge," first published in the February and March 1922 issues of *The Strand*, and reprinted in the final collection, *The Case-Book of Sherlock Holmes*, the plot had only the most vestigial relation to the American frontier. The apparent murder victim, Mrs. Maria Gibson, is the wife of Neil Gibson, a mining magnate described as America's "Gold King," who briefly served as a US Senator from an unnamed "western state." From this description, it seems likely that Conan Doyle's real-life model for Gibson is George Hearst, whose vast fortune was built on the mining of gold and other precious metals all over the West, and who was appointed to serve as a US Senator for California for five months when the incumbent died in office. If Hearst was the model, it seems ironic that the story's first American publication, almost simultaneous with its British appearance, was in the February and March 1922 issues of *Hearst's International*, which was, of course, owned and operated by William Randolph Heart, George Hearst's son. It's particularly ironic since Gibson is not depicted as a sympathetic figure at all.

As a side note, it might be noted that some Sherlockian enthusiasts have suggested that the story's heroine, Miss Grace Dunbar, the lady accused of Mrs. Gibson's murder, whom Holmes and Watson are trying to clear, eventually becomes the second Mrs. Watson, the lady with whom Holmes's "Boswell" plighted his troth around 1903, to Holmes's chagrin, around the time of "The Adventure of the Blanched Soldier" (first published in the November 1926 issue of *The Strand*, and also reprinted in *Case-Book*). This story is narrated by Holmes rather than Watson, a circumstance he explains by stating that, "The good Watson had deserted me for a wife, the only selfish action I can recall in our association." Apparently this second Mrs. Watson was not as sanguine about letting her husband abandon his medical practice to go gallivanting all over the countryside adventuring as the former Miss Mary Morstan once was. I don't endorse this theory, but I will say I find the arguments in favor of it persuasive.

Two other Holmes stories, though not precisely set in the American West, have at least the flavor of westerns about them.

"The Boscombe Valley Mystery," first published in the October 1891 issue of *The Strand*, and reprinted in *The Adventures of Sherlock Holmes*, takes, as its background, the settling of Australia during the height of the gold strikes on the Island Continent. The discovery of the precious metal in the 1850's, and the development of an Australian cattle industry at roughly the same time, led to a pioneer society that had much in common with the American West during that same period. And it led to a similar kind of criminality. "Bushrangers" like Ned Kelly, Ben Hall, and Frank Gardiner are as legendary in Australia as their American counterparts, Jesse James, Billy the Kid, and Cole Younger are in the United States. There was even an internationally popular TV series in the 1970's, *Rush*, about a colonial policeman fighting such crime. It was something of an Australian counterpart to America's *Gunsmoke*.

Inspired by the 1862 Eugowra Rocks robbery and the 1863 Mudgee Mail robbery, Conan Doyle created a backstory in which a present-day murder traces back to a gold robbery carried out decades earlier by a notorious bushranger known as "Black Jack of Ballarat." Eventually "Black Jack" changes his identity (or resumes his former identity), returns to England, and takes up the life of a wealthy, landed squire. Until his past catches up to him.

The Valley of Fear, the last full-length Holmes novel by Sir Arthur (he was knighted by this time), was first published in 1915. Like *A Study in*

Scarlet, the second portion of the book, titled "The Scowrers," is a long flashback set in the United States. Though the locale is implicitly Pennsylvania rather than a western state or territory, the rural mining community in the titular Vermissa Valley has the feel of the mining camps found in such western locations as Tombstone, Arizona, or Deadwood, South Dakota.

In fact, this whole sequence is a thinly fictionalized depiction of real-life Pinkerton operative James McParland's 1876 undercover investigation of a group of labor terrorists (or at least purported terrorists) known as the Mollie Maguires, fictionalized into the "Scowrers" for the novel. Sir Arthur had been told the story of McParland's investigation by William Pinkerton, the son of Allan Pinkerton, who founded the world renowned private detective agency.

Though Pinkerton chose to tell the story of McParland and the Pennsylvania case, he could have just as easily made it the story of another Pinkerton operative, the legendary Charlie "The Cowboy Detective" Siringo, and his 1892 undercover investigation of Mollie Maguire activity in the western mining community of Coeur D'Alene, Idaho. The resulting novel wouldn't've been substantially different. So, in a way, *The Valley of Fear* missed being Conan Doyle's last literary visit to the American Frontier simply due to William Pinkerton chancing to share McParland's story with Sir Arthur instead of Siringo's.

I love westerns, and, when I undertook to write a Sherlock Holmes pastiche, the idea of doing my own "westernized" version of a Holmes story was irresistible. My original notion was to write a story set during the "Great Hiatus" between Holmes's supposed 1892 death at Reichenbach Falls at the hands of Professor Moriarty, and his sudden reappearance three years later to capture Colonel Moran, the last member of Moriarty's organization still at large.

It would be told from the point of view of, perhaps even narrated by, a deputy US marshal working out of Judge Isaac Parker's Federal District Court, who is partnered with a mysterious newcomer to the Marshal's force named "Mike Croft." As they work together, it becomes evident to the veteran deputy that Mike Croft is someone else altogether. However, the format requirements of the *Sherlock Holmes – Consulting Detective* series of anthologies were such that this approach was not possible. But I found that I couldn't abandon the notion completely. And if a story about Holmes operating incognito during his supposed death was not possible, a story using the "detailed flashback" approach taken in *A Study in Scarlet* and "The Adventure of the Noble Bachelor" certainly was. It soon became evident that transplanting, so to speak, America's violent frontier into the heart of Victorian London made for a better story than my initial idea.

Cordrell Vance was a composite of several of the real-life marshals who rode for Judge Parker, particularly Bill Tilghman (perhaps the greatest of all frontier lawmen), and his close friend Heck Thomas (who is also a contender for that title), two thirds of the crime-fighting combo known as "The Three Guardsmen of Oklahoma." The character's name was simply an inversion of "Vance Cordrell," the name of the federal marshal portrayed by Randolph Scott in *The Return of the Bad Men* (1948), which heavily fictionalized the taming of the Oklahoma and Indian territories by federal peace officers. Scott's character, like mine, was a composite of several real-life lawmen of the era.

Rob, Matt, Elliot, and Will Bolton were thinly fictionalized versions of Bob, Grat, Emmett, and Bill Dalton, the four brothers who gave the infamous Dalton Gang its name. "Sailor Ned" Dolan fills in for real-life western desperado Bill Doolin, who took over what was left of the gang after the debacle in Coffeyville (fictionalized in my story into "Coffeeboro") left two of the Daltons dead and one on his way to a long prison term. Bill Doolin, rebuilt the gang into a notorious band known as the "Wild Bunch" (not to be confused with the identically named group operated by Butch Cassidy and Harry "The Sundance Kid" Longabaugh in Wyoming, also known as the "Hole-in-the-Wall Gang"). He soon came to be the personal "Moriarty figure" of Tilghman and Thomas, who relentlessly pursued him. "Sailor Ned" has some of the characteristics of his real-life counterpart (a penchant for steam baths, for example; Bill Tilghman actually did arrest Doolin in a steam bath while disguised as a clergyman; only it was at Eureka Springs, Arkansas, not London, England).

Bill Doolin, however, was not the son of an Royal Navy petty officer, was never an officer in the Royal Navy himself, and, according to most accounts, was never as deliberately cruel as I've made his fictional doppelganger in this story.

The murder of Marshal Dash Richards during the shootout at "Wilder" was based on the death Marshal Dick Speed, who was fatally wounded during a similarly ill-fated attempt to apprehend the Wild Bunch in an Oklahoma town that was actually named "Ingalls." In real life no one knows for certain who fired the fatal shot that I've attributed to Sailor Ned for the purposes of this story, though the only gang member apprehended at Ingalls, Roy Daugherty, aka "Arkansas Tom" Jones, is often said to be the man who gunned down Speed and two other marshals.

The murder of Marshal Marty Thomas was based on the actual murder of Marshal Thomas Martin, a deputy assigned to Judge Parker's court, who really was killed by outlaws while relaxing on the front porch of his home. In real life, it was a gang of moonshiners he was pursuing who were responsible for the crime, and had nothing to do with Doolin or the Wild Bunch.

I thoroughly enjoyed writing "The Adventure of the Manhunting Marshal," and I hope you enjoyed reading it. I have a notion for another story, set during the long extradition process, in which Cord Vance would be involved. If I can work out the plot, and this story is well-received, I may write it.

⸺ ⸺ ⸺

PETER BASILE the pseudonym adopted by Jim Doherty, the author of "The Adventure of the Manhunting Marshal," derives from the names of the two actors Jim regards as the best portrayers of the Great Detective, Peter Jeremy William Brett, who performed as Jeremy Brett, and, of course, Basil Rathbone.

"I'd never tried my hand at a Holmes story before," he says, "and felt I needed to assume a different persona in order to properly channel Sir Arthur and Dr. Watson."

Jim first discovered Sherlock Holmes at the age of 10, roughly the same age he decided to make police work his career. Perhaps there was some link.

A cop of one kind or another for more than twenty years, Jim's served American law enforcement at the local, state, and federal levels, policing everything from military bases to college campuses, from inner city streets to suburban lanes, from rural parks to urban railroad yards. He lives in Chicago with his lovely wife, Katy.

Jim's the author of *Just the Facts – True Tales of Cops & Criminals*, a collection of articles on real-life crimes, one of which, "Blood for Oil," won the WWA's Spur award for Best Short Non-Fiction; *Raymond Chandler – Master of American Noir*, a study of the work of the famed pioneer of hard-boiled detective fiction; *The Adventures of Colonel Britannia* (under the pseudonym "Simon A. Jacobs"), in which Jane Austen's romantic hero, Captain Frederick Wentworth, is reimagined as the UK's World War II super-soldier; and *An Obscure Grave*, a police procedural set in Berkeley, California, which was a finalist for the CWA's Debut Dagger award. He's also written enough articles and short stories to fill several more books.

Sherlock Holmes

in

"The Adventure of the Conundrum King"

By
Greg Hatcher

I wonder that you did not bring this to me sooner, Lestrade." Sherlock Holmes frowned at the paper he held in his hand. "It is, after all, addressed to me."

"Well, it's all very well to say that now that a man is actually dead, Mr. Holmes." The police inspector's ratlike features were even more pinched than usual—with embarrassment, I wagered. "But at the time it was one more crank letter among the hundred or so we receive every week. Since it came to us at the Yard we thought it was just another lunatic, and apart from all that we know how you feel about being confused with the official police."

Holmes sniffed. "Little chance of that." Lestrade looked stung and Holmes added, with a gentleness he rarely displayed to any representative of Scotland Yard, "I only meant that I am the only one in my singular profession: that of free-lance consulting detective. Very well then, let us consult." He returned to his examination of the letter the policeman had brought.

I found myself sympathizing somewhat with Lestrade. Holmes could be a daunting presence, especially with intellects he considered lesser than his own. It was not at all incomprehensible that the Scotland Yard detective would have preferred not to involve my friend in a matter that initially must have seemed trivial. Doubtless Lestrade had thought that it would only have been yet another occasion for Sherlock Holmes to amuse himself at his expense, which, in all fairness, was a pastime in which Holmes frequently indulged. Having occasionally been on the receiving end of Holmes' gibes myself I could not blame Lestrade for attempting to avoid such if at all possible.

For my part, I was glad of the distraction. It was late August, and the heat in London was unbearable. Every window in the Baker Street rooms I shared with Holmes was thrown open, and I had decided that even custom must bow to circumstance and spent the day collarless and in shirt-sleeves. Holmes, of course, took no notice of such mundane discomforts and his only concession to the heat had been, at my desperate urging, to eschew his planned chemical experiments and instead content himself with indexing his case records. This usually was more than enough to occupy him, but today he had been out of sorts and complained repeatedly that his talents were being wasted and he craved a genuine challenge. It was an old song with him. I hoped that Lestrade's visit was the harbinger of such a challenge, for our rooms were still barely tolerable even at ten in the evening, and the heat wave showed no sign of abating. Any excuse to get Holmes out and about upon the morrow would be welcome.

Holmes was lost in his examination. Abruptly he strode to his desk, retrieved his magnifying glass, and moved closer to the gas-lamp to get a better look at the missive. To fill what was rapidly becoming an awkward and embarrassed silence, I asked Lestrade, "How did the letter arrive? Was there any sort of postmark or anything else that might prove helpful?"

Holmes snorted briefly, which may or may not have been commentary.

Lestrade ignored it. "No, Doctor Watson, that's the devil of the thing. It appeared in a pile of other crank letters—we *do* examine each one with an eye towards detecting genuine threats, but it's a low priority. Usually it's a junior officer sorting through them with standing orders to report anything that may require us to act. But he didn't see this come in, nor did anyone else. No one remembers receiving this one or opening it, it was just suddenly there in the pile, as if by magic."

"*Tcha!*" Holmes shook his head. "Not magic. Theatrics. The delivery is part of the message itself; it was done that way to create just such an air of inexplicable mystery. This is calculated to provoke a response as surely as is a stage magician's pulling of a rabbit from a hat. Listen to this—

"*To Mr. Sherlock Holmes.*
Here now, my challenge, O Great Detective!

"*Once a year it came with no giver in sight*
Lovely and round it shone with pale light,
Grown in the darkness, a lady's delight.

"*He gave this treasure to one*
who always runs but never walks,
often murmurs, never talks,
has a bed but never sleeps,
has a mouth but never eats.
Name the thief and save his life."

I raised an eyebrow. "But that is just nonsense, Holmes. A child's riddle. How can you chastise Lestrade for not thinking it anything other than a poor joke?"

"Exactly!" Lestrade looked gratefully at me.

"Except it was no joke," Holmes said. "Because now the man is dead. It was Small?"

For a moment I thought dazedly that Holmes meant the murder itself was miniscule, but Lestrade understood. "Yes indeed, Mr. Holmes. Jonathan Small, the man that stole the Agra treasure, found poisoned in his cell at Dartmoor this morning. But how in heaven's name did you...?"

"Meretricious." Holmes waved the letter at him. "He tells us himself. The treasure sent 'once a year' and 'grown in darkness,' that was the chaplet of gray pearls, the ones detached and posted one-by-one to Mary Morstan each year, by the guilt-ridden Thaddeus Sholto. I daresay that you probably did not know all the details, Lestrade—it was not your case, though the doctor here published a full account of the matter several years ago."

Lestrade reddened a little and muttered something about not being much of a reader. I knew that my accounts of Holmes' cases were something of a sore spot with Scotland Yard, as many officers felt that they were unfairly slanted and cast law enforcement in a poor light. In my defense, I can only say that I have done my best to present these narratives as I myself witnessed them over the years. The plain truth is that everyone in the presence of Sherlock Holmes tended to seem intellectually lacking in comparison, including myself, and I have always striven to make that clear in these writings.

This phenomenon was exemplified by Holmes' next words. "Lestrade I can excuse," he said with a wry smile. He turned to me. "But I'm surprised at you, Watson. I would have expected you to recognize the reference. You did, after all, marry Miss Morstan."

"'Grown in darkness' is a deucedly obscure reference to pearls," I protested. "Anyhow, what made you so sure it was *those* pearls?"

"Apart from the line about 'once a year'?" Holmes smiled. "Again, he tells us himself, in the next stanza. The reference is to a river. A river runs, it has a bed, it murmurs, it has a mouth. Pearls sent once a year? And dumped in a river by a thief? Who else could it be? Jonathan Small, you will recall, poured the entirety of the Agra treasure into the Thames rather than let it be claimed by any heir to Morstan or Sholto. He was a driven, fanatical man."

"Yes." I remembered Small's words. "You were not with us, Lestrade, so I do not know how much of this is noted in the official record of the murder of Bartholomew Sholto, which was how the Yard became involved. *The sign of four* was Small's refrain. Jonathan Small had persuaded himself he was redressing an injustice, despite the fact that he and his three confederates had stolen the treasure themselves in the first place—to say nothing of the murders of several innocents committed during the course of that original theft." I sighed. "Certainly, Holmes, when you explain it, it is absurdly simple. Once again." I spread my hands helplessly. "But why now? Why Small? The treasure is gone, the Sholtos are both dead—Bartholomew's brother Thaddeus succumbed to heart failure three years ago," I added in an aside to Lestrade. "It was why I finally went ahead and published the account. And, of course, my own dear Mary passed some time ago as well."

I did not add that writing of the events that first drew Mary and I together, despite the death and horror that had accompanied them, had nevertheless helped soften the blow of losing her; for I still missed her keenly. Though I suspected Holmes knew—normally he had many acerbic remarks to make regarding my efforts to record his exploits in print, but this time he had not even objected to my mention of his cocaine use in the narrative I called *The Sign of Four*, though that vile practice was long behind him now. Perhaps one day I shall set down how that came to be, but not until certain august persons I cannot name will no longer be endangered by my doing so.

"So the man writing these silly riddles had some enmity toward Jonathan Small," Lestrade ventured.

"A possibility." Holmes did not sound convinced. "But unlikely. Who is left to hold such a grudge? His confederates are dead, as are the ones he felt wronged him. He made a full confession of the killings, both in London and in Agra. He was himself resigned to spending the rest of his days doing hard labor in Dartmoor prison. No, I think Small's death was merely an opening gambit, a first move in a much deeper game."

"But who would be the target? Doctor Watson is correct, there is no one left connected with the case. Even the detective assigned to it is dead now." Lestrade was growing impatient.

"Really?" I was surprised. "But that seems inconceivable, at his age. Jones was so …energetic. Was it in the line of duty?"

"Ah. Well." Now Lestrade looked uncomfortable. "That would almost have been less tragic. I'm afraid the man was prey to drink, doctor. Anyway, the point is that he has passed on as well, some weeks ago. I should prefer not to speak of it further."

"Athelney Jones never needed alcohol to demonstrate poor judgement." Holmes made the remark casually but it still caused Lestrade to raise an eyebrow. I knew better than to remonstrate with my friend: as with most societal conventions, Holmes had no time for demonstrating obligatory respect for the dead, especially towards one for whom he had little respect during his lifetime. Holmes went on, "But it seems rather obvious who the target is. The letter, after all, was addressed to me, and the victim was connected to a case Watson has made famous. It is a direct challenge, gentlemen. A duel of wits with Sherlock Holmes is what this fellow craves."

"But why?" I asked. "Why you? Why now?"

"Therein lies the challenge." Holmes rubbed his hands together in anticipation. "Tell me more about Small, Lestrade. How was the body found? There must have been another note, yes?"

Lestrade let out a mild huff of indignation. "I wish you'd just let me tell it instead of guessing. But yes, there was a note. I didn't remove it because it's evidence, but I copied down what the officer told me."

Normally Holmes would have chided the inspector for using the word *guessing*, but he was too interested in the note itself. He leaned forward as Lestrade pulled out another sheet of paper and read:

"You failed to heed my warning and now another has paid the price.
Can you save this one?
The Jew who rides the dawn DIES
Before you see your next!
Name him in time and save his life.
Your clue, as before, is through his wife."

He handed the note to Holmes and finished, "I came straight here. I am all at sea. I cannot think…"

Before Holmes could insert a cutting remark, I put in, "Holmes, if it is in connection with a past case—should we look in the index…?"

Holmes smiled and shook his head. "No need. Our man is not terribly subtle. We are still dealing with the Small affair. Think, gentlemen," he added. "The name of the motor launch Small used to escape with the treasure?"

"Of course!" I knew at once, though Lestrade just shook his head. I added, "The *Aurora*, Lestrade. Captained by Mordechai Smith."

"I still don't…"

"*Aurora*. Dawn. Mordechai. Jew." Holmes' tone was clipped as he stood. "And as it is close on eleven, we must hurry. The threat was to be made good before we see our next dawn, remember. We have until sunrise."

He would have said more, but there was a sharp *thwack!* that startled us all into silence. An arrow had thudded into the wall opposite the front window.

I made to rush for the window to see who had fired this bizarre missile, but Lestrade gestured me to stay where I was and drew his pistol as he walked slowly towards the window. "No one in sight," he reported. "I can check with the lad down below with the wagon, but..."

"He will have seen nothing." Holmes was certain. "Our man is long gone. And anyway, this was not an attack." He went to the wall and plucked the arrow from it. "Interesting. A crossbow bolt. It explains how he was able to fire this with such power. Almost as good as a pistol."

I was not as complacent as my companion. "But Holmes, if not meant as an attack, then what...?"

"Mail." He peeled a tiny scroll from the end of the arrow just below the point. "Here you go."

I read it aloud:

"The game's afoot, detective!
So detect! To find me you must first find these.
Adding two and two, there will be four in all.
The first found in fire, bright and hot;
The second begins over, never under;
The third began under, never over;
The last in a horror times three;
And closer to you than any other."

I shook my head. "I can make nothing of it."

"No?" Holmes smiled again, but there was no humor in it, and his eyes held a hard, predatory glitter. The lassitude of the day's boredom had departed; he was once again upon the hunt. "He is clearly one of your readers, Watson. 'The game is afoot,' indeed. Further analysis must wait, for we have to hurry. We still have Mordechai Smith to deal with and we cannot let this man's theatricality divert us from the threat. Come, Lestrade, let us make use of your man below, we have little time. We must be off to the docks."

He was up and moving even as he finished speaking, and there was nothing for it but to follow. Lestrade and I hurried down the stairs after him, with a brief pause for me to retrieve my revolver from the desk drawer and thrust it into my pocket. As we emerged on to the street I cast my eyes around to see if, perhaps, the author of these infernal riddles was watching to see if his cryptic taunts had provoked a response, but I could see nothing; at this hour of the night Baker Street was dark save for the street-lamps. I looked up at the building across the street from our rooms—Camden House, where Holmes and I had apprehended Colonel Sebastian Moran just two months ago. Surely our crossbow-wielding foe had shot his bolt from its roof and I said as much to Holmes as we settled into the police-wagon. "Would the roof not bear investigating? Perhaps he inadvertently left some trace of his presence that we could use to track him."

"Such trace evidence would be extraordinarily difficult to find at this hour of the night," Holmes said. "No, we must content ourselves to follow his path as he has laid it out."

"What path?" Lestrade wanted to know. "I see no agenda here. He just wants to cause a lot of chaos and waste our time, making us run hither and yon trying to prevent God knows what."

"Ah, Lestrade, there you show a lack of imagination. This man is obsessed with his agenda—we just don't know what it concerns as yet. It is too early in the game he is constructing. But he has one, never fear. Vengeance, perhaps, though I cannot name a specific cause; we have bagged some hundreds of criminals, any one of whom could have a friend or relative obsessed with the need to right a perceived wrong. " Holmes scowled. "Or he may be something even more dangerous—a madman who simply seeks an opponent for his murderous game."

"But what can this game be? What does he gain?" I confess I was as baffled as Lestrade.

Holmes leaned back in the seat, his eyes half-closed. "He wishes to demonstrate something to me personally, though as yet I cannot surmise what it must be. Certainly part of what he wishes to prove is his mental superiority. Note the jeers directed at my reputation and the challenges to my intellect. His antagonism is clearly reserved for me, his victims are mere pawns. Small, Smith, even Lestrade's officer opening the crank letters—he is attempting to move them about like pawns on a chessboard. His approach is oblique, he operates through others."

"Like Moriarty, once," I ventured. "The spider in the invisible web. That is what you called him, Holmes. Could we be facing another such?"

"Lord have mercy," muttered Lestrade. "I hope to God that is not so."

Holmes smiled. "Rest your minds, gentlemen. The late Professor Moriarty was indeed a genius but he was adamantly opposed to ever exposing his operations, it took me almost three years of the most diligent and unrelenting investigation to ferret out his role in the criminal underworld. For him it was a business. He would never be compelled to issue taunts and clues such as we have seen tonight. No, this man we are pursuing is… something different." His smile faded as he became lost in thought. "He may be something heretofore unseen in the annals of crime. For him the criminal act itself is secondary, even something as heinous as a homicide. What he relishes is the *challenge*. He is compelled to prove himself impervious to all who would oppose him. It is why he chose me as his target, I am certain. To be acclaimed England's foremost criminal he must first show his triumph over England's foremost champion of the law."

Lestrade sniffed, but he did not contest the characterization. He knew, as did I, that Holmes meant no insult. He simply stated fact. The inspector did not always like Holmes but, although he was loath to admit it in public, he respected him profoundly. My friend generally eschewed any credit for his victories, but there had been many instances where a malefactor would have escaped justice were it not for the intervention of Sherlock Holmes. It often chafed the officers at Scotland Yard that this was so, but none would deny it. At least not in private.

I thought perhaps a change of subject was in order. "What do you make of the latest riddle, Holmes?"

Holmes shook his head. "I confess I cannot arrive at a satisfactory answer for the latest one," he admitted. "Though the flamboyance of the delivery is suggestive. A crossbow bolt through our front window is dramatic, to say the least. Why undertake such an absurdly complex operation for a moment's worth of shock? I think that his compulsion towards the theatrical may well be his downfall. The riddles are merely a distraction. I must solve the puzzle of the man." He fell silent.

Rather than continue our futile attempts to engage him, Lestrade and I passed the remainder of the journey in silence as well. It was close on to midnight when we arrived at the docks where the Smith household was located. It had been some years, but the wharf looked much as I remembered it. Though slightly more weathered, the sign was still there: *Mordechai Smith, Boats for Hire by Hour or Day.* The last time we were here was when Holmes had made it clear to the police—even to the obstreperous Athelney Jones—that Jonathan Small and his companion Tonga were the villains of the Sholto affair, and arresting Mordechai Smith as an accomplice was not worth the trouble, and moreover arresting the boat captain would be placing an unfair burden upon Mrs. Smith and

*"For him the criminal act itself is secondary. What he relishes is the **challenge**."*

the four children. Finally Jones, a family man himself, had relented, since Mordechai Smith had merely been engaged to sail the criminals down the river in his steam launch. Nevertheless the blustery Scotland Yarder had forced Smith to listen to a long lecture about being more careful to whom he hired his vessel in the future, and the boat captain had meekly nodded. (Holmes later confided to me that if he had to choose between such a harangue and jail time, he might well have chosen prison as the lesser evil.) The *Aurora* had been one of the fastest boats on the Thames in its day and I wondered if it was still there. The boat-house was dark, as was the dilapidated rental office.

"Doubtless the residential quarters are in the rear," Holmes said. "We shall have to raise the household. I trust that we are not too late; I am counting on his word that our deadline is dawn."

"Surely, Mr. Holmes, you are not expecting honor from a murderer," Lestrade huffed as we disembarked from the police-wagon.

"Perhaps not. But I do expect consistency. The compulsion that drives him is to prove his own genius against mine. Therefore cheating, under his own rules, would not suffice as evidence of his superiority."

Lestrade merely shook his head and, refraining from further comment, gestured for the young constable to join him and they disappeared around the rear of the building.

I had a thought. "It is possible he seeks to confound your expectations," I suggested. "Would that not serve as proof that he had successfully manipulated you?"

"Ha!" Holmes' answering smile was rueful. "You may have me there, Watson. But your theory illustrates why it is dangerous for us to become too embroiled in attempting to solve the riddles he has posed to us, for almost certainly that is the intent, to confuse and confound our pursuit. We must not allow this man's game to become the focus. We must play our own game, and I fancy I have confounded more than a few criminal expectations myself. But look! It appears Lestrade has managed to awaken the Smith family," he added, as we saw a light come on in the rental office. "Mrs. Smith! A pleasure to see you again."

The door had flown open and we were faced with an angry middle-aged woman in a quilted house-robe. "It's indecent of you coppers to knock people up at this hour, it is, and don't you try to soften it with pretty words, you..." She paused. "Oh, it's you, Mister Holmes. And the doctor too!" I nodded at her as she waved a shyly embarrassed greeting. "And me in my night-dress! I am glad to see you too—thought it was just coppers," she added with a venomous glare at Lestrade and the constable, who had come round the front again. She went on, firmly, "Still! This is no time for us to be receiving visitors, Mister Holmes, though I am still grateful for your intercession with the magistrate that time. Whyever are you...."

Holmes raised a hand. "Please. Time is of the essence. Mrs. Smith, we think you are in some danger. Where is your husband?"

"Morts? Why, he's down in the boat-house..." She pointed to the docks behind us.

At that moment, the boat-house exploded into flame.

*   *   *

"Great heavens!" I moved at once toward the blazing structure, but Holmes laid a restraining hand on my shoulder.

"Careful, Watson. Mordechai Smith cannot possibly have lived through that, and our foe may have laid other traps." I nodded and turned to where Lestrade was standing with the constable trying to comfort the hysterical Mrs. Smith...*no, the widow Smith now*, I thought. *Once again he has been ahead of us.*

Holmes scowled. "Indeed, he has planned many moves ahead," he muttered, echoing my thought. "'*The first in fire, bright and hot*,' the note said. Some sort of bomb, on a clockwork timer.... And set for when we would be here. He wanted us here for the explosion. This man cuts deep, Watson." Only someone who knew him as well as I could have detected the suppressed anger in the words. Our foe had made a deadly enemy of Holmes now. He raised his voice. "Lestrade! We must get this fire out before it spreads up and down the river, those docks on either side are covered in pitch and creosote, and they might all go up. Quickly, man!"

Mrs. Smith, still weeping, pointed wordlessly at a couple of buckets and a tub. We at once availed ourselves of them, and the Thames itself supplied us with water. Bearing Holmes' caution in mind, we approached carefully, but there were no further hazards other than the flames we sought to extinguish. Working from the outside in, we eventually had the fire contained. The boat-house was a total loss, as was the shattered steam launch within, but we managed to save the rest of the dock and to confine the blaze to the Smith boat-yard. It was almost an hour before we were satisfied that there would be no further harm done by the fire, and by then we were all shirtless and covered in soot. I was more than ready to call it a night, but Holmes seemed as fresh as he had been that morning.

"'*Your clue, as before, is through his wife.*' A word with Mrs. Smith before we depart, Lestrade," he said. He retrieved his shirt from where he had thrown it over a piling and shrugged into it. "She is up at the house with your man?"

"She should be." Lestrade was puffing with exertion. "One of them, anyway. I sent the lad for reinforcements—and for the Fire Department, fat lot of good they did us. Where are they, anyway?"

"We did well enough," I said, turning to Holmes for confirmation, but he was already headed back up the pier to the rental office.

Lestrade laughed and gave me a comradely whack on the shoulder. "Aye, we did at that! We are old war-horses but there is some life left in us yet. Look, Doctor, Mr. Holmes is waving at us to join him. I wish he would wait for me when it's police business," he added, annoyed.

We both broke into a trot when we saw what Holmes had seen. The bloodied form of the constable lay prostrate on the boards, and Mrs. Smith's crumpled body was a few feet beyond.

"No wonder reinforcements never arrived," Holmes said. "The man was lying in wait, watching us. He has been with us all night. Fool that I am not to have realized it! Of course he would watch. He must see his games unfold. Here is his damned clue, as promised. This was pinned under your man, Lestrade." He held up a slip of paper. "He still lives, though Mrs. Smith is gone."

"Gone? Dead? That's three murders then?" Lestrade blinked.

"Three so far." Holmes was bitter. "We still have some hours before dawn. There may be more. Read this."

Lestrade read it aloud:

"The flaw is that which fails the higher it soars
The next corpse shall be the wounded who heals
The cause shall be the curse of the rose
The reason shall be that which is seen but never visible."

"This grows more impenetrable by the hour," I said. "Each of these is worse than the last."

"Indeed," Holmes nodded. "Deliberately obtuse. Lacking his mad context we can make nothing of this. Yet one part seems clear." He held up a long, thin wooden dart. The pointed end was blackened with a gummy substance. "This is what killed Mrs. Smith."

Even Lestrade recognized it. "But—that's one of those hellish blow-darts. From the Andaman Islands. I've seen the ones locked up in the Yard's museum archives."

"Yes." Holmes nodded. "Made from thorn." When we merely gaped at him, he added impatiently, "*Thorn.* The curse of the rose. And the preferred weapon of Jonathan Small's companion, the Andaman Islander Tonga. The one that murdered Sholto."

"But Tonga is dead," I protested. "Holmes, you were there, you saw it. I shot him myself."

"Indeed I did, Watson." Holmes was grimmer than I had ever seen him. "I have not forgotten. Apparently neither has our friend, because he names his next victim. 'The wounded who heals.' A healer... meaning a *doctor.* With a wound." He gestured at my bad leg, the one that had never healed properly after the bone had been shattered by a Jezail bullet back during the Afghan war. "You, Watson. He means to have you next."

— — —

It was a somber ride back to Baker Street. For one thing, we were both spent from our long day; we were another hour at the scene, awaiting the arrival of Lestrade's men to secure evidence from the Smith boat-yard and take charge of the remains of the unfortunate widow. There was some confusion when the children could not be located, for they were not in the house; but one of Lestrade's men found them at a neighbor's. The oldest boy had provided a garbled narrative to the officer. Apparently Smith had sent them there to assure their safety when a note arrived threatening his boat, and so he had sent the children away, bade his wife lock herself in the back apartment, and set himself in the boat-house with a rifle to await the intruders.

"But of course the intrusion came before the note, when he planted his clockwork bomb." Holmes was seething. His response was an impatient sniff when Lestrade ruled that the police would wait for daylight to sift the ashes of the boat-house to search for the body of Mordechai Smith. "Almost certainly whatever was left of him is already some miles down-river by now, as well as a great measure of the debris. But you are correct, Lestrade; there is nothing to be gained by trying to turn over the few smoldering coals we have left under cover of darkness." He scowled again.

I knew that what was really vexing Holmes was our failure to protect the Smiths, though I could not see how we might have proceeded differently. Holmes had us in motion the moment we realized there was to be an attack on the Smith household; the explosion and subsequent fire was a pressing danger that we had no choice but to deal with; and when we realized that we would need additional help Lestrade had promptly sent for reinforcements. In every possible measure that I could discern our actions had been the right and proper ones, carried out with all the speed we could muster. I said as much to Holmes and he responded with an explosive noise of disgust that was almost the growl of an animal.

"I do not suggest we are to blame for doing the things that were necessary." Holmes' anger was a palpable thing. "I am, however, considerably aggrieved at the ease with which our quarry so accurately predicted our actions. Consider the bomb in the boat, timed almost exactly to our arrival. The attack on Mrs. Smith and the constable, arriving exactly when we were occupied with fighting the fire and unable to see what was taking place at the pier entrance above. And these gloating riddles, meant to confound and confuse us—I have allowed them to distract me from employing my usual methods. We must not be seduced into playing this man's infernal game, for there is where he makes up the rules—if we are forced to play by them, he will win."

"But how then will you proceed?"

"As yet... I do not know."

I knew how it must have chafed Holmes to admit this, even only to me. I had busied myself with attending to the wounded constable, who, thankfully, had only suffered a blow to the head—none of the deadly Andaman poison had been directed at him. Our foe must have reserved his darts for the unfortunate Mrs. Smith. The lad was as frustrated with his own inability to confront our adversary as Holmes was himself. "No excuse for it, doctor," he said, his expression rueful. "Took me completely off-guard. He come up on us just as I was approaching the house. Mrs. Smith didn't think anything of him so I thought he must be a neighbor. Certainly didn't look threatening. Jolly fellow in a green bowler hat."

"Can you think of anything else?" I asked him. "You are the only one to have actually seen the man."

The constable, whose name was Woodrow, shook his head. "Not really. Youngish sort. Clean-shaven. Looked a bit thin. Honestly, his hat was so hideous I almost didn't look at his face. Never seen anything so green. Almost like a leprechaun's hat in a child's book. And then he whacks me with his stick and that was the end of that."

"You were extremely fortunate," I told him. "He has killed three people, casually and with no remorse, in the last twenty-four hours. Moreover, the assault on you was doubtless meant to be a killing blow as well. Nevertheless you must be careful. Light duty for the next couple of days, there might be concussion."

"We're a hard-headed lot in my family," he grinned, then winced. "But I'm grateful for your aid, Doctor, for sure."

I had pressed him further on his memory of the attack but clearly the young officer knew little more than what he had already recounted. Later, in the cab, I dutifully passed it all on to Holmes. His eyes slitted somewhat at the description of the bilious green hat, but otherwise he made no comment.

Abruptly he shook his head. "We must move forward, Watson. Regret avails us nothing. Our focus must be to prevent any further killings. If only…" Holmes fell silent, considering.

"He has threatened me, you say," I said when I could stand the silence no longer. "Can we not use that? Lay a trap, as we did for John Clay or Colonel Moran? I might draw the man out of hiding."

"No." Holmes was firm. "I considered that but I dare not take the chance. I had thought to employ a similar stratagem with the Smiths and they are both dead, before I could even begin to outline a plan. I am certain such hubris is exactly what he expects of us, but I will not allow my pride to get the better of me in this case. Not when it is my oldest friend that is under threat."

My heart warmed at such rarely expressed sentiment from Holmes, even as I was irked at his clear assumption that I was defenseless. "But, Holmes, you cannot expect me to hide under my bed in Baker Street like a frightened schoolchild. We have faced many dangers…"

"Not like this," he snapped. "Never have we been actively hunted before, attacked in our own home—note the incident of the crossbow, a clear signal that he could kill us at any time. Moreover, given his fondness for poisons I am rapidly becoming convinced that Athelney Jones' death was no accident, either. He is systematically eliminating everyone involved with the Sholto matter: Jones, Small, the Smiths. And now it is apparently our turn. We are being stalked like prey, our every move under surveillance by an unknown foe. Not even Moriarty cut this deep, for he at least was a known adversary. There were counter-strikes available with the Professor; it was possible to defend against him. This man…we have no clue to his real identity. His every move, even to the hat you describe—it is all theater. A role he plays. The real man is carefully hidden."

"Should we flee, then?" My entire being rebelled against this idea but I had never seen Holmes in such a state.

"He expects that too. At least it must be a contingency he has planned for. No, we must somehow change the game itself and extricate ourselves from the roles he has assigned us." He smiled. "We shall fort up in our rooms and get some rest tonight, and tomorrow I shall re-examine the problem. I am missing a key data point somewhere. I am certain of it. But first we must ascertain whether or not our foe has planted a bomb in our rooms as well."

It was typical of Holmes to smile ruefully at this possibility, but I was not nearly so blasé about it. "Holmes! But—Mrs. Hudson—what if he…"

"Steady on, Watson." Holmes put a hand on my shoulder. "I do not think he has been to Baker Street as yet—I sense that it is too early in his game, for first he wants to see us twist and squirm like a lepidopterist's pinned butterfly. But we dare not make assumptions. There have already been too many of those on my part. I have been treating this man like a typical criminal but he is… something else. In fact, he…" Holmes fell silent again, lost in thought.

That was all he would say until we arrived at our rooms. Mindful of Holmes's caution, I immediately embarked upon a thorough examination of our dwelling. To my relief I found nothing, and Holmes, after a brief survey of his own, pronounced our rooms free of bombs or other hazards as well.

I took it upon myself to wake Mrs. Hudson and warn her that we were in a state of siege for the indefinite future. She agreed to admit no one without our express consent and certainly that no one was to be permitted into the building at all when we were not in residence. "Not even tradesmen," I added firmly. "We must make do with the supplies on hand."

She nodded and returned to her bedchamber, though I thought I heard a muttered comment concerning something regarding us being the most difficult tenants in the history of London. Since I could not actually argue the point—the case to be made against Holmes as a difficult tenant was close to impregnable— I chose rather to simply ascend the stairs to our own rooms and retire. Fortunately the heat had abated to the point where we could close the windows and draw the blinds, and feeling that we had taken all the precautions available to us that it was possible to take under the circumstances, I undressed and went to bed. Despite my concerns about our unseen enemy, I was asleep almost instantly.

It was close on to dawn when I finally retired, so it was no surprise that it was well into the following afternoon when I at last awoke. Apart from

She nodded and returned to her bedchamber...

a slight ache in my bad leg, most likely from our fire-fighting exertions during the previous night's adventure at the Smith boat-yard, I felt quite refreshed. Once dressed, I emerged into our sitting-room to find a note from Holmes: *At Scotland Yard. Must examine some records. Await my return. Please, old fellow, do not take any action without me. Holmes.*

I was at a loss to think what records he might need to examine, save something to do with the Sholto killings and the Sign of the Four. But as to specifics, I could not imagine what Holmes had seen that the rest of us had not, to lead him in such a direction. I confess it stung a little to be left behind but I knew that he had done so out of concern for my welfare, since I had been named as the madman's next victim.

Still, I resolved that I should not just sit idly. There must be something to be done. I rang for Mrs. Hudson, and once she had provided a cup of tea and a scone, I considered the matter.

There were still the riddles. Holmes scorned them as clues but I felt certain there was something there, though it hovered just out of reach. I retrieved the scraps of paper and looked carefully over each one, trying to bear Holmes' methods in mind as I did so.

There was a knock on the door. Startled, for I had expressly told Mrs. Hudson there were to be no visitors, I relaxed when I saw it was Lestrade at our door. He glanced around the sitting room, then turned in disappointment to me. "Mr. Holmes is not here?"

"I'm afraid not, Lestrade." I raised an eyebrow. "I should have thought he would be with you. His note said he was conducting researches at the Yard."

"Humph!" Lestrade shook his head. "I appreciate the thought, doctor, but surely you know Mr. Holmes never takes lowly inspectors such as myself into his confidence. We are merely suited to run those errands which he cannot be troubled with himself."

"Oh, surely it is not as bad as all that, Lestrade."

"Well, perhaps not," admitted the inspector. "Still, I had hoped to confer with him, for I confess I have no clue how to proceed. That is to say, no clue save for those damnable riddles. Which reminds me, Doctor, I need to collect those as evidence."

"Certainly, but perhaps you would let me copy them on Holmes' chalk-board first." Lestrade nodded, and I wheeled out the large chalk-board Holmes used to work out his chemical formulas. As I wrote, I added, "But this cannot be the errand to which you refer."

"Ah. No, Doctor. Actually..." Lestrade reddened a little. "I had a telegram from Holmes earlier, requesting police protection for your rooms here at Baker Street."

"Now, really." I set the chalk back in its tray and turned to face the police inspector, my hands on my hips. "You are letting this man frighten you so as well? This is entirely too much. It is bad enough when Holmes—"

"Doctor, please." Lestrade held up a hand. "Consider. In all your years with Sherlock Holmes, has he ever asked for such a measure?"

I was forced to admit he had not.

"Well, then." Lestrade spread his hands. "I cannot say I disagree with Mr. Holmes' assessment of the danger this man represents. Look here, Doctor, I understand the insult to one's pride. No man likes to think himself helpless. But Doctor, I will say this. I have seen it demonstrated many times over the years that pride means nothing. Look at how many times Sherlock Holmes has shown me up, in case after case. Any man at the Yard will tell you. One might even say that Holmes delights in doing such. Yes?"

Reluctantly, I nodded.

"And yet we continue to consult with him. Myself, Hopkins, Gregson… even Athelney Jones, rest his soul. Because we know that it's worth all the gibes and humiliation to get a case solved and a killer off the streets. Because in spite of everything, Doctor Watson, the one thing I take genuine pride in is being a good police officer. I will never be as smart as Mr. Sherlock Holmes but by heaven, I will never be so stupid as to discount what he has to say. This man frightens him as no other malefactor ever has in the history of our association and that, Doctor…. That frightens *me*. So you'll accept the protection my department is offering without putting up an argument, yes?"

Lestrade's jaw thrust forth in such challenge that I could not but laugh and raise my hands in surrender. "The presentation of your case would be the envy of any prosecutor. I daresay Holmes himself might have wilted before it. Certainly he would be moved at hearing your opinion of his contributions to law enforcement."

The inspector smiled and waggled a finger at me. "Let's keep that part between us, Doctor. Our friend Mr. Holmes has more than enough vanity to sustain him as it is." He rose to go. "Anyway, I'm leaving young Woodrow down there on watch. He's got some pride to mend himself, after last night, and this seemed as good a way as any to let him get some of his own back. He's got quite the grudge against our man in the green hat himself now."

"As long as his injury does not trouble him unduly."

"Why, if it does, he's got a doctor right here, doesn't he?" Lestrade chuckled at his own witticism, then grew serious. "I would not leave him on guard if I did not trust in his ability. He is one of our best and brightest and he begged me for the chance to redeem his honor. I could not refuse."

"Put that way, I cannot argue the point. But you might send him up, anyway, Lestrade. I should like to introduce him to Mrs. Hudson, so that she knows he is safe to allow on the premises. And perhaps he might lend a fresh eye to these infernal conundrums."

"There you go," Lestrade agreed. "That's the way to make the best of things, Doctor. He'll be right up."

With that, the inspector took his leave, and young Woodrow was indeed up shortly thereafter. I inspected his head wound and inquired after his condition—specifically, if he had experienced any dizziness or blurred vision, or any of the other symptoms of concussion. He averred that he had not. "Just aches a little, but I told the Inspector that I'd appreciate another chance at the blighter."

"You were fortunate," I told him. "Scalp wounds bleed copiously and when you collapsed the spray of blood must have persuaded him that he had dealt you a lethal blow."

The young policeman flashed a brief and rueful smile. I could see that he was somewhat shamed still at having missed the opportunity to capture our killer, though I daresay any of us would have been similarly deceived, under the circumstances. "What's this, then, Doctor?" he asked, waving at the chalk-board.

"More taunts from our man." I scowled at the lines of doggerel I had painstakingly copied from the notes delivered so far. "Holmes thinks they are a mere diversion but I cannot but think there is some clue here that we are not seeing."

Officer Woodrow nodded dutifully and leaned forward to examine the riddles. "Well, it beats me, Doctor," he admitted after a few moments spent staring at the writing on the chalk-board. "I think I'll be more use standing guard."

"As you wish."

The officer departed to take his station at the foot of the front stairs, and I returned to my examination.

Hours passed and despite applying all I could think of to the problem I got no further. I knew Holmes was correct in his assertion that this game was meant to distract and mystify us, but I thought that perhaps solving the riddles might at least provide some direction. And—it must be said—a distraction was somewhat welcome, as the time wore on and night fell. I knew not what had taken Holmes from our rooms for such a length of time but I was determined to not spend the hours in fruitless worry.

After all, I reminded myself, of the two of us it was I that was the man of letters. Though I was no literary lion, nevertheless I was a working writer of sorts. A word puzzle was more in my territory than that of Holmes, whose expertise lay largely in chemistry and the forensic sciences.

The answer *must* be there somewhere! For the thousandth time I examined the lines on the chalk-board. This time I read it aloud, thinking perhaps the sound of the words themselves might hold the secret.

> *"The game's afoot, detective!*
> *So detect! To find me you must first find these.*
> *Adding two and two, there will be four in all.*
> *The first found in fire, bright and hot;*
> *The second begins over, never under;*
> *The third began under, never over;*
> *The last in a horror times three;*
> *And closer to you than any other."*

A child's riddle, I mused. Perhaps a pun, some sort of double meaning. And the case that was referenced in the other clues perforce might well be referenced here as well. Jonathan Small. The Sign of Four.

Four was the sum of two and two, certainly. But was there another reference? Something about the phrasing, perhaps. I stared at the words almost until they lost all meaning.

And then I saw it. The sentences themselves indeed had no meaning. It was the words, the *letters*. The juxtaposition.

I make no claim for deductive genius comparable to that of Sherlock Holmes, but I fancy that I am not a dullard. Dogged persistence from such as I could not compete with the flashes of brilliance Holmes displayed as a matter of routine, but nevertheless I was certain I had hit upon the answer. Once I realized the wordplay that lay beneath the lines I could not see any other possible interpretation. Still, I could not be certain. I pulled out my handkerchief and wiped away some of the riddle and rewrote it, then bellowed for Woodrow to join me.

"Great heavens, Doctor, what's the ruckus?" The police officer looked mildly alarmed. "Has something happened? There's been no one…"

"No, no." I grasped his arm and pointed at my revisions on the chalk-board. "Look here. See what you make of this."

I had written:

The game's afoot, detective!
So detect! To find me you must first find these.
Adding 2 and 2, there will be **four (letters)** *in all.*
The first found in **F***ire, bright and hot;*
The second begins **O***ver, never under;*
The third began **U***nder, never over;*
*The last in a ho***RR***o***R** *times three;*
And **closer** *to* **U** *than any other.*

Add 2 and 2 to the four letters
F-O-U-R! And CLOSE!
Answer - 224 Baker Street

"The first letter in 'fire'! F! The second begins 'over'! O! The third is U, and there are three 'R's in horror! And not only is the R closest to the U in the word 'four,' with the two vertical strokes in parallel, but 224 is the closest address to this one, 221B! Well?" I asked him. "What do you think?"

Woodrow rubbed his jaw. "Gorblimey! That's clever, that is. I think you must have hit it, Doctor."

"He is across the street!" I said, barely able to contain my excitement. "'Closer than any other!' More, 224 is the address of Camden House, it is from there that he fired his missile through our open window. We thought it was the roof but he was in the dwelling itself! If we are subtle we might well trap him. He must be watching the windows, waiting for Holmes to return. Let us draw the curtains and arrange a silhouette to foster the belief we are still here. Then we can exit out the tradesmen's door in the back and circle around the side streets to enter 224 from the rear."

"But..." Officer Woodrow looked dubiously at me. "Just the two of us?"

"You can send word by our boy Billy to the inspector whilst I arrange the decoy with Mrs. Hudson. We shall have reinforcements soon enough. Quickly, man!"

My excitement and triumph were contagious. The policeman considered a moment, then nodded. "All right, doctor. I'm with you." He grinned. "I owe this man something myself."

"Stout fellow!" I clapped him on the shoulder. "Let us be about it, then. This man has claimed enough victims already."

It did not take much time to coach the sorely-tried Mrs. Hudson in the placing of silhouetted objects by the window, and moving them occasionally to provide the illusion that we were still in residence. She had done such for Holmes before to deceive Colonel Sebastian Moran when he had attempted to assassinate Holmes from the same Camden House some months previously. We no longer had the wax bust we had used for that deception, but it was easy enough to improvise a figure from pillows and laundry to sit in the chair by the window. Through all this our valiant landlady never complained, but did express the hope that this would be the conclusion to all the 'terrible goings-on,' as she put it. By the time we had the stratagem worked out, Woodrow had returned.

"The lad's on his way," he said. "The inspector should be along with a squad as soon as he gets word." His eyes glittered with excitement. "Shall we be off then, Doctor?"

I nodded. "Are you armed?"

The officer looked abashed. "Afraid not, sir. We generally don't carry…"

"That's all right. I have my Webley. And here…" I handed him my walking stick with the brass knob. "It's weighted. Cored out and filled with lead."

"Penang lawyer, is it?" Woodrow hefted the stick experimentally "Aye, this would do some damage. You think it will come to that?"

"I hope not." The night was still warm, though not as unbearable as the previous one had been. I decided against a greatcoat, instead thrusting the revolver into my waist-band. After all, I reasoned, there was no need to conceal the firearm. I was accompanied by a uniformed officer. "But this man has killed three people that we know of and he tried to kill you. It is best to be cautious."

The constable nodded. Together we crept down the back stairs and out through the scullery to the alley. Within a quarter of an hour we had threaded our way past piles of refuse and other debris to emerge on the side street that curved round towards the east.

"Past that wall there," I said softly, and pointed. "I believe these rooms are largely vacant on this side. Nevertheless, stealth should be our aim. We shall have to hope that we do not inadvertently raise an alarm that frightens off our quarry."

"You know your way pretty well," Woodrow puffed a little as we clambered over the stone wall. "One would think you had done this before, Doctor."

"Once. I have not yet published the account, but it was the occasion of Holmes' return some months ago, the capture of Colonel Moran. Here now, this is the door."

I had brought a jemmy—Holmes had a fine collection of burglar's tools—but the door was, to my pleased surprise, unlocked. Together, we advanced down the darkened hallway. The stairs lay before us and I clamped a hand upon Woodrow's arm. "Listen! Was that not the rustle of movement?"

Woodrow nodded. I indicated that I should go first, handed him the jemmy, and pulled out my revolver. He followed close behind as we ascended the stairway, as silently as possible. There was a faint flicker of candlelight at the top of the stairs and I emerged to see a huddled figure on the floor.

"Good God!" I stiffened. "Holmes! What..."

"Watson...." His voice was a rasp. "Beware. Poison..."

I whirled to see Woodrow, grinning, bringing the very Penang lawyer I had armed him with in a deadly arc towards my head. Instinctively, I flung up my arm to defend myself but only partially deflected the blow. The brass knob collided with my skull and then I fell into blackness.

When consciousness returned I first became aware of a childish giggling. My head was throbbing where the blow had struck and I fought down an overwhelming nausea. *Concussion, likely.*

I opened my eyes to see that I was still in the same room in Camden House, lying upon the bare wooden planking of the floor. There was no furniture, merely scattered drop-cloths smelling of turpentine. Woodrow had lit a kerosene lamp that stood upon an upended crate, casting a pale orange-yellow light over the small room. Holmes lay crumpled in the corner still, almost unchanged from my first glimpse of him.

"Holmes!" I struggled to rise from the floor and that was when I realized I had been bound securely with stout clothes-line. Woodrow had not stinted, but wound the cord round my wrists and knees so that I was quite immobilized.

My heart sank as I realized that no help would be coming. Woodrow would not have sent Billy for Lestrade. Or, more likely, he had seen to it that the lad was off on some wild-goose chase. I glared up at the grinning madman and he, in turn, leered down at me. "What have you done to

I whirled to see Woodrow bringing the Penang lawyer in a deadly arc towards my head.

Holmes? What's it all about, Woodrow?"

Woodrow giggled again, a high, manic sound that was more madness than mirth. "What indeed? What do you think it is, Doctor?" The working-class Cockney accent was gone. Now the voice was high and reedy, like that of some lunatic minstrel. "What, who, why? Whyever can this be? Your head is full of questions, I've no doubt. Riddle me this: *Why is a raven like a writing-desk?* Answer mine and I may consent to answer yours."

"Because they both produce notes that are flat," I snapped. "Very well, I have answered, now you answer me. What have you done to Holmes?"

"Ha!" Unaccountably, my anger seemed to please him. "So! A sharper mind lurks beneath the façade of the detective's loyal amanuensis than your readers have been led to believe. Yes, flat! Flat indeed! As flat as your great detective here!"

"What have you done to him?"

"Ah, all I did was handcuff him when I found him collapsed here earlier. As a precaution. But he was already defenseless. Really, he did it to himself, Doctor. I had a trap laid for any that should reach my private sanctuary— I was prepared, naturally, because as you saw, my clues were meant to bring you here eventually. Holmes was ahead of you with the riddle, for he tracked me here this afternoon, apparently, and triggered one of several trip-wires I had prepared. I was certain the great Sherlock Holmes would unravel my clues sooner or later and I was ready!" Woodrow threw back his head and laughed.

Inwardly I berated myself for not seeing the obvious. It would have been a simple matter for Woodrow to have entered Camden House to fire the arrow into our window the night before, and then hasten back downstairs to be waiting with the wagon when we burst out on to the street. And equally simple for him to feign the head injury that I had been so foolishly concerned about, and then spin the tale of the mysterious stranger who had approached him and the widow Smith. There had never been any man in a green hat. Holmes had said it himself—the man had been watching us all along.

Woodrow chuckled and continued, in high good humor, "The curse of the rose! That is what has done for your friend. Another dart, loaded with tropical poison. This one is a paralytic, much slower than what I used on the unfortunate Smiths. Those brought death almost instantly, for the Andaman tribes are not sadistic, merely efficient and deadly. But the aboriginals of the Amazon basin prefer death to come slowly." Woodrow nodded at Holmes and smiled. "As do I. This dart was coated with a much more artistic preparation. At first comes paralysis, followed soon after by total biological collapse. His breathing will gradually slow as his chest muscles tighten and spasm, along with the rest of his body. He is helpless, unable to move or speak. Eventually his breathing will cease entirely, but until then... he can hear every word. He will witness as I mete out the punishment that you so richly deserve. Oh, how I have dreamed of this moment!" The constable leapt to his feet and capered and pranced like a leprechaun. "The criminal classes shall bow to me, the king of conundrums, for my schemes and riddles have made puppets of the great Sherlock Holmes and his loyal dogs-body!"

He twirled about as though performing in some insane ballet. "You prate of the genius of Sherlock Holmes, but you have never seen true genius, Doctor Watson, not until today. Yes, I led you with arrows and thorns and mysterious notes, knowing that such dramatic trappings were as irresistible to Holmes as opium to an addict! You both danced like marionettes for me!" Woodrow took a deep, shuddering breath, gathering himself. "And Lestrade said Moriarty was the greatest criminal London ever saw! Moriarty? Pah! A mere accountant, a mathematician with delusions of grandeur. He had no true genius, no poetry in him! Your great detective has never faced anyone like me. The criminal classes and the minions of the law alike shall cheer to be rid of the insufferable braggart! See, now, before you: the man who truly killed Sherlock Holmes! Huzzah! Huzzah!"

Abruptly he stopped and knelt before me, his eyes glittering with pure hate. "And the greatest irony of all... Holmes is the bonus. It is you I owe the blood debt, Doctor Watson. Your sin was the greatest. Hence you must go last, and watch helplessly as all the other victims precede you, knowing you are the cause of it all."

"But why, man?" I raged helplessly against my bonds. "What possible..."

"Can it be you do not know? Seriously? Are you so utterly self-involved...? But of course you are. Perhaps this will enlighten you: my full name is Woodrow Athelney Jones, Doctor Watson. You murdered my father."

"That is not—however could you..." I was sputtering with baffled indignation as I struggled to sit up. "You have been deceived, young man. Or you have deceived yourself."

"You dare to speak of deceit!" Woodrow Jones backhanded me across the face. I fell back to the floor as he continued ranting. "You who publish lies about men whose boots you are not fit to lick! Every time you take up your pen you defame the Metropolitan Police Force, the finest men to serve this nation, just to inflate the reputation of this... this pretender!" He whirled and kicked at Holmes' inert form, then returned to face me. "Your pestilent magazine accounts! My father was a respected detective, a senior officer at Scotland Yard! Your narrative of the Sholto affair made a mockery of him! He was a laughingstock! Your caricatured portrait ruined him utterly at the Yard. Old cases were re-opened, convictions overturned, and ultimately he was relieved of his rank. The shame was more than he could bear. He took to drink to ease the pain. And it killed him. You killed him. As surely as if you put a gun to his head and pulled the trigger." He paused, then intoned, "The flaw is that which fails the higher it soars...The reason shall be that which is seen but never visible. The flaw is pride. The reason is vengeance. All who you made famous in your foul, biased narrative have died now, and the world will see the great failure of your so-called genius detective to prevent any of it. Aye, the world shall witness my vengeance when it mourns Sherlock Holmes... and it will be so very sweet."

"You are premature, I think."

Holmes! *Alive!*

He stood at the far end of the room, massaging his wrists. "Even handicapped as I was by working with my pocket blade and a collar pin, I am afraid it still took longer to pick that lock than it should have," he said with a thin smile. "Fortunately, your deluded rantings provided more than enough time. I had feared that you might do more violence to poor Watson before I could free myself." Holmes' voice sharpened. "For the record, your father was a pompous incompetent who jailed at least half a dozen innocent men. The debacle he nearly made of the Sholto matter was but the tip of the iceberg. The doctor's account of the case, if anything, understated the embarrassing performance we all witnessed. The fact that a magistrate took long-overdue action to remedy the disgraceful conduct of your father..."

Woodrow Jones could stand no more and let out an inarticulate shriek of pure animal fury. He snatched up my revolver and fired, but Holmes had been ready; indeed, had deliberately goaded him in order to provoke just such an intemperate, uncalculated action. He spun away even as Jones was moving, whirling well away from the pistol fire and raking a hand across the young man's face. Jones stiffened and uttered a muffled grunt. Holmes knocked the revolver out of his hand and shoved him away. Jones, his face a mask of baffled fury, fell to the floor.

Holmes nodded with satisfaction and knelt to where I lay helpless. "I am not such a fool as he imagined," he chuckled. "I saw his trip-wire even in the darkness and disarmed it, and in the process of doing so, helped myself to his paralytic dart. Unfortunately, when he came upon me here moments afterward, with no place of concealment I could think of no other stratagem than to pretend to have fallen victim to his poison. And then I was faced with the unexpected complication of the handcuffs, else I should have been ready for his return. Certainly I would have spared you that knock on the head," he added ruefully. As he spoke he was cutting the cords that bound me, and in a moment I was standing beside him.

Holmes returned the small blade to his pocket. "Soon he will be as immobile as he imagined me to be, but by then we shall have Lestrade here and you can administer medical aid. I believe the antidote to curare is a compound of..."

There was an animal noise behind us. We turned to see that Jones was somehow, impossibly, still moving, despite the poison in his system. "Gnnn...." He struggled to rise but instead only succeeded in falling against the crate and knocking his kerosene lamp to the floor. It shattered, spraying the volatile liquid in all directions. The drop-cloths ignited and in a second the room was aflame... and Jones was, as well. Unable to move, even to roll clear of the blaze, the paralytic poison held him immobile. As the fire raced up his legs and torso he uttered a scream of such rage and horror that I think I shall ever hear it in my nightmares.

I moved towards the body instinctively, I suppose with some hope of rescuing the dying man. But Holmes grasped my arm. "It is too late for him," he said. "Quickly, Watson, or we too shall be consumed in this inferno."

We stumbled down the stairs. Eschewing the back door we had used earlier, Holmes wrapped his vest about his fist and swung it at the front window. The blow shattered the panes and we emerged on to Baker Street in a cascade of broken glass, kicking aside the fragments remaining in the frame as smoke billowed behind us. The upper floors of Camden House, dry as tinder in the August heat, were already engulfed in flame.

"I should have liked to see him stand trial," Holmes said. "But I suppose the Yard would prefer not to have a public spectacle."

I pointed. "Here comes Lestrade, in a police-wagon, and it looks like the fire brigade is close behind. You can ask him." I coughed and added, "But please, Holmes, let us do so in the comfort of our rooms. I think we both deserve a brandy."

Sherlock Holmes looked at my battered and sooty face and let out one of his infrequent barks of genuine laughter. "My dear Watson, I daresay we might have even earned two."

It turned out that when Billy returned alone Mrs. Hudson had grown alarmed and sent for the police herself. Lestrade followed us up the stairs as we left the fire brigade and the rest of the inspector's squad to control the blaze consuming the ill-fated Camden House. I procured cigars for Lestrade and myself while Holmes attended to the duties of a bartender. Soon we were settled in our usual chairs, each with the promised brandy and soda.

"It was simplicity itself, once I returned to the core principles of logic and deduction that form the basis of detection." Holmes, eschewing the cigar I had proffered, reached instead for the disreputable clay pipe that he favored in the late evening. "The riddles were a mere distraction, as I said all along."

"But what, then, pointed to Woodrow?" I asked. "He was the very picture of a well-meaning young constable. It was a performance to rival any seen in the theatre. Certainly I was blind as a beetle to his perfidy."

"And I," Lestrade added. "When he first arrived at my precinct he had asked me to keep his parentage between us, for he wanted no pity or special favors. I did not find it suspicious. Indeed, I found it admirable, even noble. I thought his father's legacy made him one of my most dependable lads, not… well, not what he clearly was," he finished, awkwardly.

Holmes ticked off points on his fingers. "First of all, recall the initial event, the murder of Jonathan Small. Remove the theatrics of the mysterious note pinned to his chest and the warning that preceded it and you are left with the simple fact that there are few individuals allowed access to a prisoner in his cell. Add to that Woodrow's fondness for poisons, especially the fast-acting paralytic agents, and it is easy to surmise the lad inventing some excuse to visit the prison and firing a dart at his victim, then disappearing from the scene before the body can be discovered. Likewise, it would be the work of a moment to insert the warning note into the pile of crank letters. Who would notice one more young man in uniform in either circumstance?"

Lestrade shook his head. He had, upon my urging, consented to accept a libation along with the cigar, but his expression remained bleak. "I feel responsible. I assigned him to this duty, for heaven's sake."

Holmes waved it away. "I am certain that our Mr. Jones would have contrived a reason to be on the scene whether or not you had given in to his entreaties to 'redeem his honor.' If there is blame, I must shoulder my fair share of it for permitting myself to be distracted by the man's games as long as I was. I should have realized that the only victim *not* to be poisoned—indeed, not to be killed at all but only clouted a blow to the head—was in itself a suspicious circumstance worthy of further investigation. And the note with the third riddle was found *under* his body, an impossible circumstance in the scenario Woodrow described unless he had put it there himself. However, his account of the sinister man in the green hat was so convincing—for it was right in line with the theatricality I was already certain our killer was compelled to demonstrate—that I allowed myself to believe the lad was telling the truth."

Holmes fell silent for a moment, then continued, "Nevertheless, the more consideration I gave the matter upon our return the more these inconsistencies troubled me, and I kept returning to the questions of access and opportunity. It seemed inconceivable that any man could commit these crimes yet remain invisible—*unless that man was a police officer.* Either Woodrow himself or a confederate, also in uniform. Moreover, it would be almost impossible to duplicate those primitive thorn weapons with the same compound the Andaman Islander Tonga used, here in the fogs of London. I was certain that the weapon used to kill Mrs. Smith was, in fact, one of the actual blowgun darts from the Sholto case."

"But, for heaven's sake, Holmes, you could have confided in me." Lestrade sounded wounded. "Surely..."

"I dared not. I had posited that a policeman must be the guilty party, but I had no way of knowing if he was working alone or with others. I could not risk it, not after Watson had been directly threatened and we still had no idea what the murderer's ultimate game was to be." Holmes shook his head. "No, I had to play a lone hand, and quickly. Therefore I determined first to visit the archives at Scotland Yard and, sure enough, the exhibit with Tonga's darts had been plundered. So then I was certain our man was a police officer, although I was not yet persuaded that Woodrow was in fact the killer. Seeking further confirmation, I returned to Baker Street—this was while you were still asleep, Watson—and re-examined the notes you had brought. It was obvious at once that the brand of paper that you, Lestrade, had used to copy the prison note was identical to the brand used to write the missive our killer had wrapped around his crossbow bolt. The same cheap common foolscap used in your police-station."

"But what led you to Camden House, then, if not the riddle itself?" I asked him.

Holmes steepled his hands. "It was a fine bit of reasoning you did with the riddle, old fellow," he said gently. "Worthy of applause. But it was a sounder strategy, and incidentally much faster, to use simple physics to arrive at the same conclusion. Upon further examination, the trajectory of the missile fired through our window, extrapolated from the hole it left in the wall..." he pointed "...and the velocity with which it hit, made it obvious that it had to have come straight across, from the opposite window in Camden House. Not the roof, as we all originally assumed."

Holmes spread his hands. "And then once he had threatened you, Watson, I surmised that of course he would have to have a base of operations to keep watch on our rooms, and what better one than the one I had established he had already used to fire his arrow? So I hastened over to investigate. It was the obvious next step and the best chance of catching him unawares. My thought was to lie in wait and surprise him when he arrived, before he could make good his threat, after wiring Lestrade to insure his men were extending their protection so that there would be no danger to you, Watson. I misjudged the timing, unfortunately. I was sure he would want the cover of darkness."

"But the police protection I assigned was the very man we were all trying to guard against," Lestrade sighed and shook his head sadly. "Not my finest hour, Doctor. I cannot apologize enough."

Holmes smiled, somewhat ruefully. "I made several dangerous mistakes as well, Lestrade. This is a case where none of us can be said to have covered ourselves with glory." Abruptly, he smiled widely and raised his glass in my direction. "None save Watson, anyhow! Let us not forget, he was the one to *solve* the riddle. And I gather Woodrow witnessed this himself. It was a blow to his self-declared genius, I daresay. If anyone is the 'conundrum king'...."

We were interrupted by a knock on the door. It was a disheveled member of the fire brigade, hat in hand. "Begging your pardon, Inspector," he said to Lestrade. "But you said there was a body."

Lestrade nodded. "Yes, indeed."

"We didn't find none, sir."

"What?" I nearly spilled my drink. "But—Holmes! We both saw Jones poisoned, collapsing in the fire—is it possible...?"

Lestrade leapt to his feet. "We'll soon have the truth of it," he said, and motioned to the firefighter to follow.

But they found no sign of Woodrow Jones, then or in the days that followed.

"Is he alive, do you think?" I asked Holmes a week later. "Or did the flames perhaps consume him so utterly that Lestrade's men simply could not find the remains?"

Holmes stood and gazed out the window at the blackened ruin across the street. He shook his head. "I am afraid, Watson… that remains a conundrum worthy of Jones himself."

The End

Afterword: From the Batcave to Baker Street

So this one started when we were watching a rerun of the television series *Gotham*; the episode wherein the future Riddler, Edward Nygma, executes his first real foray into crime. He commits a bank robbery and leaves clues cleverly designed to lead the young Lieutenant James Gordon into a trap. As my wife and I were watching this labyrinthine, malevolent puzzle unfold I said idly to her, "You know, the ideal opponent for the Riddler isn't Batman. It's Sherlock Holmes."

Then I realized what I'd said. "Oh, man. I'm *totally* going to do that story." A few minutes' thought and the plot appeared in my head as if by magic. I hastened to the computer and banged out an email suggesting what I had in mind to Cap'n Ron at Airship 27, praying that none of my colleagues had come up with something similar. He said sure, go for it, and here we are.

It's not the first time the worlds of Sherlock Holmes and Batman have intersected. (In the comic books, Holmes has actually met both Batman and his arch-nemesis, the Joker.) One of the things I like to do is to try to fill in gaps in the original Holmes saga, and one of those that has always stood out to me is that there is a dearth of truly challenging villains in the Sherlock Holmes stories. The only actual evil genius described as being equal to Holmes himself was Professor Moriarty... and he only showed up in one story, is briefly mentioned as playing a role in another, and both appearances were mostly offstage.

I wanted a real honest-to-God supervillain that was worthy of the world's greatest detective, and I wanted to see him confront Holmes and Watson directly in a battle *royale*. Reverse-engineering that idea, along with the initial notion of "Sherlock versus the Riddler," gave me the key to the Conundrum King, a vicious and amoral killer obsessed with proving he is smarter than Sherlock Holmes. Copyrights and trademarks being what they are, naturally I couldn't actually have Holmes *genuinely* go up against Edward Nygma, but that character is where the Conundrum King found his inspiration. The more astute Bat-fans reading this story might even conclude that in the Conundrum King's rant that ends with the double "huzzah," I was doing my best to channel the spirit of Frank Gorshin. It's a fair cop, guv.

My original idea was just a murder mystery that hinged on a puzzle involving linked sequential riddles, but once I was actually working on it, I realized that Sherlock Holmes would sneer at the riddles. He caught crooks with observation, deduction, and evidence. The riddles would be a distraction. But I still wanted to have the fun of posing the riddles and letting the readers play along. So I ended up constructing both a classic murder mystery with genuine clues in the story itself, and also the artificial mystery of the Conundrum King's puzzle trap. Essentially double the workload, which meant this one took quite a bit longer than usual for me to figure out, but it was an awful lot of fun—at least, it was for me. And it let Watson have a little share of the glory, since, after all, he was a writer and a word game is really more on his side of the street. So I let him solve the riddles while Holmes actually solved the case.

There were other influences too. I always seem to end up doing stories for *Consulting Detective* that are postscripts to one or another of the original Holmes adventures and this one is no exception. This story also serves as a sequel to my very favorite of all the original Conan Doyle stories, *The Sign of Four.* I'm afraid I was even nastier about Athelney Jones than Doyle himself was, but I take comfort that I did not, at least, name him as being Jack the Ripper, or make him the unwitting pawn of Professor Moriarty, or any of another half-dozen unpleasant fates proposed by various other authors for the most incompetent of the Scotland Yarders ever to appear in the Holmes canon. All I did was follow through on what Doyle suggested to the best of my ability, which is kind of our thing here in the *Consulting Detective* series.

Also, one of the minor things that has nagged at me off and on over the years is that Inspector Lestrade goes from being a bit of a jerk to Holmes in the early books to being a guy that gives him a standing ovation and a testimonial by the time we get to *The Six Napoleons.* It's a pretty deep dive into Sherlockian trivia to even worry about this kind of thing—certainly Conan Doyle himself never bothered about it—but I nevertheless decided that this story would serve as the bridge that covers that discrepancy, and I wanted to make sure that it was explained why Lestrade puts up with so much crap from Holmes most of the time. The Holmesians out there will note that I played a little fast and loose with accepted Canonical chronology here and there, as well, and I was intentionally vague about dates. My defense is that Conan Doyle didn't really bother about *that*, either.

So that's where this one came from. All that's left is to thank the usual crew of beta readers—Lorinda Adams, Brekke Ferguson, Anne Hawley, Tiffany Tomcal, Ed Bosnar, and John Trumbull. And of course my wife Julie, who remains my first and best audience.

Thank you, as well, readers, for picking up this book and checking out our stuff. I am still kind of dazed and delighted at the fact that I get to make up actual Sherlock Holmes stories of my very own and even get them published, but I'm game to keep it up as long as you are willing to read them.

GREG HATCHER - has been writing for one outlet or another since 1992. He was a contributing editor at WITH magazine for over a decade and during that time was a three-time winner of the Higher Goals Award for children's writing; once for fiction and twice for non-fiction. Following that he did a weekly column for Comic Book Resources as one of the rotating features on the Comics Should Be Good! blog for eleven years. Currently he is doing a weekly column on pop culture for Atomic Junk Shop. He also teaches writing in the Young Authors classes offered as part of the YMCA's Afterschool Arts Program in west Seattle, for students in the 6th through the 12th grade. A fan of pulp fiction ever since he discovered the Doc Savage paperback reprints from Bantam Books in the 1970s, he has contributed a number of action-adventure stories to various 'new pulp' anthologies in recent years. Likewise a lifelong mystery fan, he has also written Nero Wolfe pastiches for the Wolfe Pack Gazette and several Sherlock Holmes adventures for the Airship 27 CONSULTING DETECTIVE series. He lives in Burien, Washington, with his wife Julie, their cat Magdalene, and ten thousand books and comics.

Made in the USA
Columbia, SC
29 March 2018